SELECTED SHORT STORIES

Gwyn Jones

SELECTED
SHORT STORIES

OXFORD UNIVERSITY PRESS
LONDON NEW YORK TORONTO
1974

Oxford University Press,

LONDON OXFORD NEW YORK

GLASGOW TORONTO MELBOURNE WELLINGTON

CAPE TOWN IBADAN NAIROBI DAR ES SALAAM LUSAKA ADDIS ABABA

DELHI BOMBAY CALCUTTA MADRAS KARACHI LAHORE DACCA

KUALA LUMPUR SINGAPORE HONG KONG TOKYO

ISBN 0 19 281162 2

© *Gwyn Jones* 1974

Printed in Great Britain by
Hazell Watson & Viney Ltd, Aylesbury, Bucks.

Contents

5433l

The Publisher wishes to make grateful acknowledgement to the Welsh Arts Council with whose support this volume is published.

Introduction

Everything an author writes is part of an autobiography, by his own hand taken down, and may be used in evidence against him. But which autobiography? For in the nature of things he has two, just as he has two lives, one factual, the other fictive, the first communicable to his public (assuming he has one), the confined circle of his acquaintance, or his private audience of one, the second a very withdrawn affair indeed, not fully intelligible even to himself. His factual, or external, record of verifiable events and dated publications does not take us very far, for if we except birth, without which he is nothing, and death, with which he is nothing, verifiable events are not all that important in an author's work. It is his transformations, even deformations, of events, situations, persons, which are important. Whether what he writes about ever happened, to himself or another, matters only if he chooses to make it matter, and then only so long as his reader can be made to believe over an appropriate period of time that it could like-wise happen to him. In a context of the creative arts truth is hard to define, and fact not much better. Apart from an ability to read, the main requirement for the acceptance and enjoyment of so fantastic a commodity as narrative fiction is faith.

This applies to its writer too. When William Blake at the age of four saw God put his head in at the window, he had an experience which even agnostics must envy. Lesser men have humbler illusions; but two childhood memories of my own, of being lost on a mountain at the age of two, and of being caught in the reverberations of a pit explosion at the age of six, though in large measure self-engendered and in their details fictitious, have seemed part of my life's truth ever since. The desolate overtones of the one fortify my belief that men and women are congenitally loseable and self-destructive, so that from time to time they lodge themselves in narrowing tunnels of doubt, fear, and aloneness, from which in life they must be rescued, though in fiction they may press to the dead end. The sombre burden of the other has helped keep me on a particular course of human sympathies, and in story-telling gave me fixations on darkness underground as an ultimate horror, and fire anywhere as our most fearsome destroyer. Also, both memories are rooted in my natal soil, and pre-figure those pastoral-industrial or pastoral-paradisal settings in which my stories have always chosen to locate themselves.

These compulsive imaginings, only tenuously linked to fact, and necessarily re-shaping and transcending it, do not, if we are lucky, cease with our childhood. We could not be authors, artists of any kind, if they did. They are part of that fictive life which is more important to the author as author than the daily recitative of trains caught, opportunities missed, and the rise and fall of a bank-balance. I am speaking, need I say, of imaginings of a longer haul and deeper reach than the transient day-dreams that make men groan and dogs whimper. Powerful fictions, if they move us, and noble feignings, if they free us, once we trust to them, and sustain them, and augment them, will prove decisive influences on our thought and feeling, and so on what as creators we are and do.

The fictive like the factual life finds room for more mundane items than the presages and afterglows of imagination and memory. Every writer of fiction is by definition a born thief, and proud of it, his eyes and ears agape on acquisition. One reads that even so assured and prolific a short-story writer as Maupassant had a standing tariff for anyone who would give, lend, or sell him an anecdote or theme. To illustrate great things by small, my 'Ora Pro Boscis' started life as someone else's yarn, orally delivered, about a deservedly much-decayed South Wales county family. I supplied the noses and the law. 'All We Like Sheep' was vouched for as true by the friend who told it me, and since I would put nothing past those impassioned and gesticulating music-masters who control the ocean-swells and avalanches of three-valley chapel *Messiahs*, I believed him, and still do. 'Guto Fewel' was a present from the poet Huw Menai, an enigmatic reminiscence of how a young married woman in the

Rhondda, entirely respectable and a friend of the family, dropped her many-petalled calyx of camphorized petticoats over his darkling infant head, for reasons never stated. He thought it bad for the boy but good for the poet. I judged it would have destroyed me, and in the hope, maybe, that it yet might, he made me free of it. I add that poor wasted Guto is not to be confused in any detail with the sparse ascetic Huw, and that the rest of the story is invention.

But what do we mean by invention? Certainly not a digging down into unknown, unused, virgin seams of story, for there aren't any. Years ago, in Greenland, which ought to be far enough off, heaven knows, for some discreet, unobservable literary light-fingering, I heard the story of a storm-beset hunter forced to take shelter alongside the altar of a deserted chapel. The first night he was joined there by a he-bear, and shot it, gladly. The second night he was joined by a she-bear, and shot it, troubledly. The third night he was joined by a young bear, their offspring. I cried out, 'No. Don't go on!' and left the hut, to my friends' consternation. Surely I didn't carry my declared aversion to the needless destruction of life to this length! Nor did I. But the whole story—*my* whole story—had burst open in my chest. Chapel, altar, Father, Mother, Son, Man the Destroyer— myth, legend, wondertale—the human and the brute creation— never, I thought, was there a story so made for me. The fate of the third bear, that of the hunter, these I must work out in my own way. That same evening a kindly young Dane offered me a paperback, saying, 'Perhaps you would like to read it by yourself?' Alas, I should have known all along that it would be in print, for the unanswerable authority which assures us that to every thing there is a season, and a time to every purpose under the heaven, does so only after informing us that there is nothing new under the sun, and no novelty on the face of the earth.

In any case, those bears were not for me. The fictive life has its limits. I doubt that I could ever think myself into a bear or a hunter of bears. To write about something you have to identify with it, and you can't identify with what you don't know. Probably it is this knowledge and identification which constitutes an author's truth, so it is important for him to realize where they will most readily be found. With most there is no problem. It is a miracle that men write at all, but granted that they do, the growing-ground of their fictions is easily discoverable. Literature exists in a context, not a vacuum, and that context tends to be the scene of our nurture. In every act of creation, physical, mental, or spiritual, whatever else we do, we explore and extend ourselves according to our perceptions and powers. Genius has its private boundaries and the capacity to break through them, and literature has never lacked far-questers and exotics, but for the most part, what men are, what they know, what they feel, grows from a place or region. This can be provincial (in the literal not pejorative sense), metropolitan, or in respect of some nations national. For me, it seems unnecessary to add, this means Wales, and therein South Wales, and still more narrowly the mining valleys of Gwent and Glamorgan on the one hand, and the thirty-mile central arc of Cardigan Bay and its hinterland on the other.

Regionalism of this high and honourable definition has a status as estimable as any other form of writing, and has been a main feature of the European and American literary tradition. For his region—it can be as small as Eire, Calabria, or Berlin, or huge as the Deep South of America—the regional writer will feel an inescapable though not necessarily an exclusive attachment. He will understand its people, as no outsider will ever understand them, and be driven to act out that understanding in words: their character, personality and traditions, patterns of behaviour and impulses to action; what they believe in, their hopes and fears, bonds and severances; their relationship to each other, to the landscape around them, and the creatures they share it with. He will be closely instructed in what Hardy calls 'the seasons in their moods, morning and evening, night and noon, winds in their different tempers, trees, waters and mists, shades and silences, and the voices of inanimate things.' Of all this he will say, 'This, these, are what I have!' If his gifts are modest but genuine, his following will be small but appreciative; if he is a Hardy, Joyce, or Faulkner, by virtue of what his region has given him he will be heard with reverence throughout the world.

This is not intended as an inflated claim for regionalism, which doesn't need it anyway. It means no more than that an author's subject matter chooses him just as much as he chooses it; and that many authors find a particular compulsion and virtue in the subject matter of that region of earth they believe to be uniquely theirs. There is no question of being dictated to by your region. You can always produce a South Wales mining valley of your own—so long as you were born in one. River, railway, road on their thin ledges, snaky chains of houses, the dramatic alternation of pit and ferny hillside, the people as they are, and still more as they were—for inevitably as you seek to produce or invent you find yourself reproducing and re-ordering the reality you know, the suddenly remembered dawn voices of men, a joyous neighing of strike-freed pit-ponies kicking at the river, the dragging crack of iron-shod boots as the men on afternoons tramp homeward for supper. Equally, you can always produce your own West Wales cwm—provided you've lived there a decade or two: the narrow roadway, gorsebloom headland, drift of sheep on the hillside inland, soft blue slumber of the summer sea, noontide swoon of islands. And animals—no need to invent those. Or the people, recurrent Adam on the green land, silent, watchful, enduring, carrying you and me and the whole world on his back; and the recurrent woman, Lilith or strong Eve, blackberry-haired, foxglove-tongued, sleek in her smooth black dress as a seal in water. No need to invent those either. Recall, let them move, and they live. Not necessarily as they did, or do; but as they might, and as you and their fates would now have them.

With this we reach the highest privilege of the fictive life. The writer of stories can play God to his creation. How we can prove intellectually or by ratiocination that there is a moral order in the world, that the universe has significance, and life a meaning, I don't know. Yet most of us start off with these assumptions or struggle to acquire them, if only because their denial is so bleak and deathly. How happy then the writer of fiction, that he can impose order and pattern, law and sanction, meaning and significance, on the private creation which circumstance forever tempts him to make public. Remembering always that God makes mistakes, that Eden was marred, and that Adam and Eve and Pinch-Me show the wounds of that marring.

Gwyn Jones

The Buttercup Field

It was too hot.

Far too hot. Gwilliam went slowly down the narrow path, regretful he had left the cold flagged inn. Once only he looked at the sun. White transparent flame licked at his eyes, and then patterns of black circles dripped before him. He blinked, his eyes wet, and the black circles changed to white suns revolving in blackness. He shook his head, muttered, and forced his vision to the bright buff dust of the cracking pathway, the glinting green of coarse hedgerow grasses, and through the high climbing hawthorn and hazel the intermittent flashing of the buttercup field.

But it was too hot. He was a fool to be out of doors. Back at the Rock and Fountain there were stone floors, fresh-wiped tables, cold beer; here in the blaze he could feel a thin spray of sweat pumped incessantly through his pores, and his shirt clung to his back like a snake. The brim of his hat was sore on his forehead.

The sun was still short of the zenith. Its rays poured fluently over a gasping world; its brightness was a barrier endlessly interposed between field and stream, flower and leaf, between Gwilliam and the fretwork shadows of the beech trees. The low line of the southern hills was clear and yet infinitely distant, fringed near Tan-y-Bwlch with a delicate massing of birch and mountain ash, gently declining on the left into the unseen river valley. To the north the high bare mound of Mynydd Mawr leaned away into mid-air, the lumps of his lofty barrows as distant in space as time. It seemed to Gwilliam that if he shouted in that loaded air, his voice would stop a yard from his lips. And he felt unbelievably alone.

Then he heard a swishing fainter than birds' wings over a lawn. He was almost at the gate and paused to listen. The silence

was alive with the thousand thin voices of a summer's day: the
humming, buzzing, zooming of insects, dry rubbings of sheathed
bodies against grass and bare earth, quiet patterings in the hedges,
the marvellously sustained vibration of seen and unseen living
things. Then he heard the noise again and knew what it was—
the death whisper of grass as it meets the scythe.

He checked at the gate. The buttercup field poured like cloth
of gold to the hidden boundary stream, swept smooth and unbroken to left and right in half a mile of flowers, taking the
noontide air with the yellow radiance of angels' wings in old
manuscripts. The brightness made him unsteady. He had to
narrow his eyes, tighten his jaws, for the whole world gleamed
like the forehead of a god.

It was then he looked close right and saw the old man. He was
dressed in funeral black, most old-fashioned. His hat had a low
crown and a wide stiff brim; there were big flat lapels to his coat,
which was cut square and long; his trousers were full at the ends
and dropped stiffly to his glittering shoes—shoes with bright
brass eyelets. Though it was later Gwilliam noticed the eyelets.

He was bending away from Gwilliam, and with a small sickle
had cut a straight and narrow swathe some thirty feet long. The
buttercups had collapsed like slain infantrymen, and those nearest
Gwilliam were already screwing up their petals as the sun sucked
the last sap from their stalks. He must have finished his row, for as
Gwilliam watched he straightened his back, took off his hat for a
moment, replaced it, swung the sickle from one hand to the other,
and was setting off again at right angles to his former line when
he discovered there was a watcher.

Gwilliam had the impression he was stupified to see anyone
there. He rubbed the back of his left hand across his cheek, and
shifted the sickle uncertainly. The sun poured blackly from the
turning blade. Then he looked, as though in wonder, at his
handiwork.

To make the best of it, Gwilliam opened the gate and went
towards him, his feet tearing great gulfs in the spread flowers.

'You are looking for something?' he asked, and glanced from
the sickle to its spoils, from the flowers to the old man's face.
It was a strong, handsome, wilful face, with a hook nose, eyes

deep as midwinter, white hair under the brim of his hat, and a stiff three-inch beard under the excessive curves of the mouth. There were blackish clefts in his tough-folded cheeks. Seventy, thought Gwilliam, or more. Not less.

'Maybe I am looking for yesterday,' he returned slowly, jerking his chin forward, studying Gwilliam, who felt foolish and snubbed.

'I'm sorry. I made a mistake, I see.' He turned away brusquely.

'No mistake,' said the old man; and as Gwilliam halted, embarrassed: 'I said nothing less than truth.'

His voice was mellow but powerful, his words like rich red earth translated into sound.

Gwilliam felt the hot hand of the sun against his left side. His heart was throbbing with a slow but mighty motion. It was crazy to be standing full in the sun like this, yet his sudden sharpness lay near his conscience.

'Gold is easy enough to find here,' he suggested, gesturing around at the buttercup field; 'but that is not always as precious as yesterday.'

The old man brought down the point of the sickle thoughtfully and cautiously against his heavy toecap. 'My yesterday *is* a golden one.' For a moment they stood silent. 'I am looking for a gold finger-ring.'

'Then let me help,' said Gwilliam. He shook his head at the flowers crushed by their feet. 'Just where?'

The other still held the sickle against his toe-cap. 'Where?' He pointed to the drying swathe he had cut. 'That was the back wall of the house.'

Gwilliam frowned, puckered his eyes for the sun and puzzlement. The old man's face moved, but was far from a smile. 'You do not understand. You cannot understand. But I am telling you —the house stood there. Tŷ'r Blodau Melyn, the Buttercup House, as this field is Cae'r Blodau Melyn, the Buttercup Field.' He looked over towards Mynydd Mawr. 'But it is of no concern.'

'You mean—a house stood here?'

'A house, yes. That was the back wall.' Gwilliam saw play in the muscles of his face. 'But it is of no concern. The Buttercup House is gone.'

The words fell from him sombre and poignant, like stones into Gwilliam's hot brain. 'Tell me——' he began, but—'Listen,' said the old man. 'Listen!' The urgency of his tone made Gwilliam strain for some noise around them, but he heard nothing save the gush of his own blood, and, once, the dry black voice of a crow, till the old man spoke again.

'You never heard tell of Ann Morgan of Llanfair. Lovely Ann Morgan was what the whole world called her. You never heard tell of her? Fifty years ago it would be, now.'

'She lived in the house that stood here?'

'Where we are standing now. But I forgot. You are a stranger. You could know nothing.' Gwilliam saw the sweat jerk down his cheeks.

'Tell me about it,' he said.

'Tell you about what?'

'Tell me about Ann Morgan and the house and the gold ring. There is a story?'

He nodded, looking to the sickle. 'A story,' he repeated. 'I have not forgotten it. Nor,' he almost whispered, 'lovely Ann Morgan.'

Then, like the pouring of water from a jug he began. Gwilliam wanted to move towards the shade of the beech trees, for the sun had now reached the top of his climb and hurled his beams from behind Tan-y-Bwlch as though to burn and kill, but the old man was staring past him as he talked, he could not catch his eye, and so must stand in the trembling air, whilst honey-heavy bees made their broken flight from flower to flower, and the pollen fell in yellow dust about the brass eyelets of the old man's boots.

'Ann Morgan was the daughter of Gwynfor and Jane Morgan, who lived in this house as Gwynfor's parents and grandparents had done. She was their only child, and would take all they had to leave, which was much. So without her beauty she would not have lacked for a husband—and she was lovelier than the falls of the Teifi at Cenarth.

'There was a man living at the stone house beyond Llanfair Bridge who fell in love with her. Fell in love with her early, when she was ten and he twelve years old. His father was black-smith to the parish, and shoed horses, repaired waggons, and kept tools as sharp as this sickle. So far as he and the world could judge she too fell in love with him, but later, when she was seventeen or more, and he full man. The parents on both sides were against them: hers because he was poor and a wild young man besides, his because they resented Gwynfor Morgan's notion of his daughter being too good for the son of a blacksmith. Eos y Fron! The Nightingale of the Fron was the name the people of the county put on him, for he sang lovelier than the thrush in April. Had he been born a prince a thousand years ago, we should read how he drew the stars out of heaven with the silver wires of his songs.

'Yet his voice was his danger. There was always open house and free drink for Eos y Fron. That was why he ran wild when very young, and wilder when old enough to know better.

'It was his voice that won Ann Morgan's heart. Jane, her mother, died in the winter of one year and Gwynfor in the spring of the next. The suitors were thicker than these flowers: a man to a buttercup in June, and twice as many in July, and all with a house, a trade, a flock of sheep, or a bag of golden sovereigns. And all, so they said, willing to take Ann Morgan in her shift. Though her house and her money, they admitted, would come handy. But one night Eos came down the narrow path, just as you came to-day, and so to her window, standing ankle deep in flowers. The drink was in him, maybe, but he sang that night to justify his name—and he sang many nights after. No need to be surprised the dog was not set on him. It was a time of full moon, and the field in its light a pale paradise. The quick hour was too beautiful for earth.

'A fortnight later he met her one evening on the road to the quarry. They stopped and talked, and he saw her home. The same night next week he saw her again, and often after that, and by bragging, flashing his white teeth, and by singing quietly the songs of the countryside, he made her fall in love with him for all the world to see. He went to work like a slave at the harvest, hoarded his wages though his fellows laughed at him, and before November was out she was wearing his gold finger-ring. They were to be married at midsummer.

'Eos gave up his pot companions. He accepted no more

invitations to houses and taverns, but stayed at Llanfair in his father's house and learned all he could of his father's trade. It dumbfounded the village that a girl could so change a man, and there were plenty to bring up the old proverb: 'Once a lover, twice a child.' But he did not care. For lovely Ann Morgan he would have done all things under the sun save one, and that one—give up Ann Morgan.

'Before the turn of the year he was oftentimes at Ann's house. Sometimes the old servant was there in the room with them, sometimes it was his own mother who went with him, for though he had smutted his own reputation twice or thrice he would have burned in hell before a bad word came on Ann Morgan.'

For the first time his eyes found Gwilliam's. They frightened him. The old man swallowed, nodded several times with harsh movements of his head, and for a moment seemed to arrange his thoughts in order.

'Lovely Ann Morgan!' he said. 'A lovely name for the loveliest woman who ever set foot in a field of golden flowers.'

'You knew her well?' Gwilliam asked, knowing his question a foolish one.

'I knew her well. But the tale is of Ann Morgan and Eos y Fron, and John Pritchard the bard of Llanbedr. You must hear the rest of it now.' For Gwilliam had put his hand to his forehead. 'Listen! For three months Eos found himself in God's pocket, and then, four days after Christmas, John Pritchard came to Llanfair. He was a relative of Jane Morgan, Ann's mother. As was to be expected, he called at the Buttercup House. As was to be expected, he fell in love there. No one out of childhood would blame him for that.'

'But if he knew she was engaged to be married to Eos y Fron?'

The old man stared. 'If you were John Pritchard—if Eos y Fron had been John Pritchard—it would have gone the same. I tell you, no man in this world could see her as she was that winter at the Buttercup House without throwing the world at her feet.' He looked from the field to the horizon. 'There is nothing in Wales to-day that can give you a notion of Ann Morgan's loveliness.'

'But what did Eos y Fron do?' asked Gwilliam.

'He knew at once. Within an hour. From the way he looked, the way he talked. And John Pritchard knew that he knew, and he cared not a buttercup for all his knowing. He was a bard, as I said, from Llanbedr, and if Eos had the nightingale's voice, John Pritchard had the language of heaven. In a full room, you'd see as many men cry at a poem of his as at a song of Eos y Fron's —and more men laughed when he changed his tune. They reckoned at Llanbedr that John Pritchard knew the metres better than a kite his wing-feathers, and if he recited to the weasels he could lead them from the burrows.

'He set himself to win Ann Morgan. Eos had to work in the daytime, and it was then John Pritchard did his courting. He sat with her for long hours, and from his lips came words finer than Taliesin's. He could talk like the little waves on the shore at Tresaith, with a music that lapped into your soul; his poems imprisoned the mountain brook; and when he wished his voice was serene as meadows under snow.

'Soon Eos knew he was losing Ann Morgan. Not that for months she did not keep face with him, but that is one knowledge native to all lovers. In March there were bitter scenes between them. He struck John Pritchard, who did not strike back. One night he struck Ann Morgan. And for that may God hate him through all eternity!

'That was the end. He did not see her for a long while. I have said that he was a wild young man until the last autumn, but now he seemed mad in his wickedness. He went back to the drinking, was out mornings with the mountain fighters, grew foul mouthed enough to disgust the foulest, and in less than two months was packed from the house by his father. This was a heavy blow to his mother, but he made it heavier by cursing both parents as a man would not curse the dog that bit him, and swearing he'd burn the smithy over their heads when next he set foot in Llanfair. That night he went to the Buttercup House with a short iron bar in his hand, and when they refused to open the door, smashed in the biggest window frame and would have done who knows what damage inside had not the labourers run up from the village and bound him. For a month he was in gaol in

Cardigan, and then came out to terrify all who met him.' The old man looked square at Gwilliam. 'He was a brute, and he lived like a brute. It would be better had he died like one, then.'

'I thought——' Gwilliam began. He was dizzy with the glare. The buttercups seemed to his aching eyes a pool of metal from the ovens, a-flicker, cruel.

'Don't think,' said the other. 'Listen! John Pritchard stayed on at Llanfair. He went to the house almost every day now. He was a man reckoned handsome, much my height, and had grown a beard as a young man. He was a kind man—the whole world would grant him that. And he loved Ann Morgan as much as man can love woman. No one can tell, but it might well be that between his love and Eos y Fron's there was no more than a pinhead. But while his rival was giddy and fierce-tempered, even savage in the end, John Pritchard was kind and gentle and yet impassioned. So with time Ann Morgan did not forget her first sweetheart but was glad she had been saved from him. For his name was now filth throughout the countryside.'

The sickle had slipped to the ground. The old man stood there like a black statue, grotesquely still in the blaze of afternoon. To the heat he now seemed indifferent. Even the sweat had dried off his cleft cheeks. The square-cut coat set off his stooping shoulders, as though they were carved from wood. His brow was shaded, but a shaft of yellow light lit the dryness of his lips.

'John Pritchard and Ann Morgan were married on the twelfth day of June.' Gwilliam lifted his head at the date. 'As it might be— yesterday. They were married at the chapel in Llanfair. There was a great to-do in the village, and a feast all day at the Buttercup House. They walked back to the house in the buttercup field, all flaming with flowers as you see it now, men and women, boys and girls, two by two, and John Jones's fiddle to keep their feet and hearts in tune. The guests stayed on late, as they still do in these parts—later by far than John Pritchard wanted them to. For if Ann Morgan had been lovely before, that day she was enough to give eternity for.

'It was eight o'clock when the last guest arrived. It was Eos y Fron, not too drunk. If John Pritchard had killed him then as he crossed the threshold from the buttercup field—— But inside he came, and for a while was civil. Most there were afraid of him, the women all. He took the colour from Ann Morgan's cheeks, which before carried such red as Peredur's maiden, like drops of blood on snow. She was Ann Pritchard now, but who would ever think of her as that? Lovely Ann Morgan!'

He fell silent, and Gwilliam, his head a-throb, the hot blood shaken through his bursting veins, was silent with him.

'He came at eight o'clock. Soon after the guests began to take their leave, but he settled himself into the ingle and went hard at the drinking. Some who were there dropped a hint, some were blunt, but Eos stayed on. At last the only folk there were John Pritchard and Ann Morgan, Eos, and Abel Penry the mason and his wife, who did not wish to leave the three of them alone. Then Abel said outright that they must all be going, and shook Eos y Fron by the shoulder, but he dashed his hand aside and said angrily he'd go in his own time. Abel then made it plain they would be going together—and Abel was craggy as his trade and not a long-suffering man. It was when he found himself slowly levered upright by Abel that Eos told why he was there. He wanted his ring back. This amazed John Pritchard, for Ann Morgan had seen no reason to tell him that the ring now caught below her knuckle was the other's gift. But he was a reasonable man; he pointed out that the ring could not be buttered off that night, but that it should be sawed off the next morning. This calmness of his maddened Eos y Fron, who swore she'd not go into the same bed as John Pritchard wearing his ring. He'd see the pair of them in hell flames first. He raved, but as he grew grosser than the sty Abel struck him so hard on the mouth that the teeth cut through his lips and from nose to chin he was a mess of blood. Then he went, and what he said at going was known only to himself.'

The old man, still as a stone, watched his listener. 'There is little left to tell. Not long after midnight a fire broke out in the Buttercup House. It burned with a terrible fierceness, as though it fed on oil and fats and bone-dry wood.' His voice came deeper from his chest. 'John Pritchard and Ann Morgan were trapped in their room at the back of the house. They found the shutters of their window barred from outside, though they had left them open, and John Pritchard lacked strength to burst them apart till the flames spurted up the wall to help him. By that time the clothes were burnt off his body.' He pointed with the sickle, which he had picked up. 'The back wall was here; the window here. The buttercups grew to the very stone. He fell through it, still alive, but the yellow fire took Ann Morgan. All her loveliness went out like a moth's wings in flame.' His hard fingers ripped the rigidity from his face. 'Lovely Ann Morgan!' he sobbed, and crouched into the buttercup field.

The angry sunshine ribbed his black coat with yellow. Sickly, Gwilliam saw how the buttercups threw their pale reflection on the mirror of his polished boots. He swayed a little, hearing him from the ground, brokenly. 'They found John Pritchard that night and took him to a house in the village. It was late morning when they found Ann Morgan. Neither John Pritchard's nor Eos y Fron's ring went into the coffin with her. A beam had crashed on to her left side, and the dust of her hand and arm lies somewhere in this patch of earth. Where I seek my yesterday.'

An age passed for Gwilliam while he did no more than swallow drily. Then he moved nearer, set a hand to the old man's shoulder, to raise him. 'Mr. Pritchard——'

'Pritchard! You fool, you fool!' cried Eos y Fron, and his hand sought the sickle. 'John Pritchard died that day, good riddance to him! What was his loss to mine? Fool!' He glared up at Gwilliam. 'And what if I did it?' His voice was cut off, his mouth gaped. 'Listen!'

In his eyes Gwilliam saw the chasms of hell. He stumbled backwards, and as his head rocked the buttercup field flashed into living flame. It tilted, flaring past the horizon, licking the mountain tops, filling the sky with masses of unbearable yellow. Then to his unbelieving ears came the hoarse crackling of fire, the snap and splinter and fluttering roar of a conflagration, and through it, for one moment of agony, the screaming of a woman in terror and pain. He shut his eyes, clasped his hands over his ears, and fell backwards to the ground as red-hot pain welted his cheek. Then, his eyes open, his hands from his ears, he saw Eos y Fron with his sickle and heard his dry cracked laughter. He stepped nearer for a second blow, but Gwilliam lost his faintness under peril, and lightheadedly ran for the gate. Into the overgrown path he went, running like a maniac from the sun, hearing a maniac's shouting behind him, and feeling the drip of blood from his jaw to his chest.

His footsteps were set to a tune, and the tune went: 'Eos y Fron is looking for his ring.' But his heart pumped blood to a different rhythm, and the rhythm was: 'Lovely Ann Morgan!'

All on a Summer's Day

A woman stood outside the black-hasped door of the farm Greenmeadows, listening into the north. She stood very still, her neck rigid, her chin a little lifted and aligned on her right shoulder. She had set down a bucket of swill before her; some liquid and boiled potato peel had splashed over her boots, but within the bucket the swill had lurched to rest under its mesh of odorous scum.

It was the declining hour of afternoon, with a first paleness infusing the high blue sky, and brown shadow standing against the back wall of the house. To her left, on the south side of the valley, the ground billowed up in soft timbered rises, with fields of grass and green oats stitched in amongst them. Northwards was a flat and luscious river bottom extending almost a mile to hills that were taller but no less cushioned with oak and ash and rowan. The river flowed sluggish and unseen in its sunken channel, bridged only at the lower Fonlas meadow. Fonlas itself, the great stone house, lay back against a crescent of elms, whence its masters had surveyed and controlled the valley for five generations. Her brother Job was up there now, for some of the elms had perished in the bole and were to be felled, and with him was her grandson, the five-year-old Wyndham. The boy's mother must be at this moment coming home by way of the bridge. In the long field further down the river the red-and-white Fonlas herd would be starring the rich grass; she knew exactly where they were, though she could not see them from Greenmeadows. Fonlas Pride, the huge swinging Fonlas bull, had for days been bellowing grossly from his fenced and wired padlock, but now he was down in the lower meadow. The listening woman was the only person in the valley to know this. She knew it because a

short time earlier she had untwisted the wire and pulled the bolt
and dragged back the gate which gave him his freedom.

She was listening hard. This moment, her blood told her, it
must be. Now, oh now!

A thrush's song dripped from the nearest hawthorn. Her foot
rasped on the dry earth. She put her hand to her mouth. Let it
be now, God, she prayed. Let it be now!

Then she heard it, a screaming from the meadow. Scream upon
scream, so baffled by the summer air that it might have been
laughter or the crying of birds. And it seemed to her that she
heard the roaring of the Fonlas bull.

Time snapped. Now she heard only the thrush in the hawthorn,
the jet and tumble of his notes, and her own heart sucking in her
breast. Picking up the swill-bucket she carried it over to the sty
and emptied it into the trough. Her hands were unsteady, and
small dribs of swill spattered the yard behind her. She avoided
setting foot on them as she went back to the house, set the bucket
down carefully alongside the water butt, and stood for a moment
listening in the direction of Fonlas. Was that the shouting of
men? The corners of her mouth moved downwards, she caught
her hands together; then she hurried into the house and closed
the door behind her.

I'm married, Mam, he had written, married to a girl in England.
And from that first moment she knew her world in peril; knew
it with a threefold jealousy and suspicion—as mother, her heart
answering every impulse and sensation of his being; as peasant,
frantic for the possession and transmission of her fields; as a
remote and lonely woman, frightened of the stranger. She had
long forgotten how to write more than her name, and it was her
brother Job from the cottage past Fonlas who painfully set
down her few sentences of inquiry and anxious caution. 'Not very
war-r-rm, is it, Esther?' he had asked, rolling the adjective across
the roof of his mouth. 'Not quite the thing, p'raps. Shall I read
it out now?' She listened, coldly. 'It will do. And I can put my
own name, thank you.'

He need never have been in the English Army at all. But he had
gone off one afternoon, three months before the war started, and

joined up with two other young labourers, friends of his. He came home, half-sheepish, half-defiant, smelling of beer, and felt the rough edge of her tongue even before he told his news. 'What's here for me?' he retorted. 'Not a damned thing from one year's end to the other, except a cow calving and a kids' treat at Whitsun.' 'Your home is here, isn't it? I'm here, aren't I?' 'Aye,' he agreed sullenly, 'aye.' And then, stupefyingly, 'I'm clearing out, Mam. I've joined the Army.'

How distant, how hostile, seemed England to her who had rarely ventured to the next county. And war, when it came, how frightening and unfair—her own son taken, the sons of her neighbours hard-rooted in their soil. London she's from, he wrote; a Cockney girl. Her stomach sickened to hear it read. 'You'll like her, Mam. She don't talk the way we do.' 'Wait and see,' her brother advised her, worriedly. He saw the world, over at Fonlas. 'I knew an Englishman once, a man I met where-would-it-be; he was all right, he was—as good as us any day. Don't be hasty-thoughted, Esther.' 'And they called him Job!' she said sharply, and frowned at his inoffensive grin.

But when Luke came to Greenmeadows he came without his wife. Her suspicion leapt again. 'But you didn't ask her, Mam,' he explained. 'And the journey—her the way she is. There'll be a baby, Mam, soon.' 'It can't be that soon,' she said, excited and angry. 'You've only been married since autumn.' He rubbed his hands in patience over his knees. 'Look, Mam, the world's changed. There's this war on, and I'll be going overseas any time now. Does it matter?' 'It always matters to be decent,' she told him stubbornly. 'But I'm not blaming *you*, Luke.' It was what she had thought all along. 'No, no, it's not your fault.' He stood up brusquely in the dark kitchen. 'Don't say it, Mam—whatever it is. She's all right, is Addie. If there's any blame, I'll take it, see? I love her, Mam. It's my kid she's having and I'm happy about it. That's all that matters.' Then he smiled. 'Don't you want a grandson, Mam?' 'Yes,' she said fiercely, 'always I've wanted you to marry and have children—but here!'

Uncle Job was ready with the Fonlas trap early the next morning, to take him five miles to the railway station. A silver web of dew clung to the grass, the valley was smudged and hazed and so deadened that the coral-combed cock led his hens in silence across the yard. 'It's good here,' he said fondly before exile, 'and when the war's over I'll come back for you, Mam.' His haversack was already bulging with food but she pressed a further package of her round cakes into his hand. 'If she'll let you. She'd never come to a place like this, Luke.' 'But she will, I tell you! And there's one thing: if they start bombing London, she's got to come here with the baby. I've told her, for the kid's sake. Mam,' he pleaded, 'if she comes, her and the kid, will you be kind?' She nodded, staring at the fidgeting Job. 'That's the one big thing you can do for me, Mam, because I'm going a long way off, for a long, long time.'

At his going there were tears of blood in her breast but her eyes were dry. It was only when the trap had disappeared that she cried quietly before turning to the day's work, desolation a clawing thing inside her. Soon she heard of the birth of her first grandson, and then of Luke in Asia. 'Be good to Addie,' he wrote, 'and our Wyndham. I've told them to come.'

Wyndham! He won her deep and selfish devotion from the moment she saw him. She had not loved even Luke more. 'Yes,' she said, seeing the green eyes, the soft clusters of brown hair, the long cheekbones, 'he's Luke's boy all right.' Her daughter-in-law stared, and went on staring at the iron-grey hair over the low forehead, the guarded eyes and severe mouth. She had not put on her best to meet them: let them take her as they found her, let them find her as she was, in her thready black blouse and rubbed black skirt, the stained black apron and the scratched black boots. 'We are rough down here,' she said, almost tauntingly; 'this isn't London, is it?' She saw Addie glance away to the woodlands enclosing the valley, with mingled admiration and misgiving in her pretty, silly face—Addie in her blue costume with the short skirt, the yellow scarf tied over her bleached and shiny hair, the shoes of imitation lizard skin, the thin stockings now bagging at the knees and ankles. Her skin was sweaty under the powder and her made-up eyelashes were stiffened as with alarm. 'He'll be safe here,' said Esther, taking the child from her. 'He'll be well looked after now.' 'It's the bombs,' said Addie, in mild protest. 'He's always had the best of everything.' The child laughed merrily, gripping his grandmother's forefinger, and with it her heart.

She was a cheap and shiftless thing, that Addie, as she had guessed from the beginning. How Luke had come to marry her—but there, that was only too clear. Useless about the farm, frightened if a goose hissed, each heifer was a bull to Addie. And soft—even the dog had his meal put out each day and straw set for him to lie on in the shed. And her clothes—'That blouse,' said Esther brutally one day, 'the way it shows—with men about it's not decent.' 'Men?' asked Addie, flushing. 'Are there men about here?' 'There are eyes,' said Esther, 'and tongues.' 'Then that's all,' Addie cried. 'What a crib! Not a pictures, not a wireless, we don't even get a newspaper till it's too late. I'm sick of it I am, sitting about knitting socks and mittens!' 'Only lazy people get bored. And why shouldn't you knit socks and mittens for Luke?' 'He's in Asia, Asia, Asia—if you've ever heard of it. They don't wear mittens in the jungle,' said Addie scornfully. 'And leave my clothes alone. They were good enough for Luke. My God,' she burst out, 'what wouldn't I give for an evening in a pub and a talk and a glass of beer!' 'There's only one sort of woman goes into a public,' sneered Esther; 'I'm learning fast.' 'There's lots you could learn,' said Addie heatedly, 'and do yourself no harm. Isn't a girl ever to have a bit of fun down here?' Her words carried only one meaning for Esther; it was as she had all along thought, Addie talked like a streetwalker because she was one. Soon she could not remember when she had not *known* that Addie was bad.

The cleavage that resulted in her mind was both deep and ugly. For the child all was love and worship; she doted on him; his whim was her law. And the little tyrant knew and enjoyed his power to the full. *Mamgu* he was calling her now, the soft Welsh for grandmother, and she was winning him to the language. When he hung at her skirts about the farm and she talked of tools and places and animals, it was the Welsh words she used. For the only time in her life she would leave the work to look after itself while she talked and taught till he thought more in Welsh than in English. 'When your Dad comes home,' she told him, 'you'll be a proper little Cymro for him.' All that was English, alien, tainted in him must be exorcized. And so Addie must sit many a trying hour without understanding his prattle, and wonder from what secrets and confidences that slippery maddening tongue shut her out. 'Talk in English, can't you?' she cried, and when in mischief he refused she slapped him. He turned weeping to his *Mamgu*, and in her weak and foolish way Addie was frightened by what she saw in Esther's face. And the grandmother was crooning in the unknown tongue: 'When she beats him, when she frightens him, the dove, the darling, the mannikin, he will always come to his *Mamgu* who is good and kind and will protect him.'

At what point, and for what last reason, will hatred grow from dislike? Esther could not have said. 'Why don't you go back to London for a change?' she asked one day during the second great bombing. 'You are always grumbling about it here.' 'You think it safe?' asked Addie. 'Oh,' said Esther, 'if you are afraid!' 'Safe enough for Wyndham?' Esther stiffened. 'Oh no! Wyndham must stay here, for his Dad's sake.' 'Then so must I,' said Addie spiritedly. 'He doesn't think less of me than the boy.' But for days she was silent and moody. London! A bit of pleasure, even if there was danger, might be better than this dreary life among fields and cows and nothingness. The streets, the people, the pictures—she shut her eyes to see them. Christ, she groaned, I'm bored. You'd think they'd have a pictures or something in a wet place like this! And the old woman hating the sight and smell of her. But it's life, she concluded perkily, and can't go on for ever; better eat grass than have a headstone of jasper. She would stick it for Wyndham's sake, and Luke's, and to spite that old bitch his mother—but oh, it would have been nice! And so thought Esther, setting the dream behind her, it would have been nice just she and Wyndham at Greenmeadows. For Wyndham belonged. He was bone of their bone now. The farm was freehold: when she went, Luke; when Luke went, Wyndham. But Addie? She hated her about the place, that slut who had trapped her Luke. The more cruel her unspoken words, the sweeter their taste on her tongue.

The women spoke less and less together, which weighed the heavier on Addie, for Esther had always been a woman given to silences and brooding. In one thing only were they in league together: they let Luke guess at nothing of their true feelings for each other. 'I'm glad, Mam,' he wrote back, 'that you and Addie are getting on fine. And our Wyndham can talk Welsh then! They call me Taffy in this mob. We've got you-know-who just about taped by now, and believe me, dear Mam and Addie, I'll be home sooner than you think.'

Luke home! She looked suspiciously at Addie who had read the letter to her. 'Is that all it says? Doesn't it say when?' Addie shook her head. 'Give me the letter!' But Job read it out exactly the same. 'When he comes home', said Esther, 'all the place will be different.' She drew her fingers along the stone wall. 'A farm needs a man. He never ought to be in the Army. There'll be a lot for him to do.'

'He won't be doing it,' said Addie.

Esther's fingers were suddenly still.

'He won't be doing it, I said. He won't be staying here. We'll go back to London, the three of us. Greenmeadows! Who'd stay in a dead end like this unless they had to? Not me for one!' She grew shrill with triumph and contempt. 'You've got to be born to it to stick it. And even then Luke ran away.'

'He didn't run away! You little carrion!'

'Go on,' shrilled Addie, 'call me names! Of course he ran away. And he will again. I'll make him, and Wyndham and me, we'll go with him. I'll dance all that day,' she cried. 'Oh, life will be lovely then!'

Life, said Esther into her pillow that night, would be no better than death then. She rose silently and went to the other bedroom where Addie and the boy lay asleep. There was moonlight but the window was small, and she could no more than distinguish their shapes in the big bed and the little. She stood there till her feet were cold as stones, the long white folds of her nightgown stiff and still, and when she went back to her own room it was to pray at her bedside to God that Addie should never take Luke's boy away from her. Even if it meant—but there was no need to put one's thoughts in words to God. He knew, and would do what was right.

It was in the summer following, almost four years since they had come to Greenmeadows, that vanity, good nature, and

boredom dug a pit for Addie's feet. She had been into the market
town with Wyndham, and as she faced the weary walk home from
the station was passed by a car whose driver stopped and offered
her a lift. He was a soldier with a scarred forehead, on leave from
Normandy. He was recovering from his wound. His home was
at Maeshelig, ten miles away. He got all the petrol he wanted from
the local farmers. 'If you would like a drive round one afternoon,'
he said, and nodded at the drowsy boy, 'bring him too. It will
do him good.' He was full of chaff and slang and laughter, and
her spirits freshened to hear him. 'Stop here,' she told him, a
quarter of a mile from Greenmeadows. 'You'll come?' he begged;
'I've got another ten days.' There could be no harm in it, and
swiftly she nodded. 'Here,' she said, 'at three. Just for an hour's
drive. But if I don't turn up, please don't call for me. Will you
promise?' His answering nod established a conspiracy between
them.

And now her life which had been so drab and tired tingled
with excitement. On the third afternoon of their companionship
this became a guilty ecstasy when he lay with her under the trees.
She was lost at the first touch of his hands; her starved body
craved the act of love, she flowered and glowed with that delicious
relief. And later, walking home by way of the Fonlas bridge, 'I
have done no harm,' she told herself. 'We are young and lonely,
and I love Luke just the same.' She met him each afternoon
thereafter, for the week that was left to him, and always by half-past
five she was crossing the Fonlas bridge. 'Soon he may be killed,'
she said, 'and I have given him what I could.' And more frankly:
'I was desperate to be loved. I was frozen inside me. Four years
it's been—and who can ever know?' She felt sleek as a cat, and
cunning as one. Esther had not once asked where she went of an
afternoon; only too glad to be rid of her, she thought. And now
that it was all over, and tomorrow he would be gone, she felt
neither sorrow nor guilt nor regret. 'It's done me good,' she
said, patting her hair. 'I can stick the old bitch now till Luke
comes home.' How warm the sun was still, how brown and slow
the water! The Fonlas bull was bellowing as usual, except that
he sounded louder and nearer. 'Poor old fellow,' said Addie. 'It's
not much fun being tied up, don't I know it!' Some shameless

recollection of the afternoon made her smile, stepping on to the bridge.

I did not let her see that I knew anything, said the woman waiting inside the house. She thought she was deep, but I was deeper. The child talked to me, her own child, and so I knew. Washing and ironing she was, bleach on her hair again, and her eyebrows skinny as a fowl's—and the different look on her all the time. Sleek she was, contented as a cat. The house stank of her wickedness; it rose about her like a cloud of flies. But Esther could be as free of anger now as she was of pity. Soon they would be knocking at the door, and she would go out to them. It was wise to send little Wyndham up to his Uncle Job—she would always keep from him what was hard and ugly. Nothing would be too good for her grandson. And all that lovely future for Luke, for Wyndham, and for her.

Now! She heard the rolling of trap wheels from the home field into the yard. Suddenly she was suffocating, there was no strength in her legs, and her bowels were dissolving within her. She was looking into the red-rimmed eyes and scarlet nostrils of the bull; his upcurved horns and pounding knees were into her; his breath was sweet and rotten as death. 'Oh, no,' she whimpered. 'Frighten her I meant. No more, before God!' The door lurched open and her brother was there, looking in at her. 'Esther,' he said, his voice broken as his face, 'Esther!'

She stood up and went outside the door. It lay there in the back of the trap where last she saw Luke, unexpectedly small under the white sheet. 'He went down to meet his Mam at the bridge,' Job was sobbing. 'And I let him. Oh, why did I let him!'

'The bull was free,' said the man who led the pony. He held out his arms. 'You mustn't look. We heard his Mam screaming.'

Then Addie screamed again, tearing at the sheet which covered her son. 'For Christ's sake,' said the man with the pony; 'For Christ's sake!' He looked to them for help, and Job ran forward and caught at Addie's shoulders. 'Esther,' he pleaded; 'please help!' But the older woman, her face grey as ashes, tottered into the house, and in the first ring of silence they heard the weaker scream of the thrusting bolt which shut her cowering from them.

Guto Fewel

Three men and a woman were sitting in the black-raftered kitchen of Pen-rhiw-gwynt, which in English is Top of the Windy Ridge. As they sat, they discussed in low voices the life and misdeeds of Guto Fewel, who lay dying in the next room. The woman, a hard-faced woman, was his sister; the fattish man nearest the fire was her husband, who farmed the wind-scraped acres of the Rhiw. Their name was Mardith. The second man wore a minister's collar and had kept his overcoat on indoors; the third, a wizened creature at once abashed and ingratiating, sat with his cap on his knee. The minister was in his late twenties; the others had little rent to draw from three-score and five.

'I just been in to him,' said the woman, her lips thin and blue. 'It's good of Miss Mabli to sit with him, I must say. Well, it can't be long now.'

The minister's throat and mouth moved with something between a cough and a benediction. 'It has been a great burden—a great burden.'

'None can say we haven't done our share,' said Mardith. He looked round the fire-masked faces for approval. 'I reckon we done our duty by him. There's some as wouldn't have.'

The wizened man with the cap squirmed on his chair. 'He got a good friend in you, Mr. Mardith. I reckon you acted like a Christian all right.'

'There's many as wouldn't have,' said Mardith again. His heavy face soaked in their praises. 'I always been a God-fearing man, and be what he may, he's my wife's kin. I don't hold with him, I never did hold with him, but I know my duty as one Christian to another.'

'You have both been very kind,' said the minister. 'Is it—would it be three months now?'

'Come next Wednesday,' said the woman. 'We hadn't seen him to talk to for nigh on thirty years. You know how it was——' Her husband gestured with his arm, and the firelight flung the shadow of it against the wall behind him. 'All them goings on! We every one of us finished with him. We had to, him being the kind he was. And then three months come next Wednesday, what was to happen? I went out after tea to the milking, and there he was, hanging on the door-frame. I never said a word. But I knew him for all he was altered.' She shook her lean head. 'His sins had come home to roost all right. I never seen a man so changed. And I'd heard too—I'd heard he was changed these years it would be—yet I never expected——'

'He got a friend in you all right, Mrs. Mardith,' said the wizened man.

'She come back in,' said Mardith, 'as if she seen a ghost. "It's my brother," she said. "It's Guto." "Then he don't come over no threshold of mine," I told her. "Didn't I tell him, haven't I told him," I said, "that if ever I see him on my land again I'll set the dogs on him?" That was after that affair with the girl over in the Nant—you've heard of that, Mr. Gideon?—she went in the river for him, right enough.'

'A dreadful affair, dreadful!' murmured the minister.

'Ah,' said the wizened man, 'he was always one after the women. Glands, I reckon. Even when he was a kid——'

'So that's what I told her,' said Mardith. '"Don't bring no Guto of yours in here," those were my words. "I know," she said, "I know, but he's fallen on the floor outside. I'd hardly a-known him." "No more you'd expect to," I took her up. "A man that gives his life over to women and the drink. And I'll tell you another thing, my girl—it's a poor chance he stands to be known by One who is more important than you or me by long chalks." That's what I told her, Mr. Gideon.'

'No doubt, he had his points,' said the wizened man. 'There's good in the worst of us, eh, Mr. Gideon?'

'What happened then?' asked the minister. 'You brought him in?'

'I known life in my time, and I known death,' said Mardith. 'And I reckon I know my duty. But if ever I seen an old ram ready for the draft! "Well," I said, when I seen him, "if I know my two-times-two, I know something here too. And I'll tell you what it is, my girl—he's as good as a goner. And the miracle to me is that he's lasted so long. So there it is," I told her, "and you may as well face it. It's up to you," I said. "He's your brother, and I'll do what you say. For I wouldn't like it to be said as any of our lot, not the worst of them, died in the poor-house, and if you want to, and on one condition only, he can have his time out here.'"

'On one condition?' prompted the wizened man, though he had heard the story a dozen times already.

'I'm a farmer, Mr. Gideon. No la-di-da about me, but I make it pay. I don't give stable room to greasy-heeled horses, and there's no place in pen of mine for a maggoty wether. "So long," I said—and you understand me, Mr. Gideon—"so long as he *got nothing*, he can have my Christian duty.'"

'Ah,' nodded the wizened man, 'gallivantin' and all that.'

'He's my brother,' said the woman, 'but the truth's the truth. We all finished with him. At least, Dad finished with him, leathered him out of the house twice before the last time; and my sister Meri she finished with him; and Mardith and me we finished with him too. And if Mam had been alive, she'd have had to finish. But she went on before it grew too bad, and she was spared that much, thank God.'

The young minister drew a hand down his troubled face. 'It's a sad story. It is difficult to judge. If it is our business to judge. We may well leave it to the Tribunal before which he must soon appear.'

'Funny though,' said the wizened man, 'I never knew him mean.'

'You didn't now?' asked Mardith, with ox-like irony. 'I wonder what you call mean? P'raps they done wrong to put him in gaol that time? And p'raps he wasn't mean to that poor girl over in the Nant?'

'I was only thinking——'

'Some,' said Mrs. Mardith through her thin lips, 'ought to think twice before they say too much.'

The minister watched the fingers twist in the cap. 'I think

perhaps——' he interrupted. 'How old is your brother, Mrs. Mardith?'

'He was the youngest of us. I was working it out the other day. There was me the oldest, then Llew who went to America, then Meri, and Guto came the last. It's a terrible thing to say of your own flesh and blood, but I often heard my poor Dad vowing it would be better if he'd never been born.' She began to ramble from the question. 'He come of a good home, and good stock even if I say it, but something got in him, I don't know what.'

'The Gadarene swine like,' said the wizened man. 'When they rushed down-hill there he was, waiting at the bottom.' He wriggled further into the firelight for the minister's approval.

The minister glanced anxiously towards the door into the passage and the next room. 'I don't think we ought——'

'Ah, it's all right, never you worry, Mr. Gideon,' Mardith assured him. 'He can't hear, and if he did he wouldn't understand. He's just lying there, past everything. We don't have to bother. If there was any change, Miss Mabli would come out and tell us.'

'That's a good woman for you,' said the wizened man. 'That's a Christian if you like, minister.' He sat forward, squeezing his cap in exultation at the goodness of Miss Mabli, but as he encountered Mrs. Mardith's eye sat back again.

'She knows her duty all right,' admitted Mardith. 'And that's the sort of people I appreciate, Mr. Gideon. If we all done our duty always, the world would be a better place. That's what I told my wife that night. "If he's dying," I said, "it's different. We have a duty by him, be what he may. And on one condition——"'

'Yes, yes,' said the minister, and got to his feet. 'I am afraid, Mrs. Mardith, I must be going now.' His swollen shadow billowed up the wall and on to the ceiling. 'There is nothing I can do for your brother save pray for him.' They all stood as he closed his eyes and muttered more to himself than to them. 'And I have other calls. If I can be of service later——'

'You shall have the burying of him, never fear,' said Mardith. The minister flushed, catching up his hat from the table. 'We'll see him into Christian ground all right. I don't begrudge him.'

'Though there's many would,' said the wizened man. 'There

was good in him, no doubt, and bad. Only the tares strangled the wheat, that's about the size of it.'

'You talk too much,' said Mrs. Mardith loudly. 'We haven't lost our memories, thank you.' The wizened man screwed himself downwards to his chair, nodding sheepish good-nights after the departing minister. As Mardith sank the latch home, his wife took a yellow-edged cloth from the dresser drawer and shook it out over the table. 'He's a good man,' she said, 'but I thought he'd never go. It hampers a woman, and me with him in there hanging on as helpless as a child. If he was married he'd have more sense.'

'He means well,' said Mardith. He tapped his forehead. 'We can't all have it up here. And he's got a lot to learn. I suppose,' he continued sideways, winking at his wife, 'you won't be leaving before you take a bit of supper?'

The wizened man grinned between brazenness and shame. 'If it wouldn't be too much trouble, Mrs. Mardith—just a cup and a bite, p'raps.' He hastened to ingratiate himself. 'Now that Miss Mabli—any minister could learn a thing or two from her.' An indefinable but exciting edge came to his voice. 'You wouldn't think a woman like her would give the black of her nail to a feller like Guto. Her being so good, and him so bad.' He sighed. 'Not that any of us are perfect.'

The Mardiths looked one at the other. The wizened man was a famed repository of gossip: it was only right that he should earn his meal.

'No,' said Mardith, sitting to table, 'it wouldn't do for any of us mortals to claim to be perfect. There's an Eye that sees too much of us. Still,' he added invitingly, 'I reckon if there's ever been a middling perfect one around here, Miss Mabli might well be her. Eh?'

'I wouldn't want to hear nothing against her,' said Mrs. Mardith thinly. 'Nothing as wasn't true, that is.'

'I'd be the last to try a thing like that,' said the wizened man. He speared a pickled onion. 'But it's funny!'

'What's funny?' asked Mardith. 'Come on now, don't talk in riddles or we'll be thinking you got something to say against Miss Mabli. Here, have some cheese.'

'Ah,' said the wizened man, 'it's nothing.' Mrs. Mardith licked her lips, turning up the lamp. 'And it's so long ago. I don't know as I can rightly remember.'

'Not about Guto, is it?' asked Mrs. Mardith. She quietly closed the passage door. 'We don't want everybody knowing our business. Not even Miss Mabli. It wouldn't be our Guto, would it—and her?'

'No, no, fair play now,' cried the wizened man. 'But that's the worst of a smelly name—it draws the flies right enough. But there was never nothing like that—you can take your oath in heaven on it. No, it was just something I happened to notice once'—he let them wait on his words—'in Trisant.'

'Hm, down in the village?' Mardith pushed the butter-dish across the table. 'Go on, man, help yourself. We don't begrudge a man his vittles. In Trisant, eh?'

'But this'll surprise you,' said the wizened man. 'It was forty-six-seven years ago, I reckon, after fair-day. She's a fine woman to-day for her age. She's always been a fine woman——'

'If you like that style of woman,' said Mrs. Mardith, her eye like acid on her husband's face.

'She's big, there's no denying it,' said Mardith slowly. 'Heavy like.' He laughed uneasily, pillowing out his hands. 'I never liked them Flanders mares myself.'

'That's enough of that!' snapped Mrs. Mardith. 'That's no talk for a decent table.' But she was smiling as she turned to the wizened man. 'In Trisant, eh—after fair-day? I wouldn't want to hear no lies, remember.'

'If I tell a lie, Mrs. Mardith, may this mouthful choke me.' He swallowed, grinning. 'Remember young Richard Lewis of Steddfa? The one that left for the big job in England? It was the day after that fair in Trisant he went. He was a handsome young feller, there's no denying, and she was a handsome piece, ah, my word she was! I never—no offence, Mrs. Mardith—minded them big myself. It's different for Mr. Mardith, I can see.' He sniggered. 'Well, to cut a long story short, it was about nine that evening I had a reason to go round the back of the White Lion, and as a young lump of a feller will, if there's a light in a window and a crack in the curtain, he'll be sure to look in—and so I did. Now this is something I wouldn't tell to nobody else, and I know it'll go

no further than this table.' The Mardiths nodded. 'Who d'you
reckon was in that room? Yes, you got it, I can see: young Lewis
and Jane Mabli. Whether it's right for me to say any more before
Mrs. Mardith here, that's a question.'

'I'm a married woman, ain't I?' said Mrs. Mardith. 'I wasn't
born yesterday. Don't you worry about me.' Her tea was growing
cold, and she had forgotten to put milk in it. 'So long as it's the
truth. Were they—eh?'

'Not exactly,' said the wizened man. 'But very near to it.
Nearer than Christians ought to who haven't been before the
parson, if you take me, Mrs. Mardith.' He sucked in his lips,
savouring their attention. 'I reckon that kind of thing's just
putting yourself in the Devil's hand, and you can't wonder if the
fingers close in on you. But I'll say this for her: she wasn't having
any when he started to try his damnedest. She was as tall as him
and strong as a horse. I never,' he said cunningly, 'seen a woman
with such fine white shoulders on her.' More cunningly still, he
fell silent.

'What happened then?' asked Mardith. 'Wasn't he able to——'

'No,' said the wizened man regretfully, 'she was too strong
for him, I reckon, and in a blazing temper at the end. The fur flew
and away she went. But it was a fight all right, and if he'd looked
like winning I don't rightly know what I ought to have done.'

'You got to keep out of things like that,' said Mardith. 'Otherwise you grow like Guto there. It's bad though, that sort of
goings-on. I wish I'd been there!' But he felt the cut of his wife's
glance. 'I mean, to give him the belting he wanted. Young swine!'

'It's never mostly the man's fault,' said Mrs. Mardith angrily.
'She must have known what she was doing. I've often wondered
about her, and all the place singing her praises. I want to sift
this proper. Tell me,' she ordered, 'when you looked in—what
did you mean about her shoulders?'

'A cupper tea's a lovely thing,' said the wizened man, reaching
forward. 'Ah, thank you, thank you! I'll start at the beginning.
As I was saying——'

In the downstairs back room of Pen-rhiw-gwynt, Guto Fewel
was lying straight and silent down the middle of the third-best

bed. He lay on his back, his uncut hair and pale-whiskered face against a high pillow. The sheet had been turned down under his chin, and the bedclothes went with hardly a wrinkle from there to the foot of the bed. His mouth hung a little open, and from time to time he made a gasping contraction of the throat. He was in the early fifties, but was dying of exhaustion and old age. The creased blue lids had fallen over his eyes, and he lacked strength to lift them again.

He knew that he was dying. He knew too that he had no wish to live. He knew this in periods of suffused recollection welling like moonlight through the surrounding dark. He judged he was nearer death because the nightmares had ended. Or were they memories? In either case, they were terrible.

It seemed to him that he was speaking aloud and audible to all creation. There was an audience, unseen, unknown, to whom he was for ever recounting the story of his life. But he could not get past his first sentences, for these were so important he must repeat them again and again so that never a hearer but would understand. 'I have never been a child,' the voice was saying. 'They thought me a child like the rest, but I was born an old man. Why didn't they hide things from me? I saw everything. God, oh God in heaven, I saw everything! "He's only a child," they would say. "He won't notice—he won't understand." But I have never been a child. They thought me a child like the rest, but I was born an old man!' Surely he was not speaking now: he must be crying, shouting, babbling along the rivers and the hill-sides, his voice a vast compelling instrument of sorrow sounding his woes throughout the earth and the firmament. 'I have never been a child. Why didn't they hide from me their horrors and their lusts? Great God in heaven—for I was born an old man!'

The woman watching from her chair at the bed-end saw his mouth move and heard him gasp and swallow. She was a tall and powerful woman crumbling in age, the hair gone thin and white, the shoulders grown round, the heavy bosom fallen. I wonder, she thought, I wonder! He is dying an old man, and he twelve years younger than me, and his name a by-word over the country-side. 'Listen,' she said suddenly, urgently. 'Do you hear me?' But he made no stir, the lids hung crinkled and worn over the unseeing eyes. She sat straight up on her chair, her thoughts moving through nearly fifty years to the fair-day in Trisant when she last saw Richard Lewis and first saw Guto Fewel. The firm-set puritan mouth set harder. What madness had possessed her? 'I was on the edge of the Pit,' she whispered, and the Pit for her was real and seen, like a crack in the mountain-side, from which her feet drew frightenedly back. By the mercy of God it lasted but an evening. No one knew, she had come to tell herself; no harm was done, she had come to hope. A lifetime of good works, with little of her own happiness: she could think back to it without complacency, and if her conscience still charged her with a great fault, she had made no small atonement. But her face grew sterner yet, and self-accusing, as she watched the movements of Guto's throat. If only she might know!

Guto could hear his voice booming between earth and heaven. Each sentence he uttered filled centuries of time. The unseen listeners waited on new words to come. But the words would not come; always the revolution of his thoughts flung him back on those same tremendous sentences. An unendurable anxiety pierced him, to think that they might not hear the thing he had to say. Miss Mabli saw sweat wet his forehead, the eyelids twitched, there was a tremor in the bedclothes from his arms. She moved round the bed to wipe his face, and at that moment he opened his eyes.

How clear and sweet the evening was! He was almost light-headed as they went to fetch the pony and trap from the stable behind Trisant Cross. Oh so happy, he thought, so happy; closing his eyes as he hung on his mother's arm. The painted stallions galloped out of blackness into the yellow light, rose and sank on thick golden rods, their nostrils blew out blood and steam, and oily manes swung on their swelling necks. Flowers of tawny flame roared and trembled from the flare boxes, saturating the night with sweet and greasy perfumes; the air was a blare of red-and-white music. And there had been black-eyed, black-haired girls with long silver ear-rings coaxing wary young labourers to the rifle-range and cockshies; the swing-boats were rushing skywards with their screaming crews; on the edge of darkness a lion grumbled in his deep African throat. And when at last they left the smell and the glare of it, there was the magic street along which they walked past kings and princes and the executioners of the East. 'Happy?' he heard his mother ask, and rubbed his face along her camphored sleeve. Coming into the lamplit stable he stumbled and yawned and the smell of clean horses and polished leather washed his nose and mouth. Importantly he held on to a shaft while his father backed the pony in; he tightened a strap or two but his father went over these after him. They were ready to start when Miss Mabli came round from the Cross and asked whether they could take her home their way. He couldn't take his eyes from her face. He had never known a woman could be so tall and noble and worshipful. Her parents, she said, would grow anxious if she were not home soon, and after some politeness it was agreed that she and Guto should share the back of the loaded trap, and the others be in front. There was only the one seat and Guto must sit on the floor-boards. As she settled herself near him, her skirts brushed his face, warm, sweet-scented, and soft as doom.

Most of their way lay down the valley, and the pony settled briskly to his load. It had grown dark, there were stars but the moon was down; their lamps threw a weak brown light ahead of them. On the close-metalled winding road the pony's hoofs tapped out a gentle clop-clip, clip-clop. The hedgerows were a moving blur, but the tops of the tree-less hills showed hard against the faintly-twinkling sky. The night hazed, grew dream-like, his head nodded with the trap, soon he was leaning heavily against Miss Mabli, with his right arm thrown across her lap. It was then it started. He began to shiver with an excitement he dreaded but could not control, a shivering as much of his frightened soul as his body. He felt Miss Mabli stiffen and hold her breath unnaturally long. 'Push me away,' he wanted to pray, 'oh, push me away!' But: 'Are you cold?' she whispered and put her hand to his head and pressed it hard to her thigh. And then he felt the same soft shiverings in her. 'He's only a child,' the great voice intoned; 'he won't know—he won't understand.' But how terribly he knew the use to which he was being put, the fury of the appetite he must now satisfy. Why didn't they hide such things from me? The horrors and the lusts they made me see! Why could I not be a child like the rest?

He heard himself groan with ecstasy and grief. It was safe now to groan. But then, that night, all that happened happened in the unnatural silence of guilt, reaching up from the trap-floor to the stars. He was drowning in the memory of it, the warm musky smell of the night and the lavender of her petticoats, the feel of the soft flannel and the softer flesh. And through the silence that guarded them from his parents he heard still the crunch of the wheels on a gravelly corner, the hoof-clops of the horse, the pantings of her breath.

'Listen,' said Miss Mabli. 'Can you hear me?'

All my life, he was crying aloud, all my life it was so. What could I do? I had seen, I knew too much. And at that age, at that moment, I lay as in the embraces of Eve. God, he shouted, oh God, have pity on me! I have never been a child. They thought me a child, but I was born an old man.

He was back in the trap. The woman, watching, saw the pillow darkening with sweat, the death-rattle had begun in his throat. I should call the others, she thought; but she did not move. His eyes opened again, but she could read nothing into them. 'Can you hear me?' she asked again, in a whisper.

The wheels were whining over the hard roadway, the hedgerows fled into the dark. Below them the earth, above them the heavens, streamed backwards to the void. He felt himself and Miss Mabli caught up in the rhythm that rolled the planets and swung the tides. This is death, he thought, and longed for it. Her limbs opened for him, he was floundering in seas of bliss and pain. I was born an old man, he mumbled, and I die as a child. Oh God, have pity! Give me rest and the dark.

And then he was falling into untellable depths, and the dark was all about him.

Miss Mabli came out into the kitchen. Their shadowed faces turned up at her, curious, furtive, hostile. 'He is dead,' she said harshly. 'I shall never forgive myself.'

'Don't you worry,' said Mardith, but his wife's face was snaky with pleasure and malice. 'We all make mistakes at times,' she said. 'All of us, Miss Mabli.'

'I was sitting there,' said Miss Mabli, 'and then it had happened.

I should have been more careful.' She's grown an older woman, thought the wizened man. 'I am much to blame.'

'Times when we all ought to be more careful,' said Mrs. Mardith. 'Even the so-called best of us.'

'They say Death pays for all,' said the wizened man, mocking all three of them.

'Only some,' pursued Mrs. Mardith, 'gets away with it better than others.'

'No one can say we didn't do our duty by him,' said Mardith. 'But it's out of our hands now.' His glances slimed her. 'Life,' he speculated, 'is a very funny thing.'

Miss Mabli moved heavily to the door. Her face was working. 'I shall never forgive myself,' she said again, brokenly. And with that she was gone from among them.

The men nodding, the woman smiling, the three who remained went into the back room, and Mardith took a clean white scarf from where it lay against the big Bible. 'The Lord's been kind,' he told them, tying up the dead man's jaws. 'It's a good riddance, I reckon. I seen many an old tup look just like him.' For once he over-rode his wife. 'He's a goner, ain't he? He can't hear, and if he did,' he added, knotting the scarf, 'he couldn't answer back.'

'Now what makes some good?' asked the wizened man, smarming the Mardiths. He looked at Guto Fewel. 'And what makes some bad?'

'He was bad from the start,' said Mrs. Mardith. 'He never was a child like you and me. And he's died an old, old man.'

'Old he might be, and wicked he was,' said her husband. He took up the night-light, motioning them out before him. 'But he can't be needing this any more.' And nipping the still flame, and leaving Guto Fewel in silence and the dark, they returned with relish to their talk in the firelit, shadow-filled kitchen.

Shacki Thomas

Shacki Thomas was fifty-two, shortish, and bandy from working underground. Unemployment was straitening his means but could do nothing with his legs. But play the white man, he would say—though I'm bandy, I'm straight. It was his one witticism, and he was not using it so frequently now that his missis was in hospital.

He was going to see her this afternoon. He gave a two-handed pluck at his white silk muffler, a tug at the broken nose of his tweed cap, and so went out the back way to the street slanting sharply from High Street to the river. The houses were part soft stone, part yellow brick, and grimy; the roadway between them was decorated with dogs and children and three new-painted lamp-posts, and each parlour window showed a china flower-pot nesting an aspidistra or rock fern. He passed his own window, and saw that the fern was doing famous, though he'd forgotten to water it since Gwenny—oh, Gwenny, Gwenny, he was saying, if only you was home in our house again!

Twenty yards in front he saw Jinkins the Oil and hurried to catch him up. Owbe, they said.

''Orse gets more human every day,' said Jinkins from the cart, and to forget his troubles Shacki made a long speech, addressing the horse's hindquarters:

'Some horses is marvellous. Pony I used to know underground, see—you never seen nothing like that pony at the end of a shift. Used to rip down the road, mun, if there'd a-been anything in the way he'd a-hit his brains out ten times over. Intelligent, Mr. Jinkins? You never seen nothing like him!'

As they approached the railway bridge, the two-ten to Cwm-cawl went whitely over. The horse raised his head.

'Now, now, you old fool,' cried Jinkins. 'It's under you got to

go, not over.' He turned to Shacki and apologized for the dumb
creature. ''Orse do get more human every day, see.'

But Shacki couldn't laugh. It was Gwenny, Gwenny, if only
you was home with me, my gel; and fear was gnawing him,
wormlike.

Turning away beyond the bridge into High Street, he found
the old sweats around the cenotaph. For a minute or two he
would take his place in the congregation. A lady angel spread
her wings over them, but her eyes were fixed on the door of the
Griffin opposite. GWELL ANGAU NA CHYWILYDD said the inscrip-
tion. 'Better death than dishonour'; and as Shacki arrived, the
conversation was of death. 'I once hear tell,' said Ianto Evans,
'about a farmer in the Vale who quarrelled summut shocking
with his daughter after his old woman died. Well, p'raps she
gave him arsenic—I donno nothing 'bout that—but he went off
at last, and they stuck him in the deep hole and went back to hear
the will. Lawyer chap, all chops and whiskers like a balled tomcat,
he reads it out, and everything in the safe goes to Mary Anne and
the other stuff to his sister. So they has a look at the safe, and what's
inside it? Sweet fanny adams, boys, that's what.' By pointing a
finger at him, Ianto brought Shacki into his audience. '"And
what'll you do with the safe, my pretty?" asks the sister—like
sugar on lemon, so I hear. Mary Anne thinks a bit and then brings
it out very slow. "If it wasn't for my poor old mam as is in heaven,"
she says, "I'd stick it up over the old tike for a tombstone".' He
scratched his big nose. 'What's think of that, uh?'

His brother Ivor picked his teeth. 'Funny things do happen at
funerals. I once heard tell about a chap as travelled from Wrexham
to the Rhondda to spit into another chap's grave.'

'Might a-brought the flowers up,' said Ianto.

'No, not this chap's spit wouldn't.'

'I mean, there's spit and spit,' said Tommy Sayce. 'I mean,
f'rinstance——.' A moist starfish splashed on the dust, and he
changed the subject. 'How's the missis, Shacki?'

Shacki looked from Ivor to the lady angel, but she was intent
on the Griffin. 'Thass what I going to see, chaps. Fine I do hope,
ay.'

They all hoped so, and confessed as much. But they were all

fools, and the worm fear was at Shacki's heart like a maggot in
a swede. 'I got to go this afternoon, see,' he said, hoping for a
chorus of reassurance and brave words, but—'I remember'—
Tommy Sayce took up the tale—'when little Sammy Jones had
his leg took off at the hip. "How do a chap with only one peg
on him get about, doctor?" he asks old Dr. Combes. "Why,
mun," doctor tells him, "we'll get you a nice wooden leg,
Sammy." "Ay, but will I be safe with him, doctor?" asks Sammy.
"Safe? Good God, mun, you'll be timber right to the face!"
Thass what doctor told him.'

'Ah, they'm marvellous places, them hospitals,' Shacki assured
them, to assure himself at the same time. 'Look at the good they
do do.'

'Ay, and look at the good they don't do! Didn't they let
Johnny James's mam out 'cos she had cancer and they was too
dull to cure it? And Johnny thinking she was better—the
devils!'

The worm went ahead with his tunnelling. 'I carn stop,
anyway,' said Shacki, and low-spiritedly he left them to their
talk. Not fifty yards away he cursed them bitterly. Death, death,
death, cancer, cancer, cancer—by God, he'd like to see that
big-nosed bastard Ianto Evans on his back there, and that brother
of his, and Tommy Sayce, and every other knackerpant as hadn't
more feeling than a tram of rippings. From the bend of the street
he looked back and saw the lady angel's head and benedictory
right arm and cursed her too, the scut of hell, the flat-faced sow she
was! Nobody have pain, or everybody—that was the thing. He
cleared his throat savagely and spat into the gutter as though
between the eyes of the world. Self-pity for his loneliness brought
too big a lump to his throat before he could curse again, and then
once more it was all Gwenny fach, oh, Gwenny fach; he'd like
to tear the sky in pieces to get her home again. If only she was
better, if only she was home, he'd do the washing, he'd blacklead
the grate, he'd scrub through every day, he'd water that fern the
minute he got back—he was shaking his head in disgust. Ay,
he was a fine one, he was.

Then he went into the greengrocer's, where the air smelled so
much a pound.

'Nice bunch of chrysanths,' he was offered, but they were white and he rejected them. 'I ain't enamelled of them white ones. Something with a bit of colour, look.'

He bought a bunch of flowers and three fresh eggs for a shilling and fivepence, and carried them as carefully as one-tenth his dole deserved to the Red Lion bus stop. Soon the bus came, chocolate and white, with chromium fittings. He found the conductor struggling with a small table brought on by a hill farm-woman at the Deri. 'Watch my eggs, butty,' he begged, and stood on the step till at last they fixed it in the gangway, where it lay on its back with its legs up in the air like a live thing gone dead. Through the back window Shacki saw a youngster running after the bus. 'Oi, mate——' 'Behind time,' said the conductor hotly. 'This here blasted table——.' He came for his fare and to mutter to Shacki. 'I never had this woman on board yet she hadn't a table or a hantimacassar or a chest in drawers or a frail of pickled onions or summut. Moving by instalments I reckon she is, or doing a moonlight flit. Iss a 'ell of a life this!'

As the bus went on up the valley, Shacki made a gloomy attempt to put in proper order what he had to tell Gwenny. The house was going on fine, he himself was feeling in the pink, there was a new baby at number five, he'd watered the fern—and he must tell her summut cheerful. Like what Jinkins said to the horse, and this here conductor chap—proper devil-may-care this conductor, you could see that with half an eye. Near Pensarn he saw lime on the bulging fields, like salt on a fat woman's lap. The grass under it looked the colour of a sick dog's nose. He saw farming as a thin-lined circle. If you hadn't the grass, you couldn't feed the beasts; if you couldn't feed the beasts, you didn't get manure; if you didn't get manure, you had to buy fertilizer—which brought you back to grass. All flesh is grass, he heard the preacher say, and all the goodliness thereof is as the flower of the field. The grass withereth, the flower fadeth—duw, duw, what a thought! It made a fellow think, indeed now it did. Yesterday a kid, today a man of fifty, to-morrow they're buying you eight pound ten's worth of elm with brass handles. Oh, death, death, death, and in life pain and trouble—away, away, the wall of his belly trembled with the trembling of the bus, and the worm drove a roadway through his heart.

At Pensarn a girl stood at the bus stop and said: 'Did a young man leave a message for me at the Red Lion?'

'Yes, my dear,' said the conductor. 'He told me special you was to let me give you a nice kiss.'

'Cheeky flamer!' said the hill farm-woman, but the girl looked down in the mouth, and Shacki felt sorry for her. He explained that a young man had run after the bus at the Red Lion. Ay, he did rather fancy he was a fairish sort of chap 'bout as big as the conductor, so—— 'It must a-been Harry,' the girl concluded. 'Thank you,' said Shacki, as though she had done him a favour. Indeed, she had, for he could talk about this to Gwenny.

Later a collier got on. 'Where you been then?' the conductor asked. 'Why you so dirty, mun?'

'I been picking you a bag of nuts.' He took the conductor's measurements, aggressively. 'Monkey nuts,' he added. He did not enter the bus and sit down, but stood on the step for his twopenny ride. 'We got to draw the line somewhere,' the conductor pointed out.

Shacki was cheered by the undoubted circumstance that all the wit of the Goytre Valley was being poured out for his and Gwenny's benefit. What Jinkins said about the horse now. And this about the nuts——. And that gel at Pensarn! What funny chaps there was about if you only came to think of it. He began to think hard, hoping for a witticism of his own, a personal offering for Gwenny. She had heard the bandy-straight one before, just once or twice or fifty times or a hundred, or maybe oftener than that. Something new was wanted. A fellow like this conductor, of course, he could turn them off like lightning. Here he was, looking at the flowers. Shacki waited for his sally. They were his flowers, weren't they? Diawl, anything said about um was as good as his, too.

'I likes a nice lily, myself,' said the conductor.

'You look more you'd like a nice pansy,' said the collier. He grinned, the slaver glistening on his red gums, and winked at the hill farm-woman. 'Cheeky flamer!' she called him.

'You askin' for a fight? 'Cos if you are——'

'Sorry, can't stop now.' Still grinning, he narrowed his coaly eyes. 'But any time you want me, butty, I'm Jack Powell, Mutton Tump. That's me—Jack Powell.' He prepared to drop off, and the conductor kept his finger on the bell, hoping to fetch him a cropper. 'Oh no, you don't, butty!' They heard his nailed boots braking on the road and then through the back window saw him fall away behind them, his knees jerking very fast. 'I'll be up here Sunday,' threatened the conductor, but Shacki didn't believe him. He'd lay two-to-one Jack Powell any day, and was glad a collier could lick a bus conductor.

'Don't forget to stop at the hospital,' he said by way of reminder, and the conductor, as though to recover face, told a tale about the patient who wouldn't take a black draught unless the sister took one too. To please him, Shacki smiled grimly and wagged his head and said what chaps there was about, but he now thought less highly of the humorist, and as they came nearer the stopping place he could feel that same old disturbance, just as though he wanted to go out the back. Bump, bump, bump, the driver must be doing it deliberate, but try to forget, for he might be going to hear good news. She might even be coming home. He grovelled. Home, like Johnny James's mother, hopeless case, cancer of the womb—not that for you, Gwenny fach, he prayed, and Ianto Evans, for speaking of it, he thrust into the devil's baking oven. Bump, bump, bump, if he didn't get off this bus soon he'd be all turned up, only too sure. He felt rotten in the belly, and the worm turned a new heading in his heart.

He alighted.

Inside the hall, he found from the clock that as usual he was five minutes too early for the women's ward. 'Would you like to see anyone in the men's ward?' He thought he would, if only to pass the time. So down the corridor he went, for it was a tiny hospital, run on the pennies of colliers like himself. The men's ward had a wireless set, and the patients were a lively lot. Bill Williams the Cwm borrowed Shacki's flowers. 'Oi, Nurse,' he shouted, ''ow'll I look with a bunch of these on my chest?'

It was the sporty probationer. 'Like a big fat pig with a happle in his mouth,' she suggested.

'There's a fine bloody thing to say, Nurse! Don't I look better'n a pig, boys?'

'Ay,' said Shacki, thinking of the flowers of the field. 'You looks like a lily in the mouth of 'ell.'

Bill started to laugh, and the other men started to laugh, and, seeing this, Shacki became quite convulsed at his second witticism. The blue small coal pitting his face grew less noticeable as his scars grew redder. It was a laugh to do a man's heart good, and it came down on that tunnelling worm like a hob-nailed boot. 'You'll have matron along,' the probationer warned them.

Then Shacki took his flowers from Bill, and grinning all over his face went back through the corridor to the entrance hall. He'd make his lovely gel laugh an' all! He felt fine now, he did, and everything was going to be all right. He knew it. Tell her he'd cleaned the house, and about the baby at number five, and about Jinkins and the collier and the girl and the conductor and Bill Williams the Cwm and him—it'd be better than a circus for Gwenny.

Into the women's ward. Nod here, nod there, straight across to Gwenny with all the news between his teeth and his tongue. Then he swore under his breath. Matron was standing by Gwenny's bed, looking like a change of pillow-cases. She was so clean and stiff and starched and grand that he felt small and mean and shabby before her, and frightened, and something of a fool. Respectfully, he greeted her even before he greeted his wife, and when she returned his good day, thanked her.

'We've got good news for you, Mr. Thomas. You'll be able to have Mrs. Thomas home very soon now.'

'Oh,' he said. He was looking down at Gwenny's white smile. A murderous hate and rage against all living things filled his heart, and he would have had no one free of suffering. ''Cos she's better?'

'Of course. Why else?'

He put the eggs down carefully, and the flowers. Then he fell on his knees at the bedside. 'My gel!' he cried out hoarsely. 'Oh, my lovely gel!' With her right hand she touched his hair. 'There, there, little Shacki bach! Don't take on, look!'

'You are upsetting the patient,' the pillow-case said severely, 'and you are disturbing the ward. I shall have to ask you to go outside.'

It was a quarter of a minute before he got to his feet, and then he was ashamed to look anyone in the face. He snuffled a bit and rubbed under his eyes. 'All right, matron,' he managed to say. 'You can send for the pleece, if you like. I'm that happy, mun!'

He saw his old Gwenny looking an absolute picture there in bed, and thought these would be her last tears, and such happy ones. And with the thought he looked proudly around, and could tell that no one in the ward thought him an old softy. He didn't hate anyone any longer. He was all love, and gave old Gwenny a kiss as bold as brass before he walked outside. He knew they'd let him in again soon.

Kittens

She wasn't waiting at the corner. He halted at the edge of the pavement, peering anxiously to and fro, and then saw her white glove beckon from shadow. He crossed over, his relief still tinged with uneasiness, touched the brim of his hat. 'Hullo,' he said, 'hullo, Glenys.' She was shorter than he, just the loving height, between slender and thin. Her mouth and eyes blotched her face viola-fashion, the smooth contours of her cheeks fell through a shallow curve to a slightly blunted chin, the nose was pretty, straight-bridged, and in harmony with the chin, a little squared at the nostrils. The nicest face in the world, for someone else's sweetheart. Her costume was dark, black it looked to him, she had a silver-fox stole loosely on her shoulders, her blouse like her gloves was white—he could see it gleaming, and the big buttons with the flower pattern on them—his eyes kept returning to them. That she was older than he pleased and flattered him, as he was pleased and flattered by her make-up, her clothes, her style, by all that made her different from the girls and women of the village. She belonged to a setting of advertisements, shop windows, motor cars, men dressed like bank managers, and this flattered him most of all. And yet, he thought, I'm here with her. Of all the men about here I'm the one. The one she chose.

'Been waiting, Morri?' Her voice too was different; a voice with class. His tongue felt fat and loose when he began to talk.

No, no, he said. Not he. Only a minute, anyway. 'Had to call in the Institute,' he told her, watching her face. 'See the team for Saturday, you know.'

'You'll be playing?'

'Got to.' It wasn't a pressing question, but it gave him something to say as he took her arm. 'Shove um right off the field without me. Strength in the middle to hold um, see.'

'Oh, I know. And you are terribly strong, Morri, aren't you?'

'Oh I donno. Average, about.'

She looked up into his face as they passed the hanging light where the mountain road starts its climb. He was a haulier from the Red Vein, hardly more than twenty, well-clamped and supple. Between the temples his face was white and broad, but it narrowed downwards like an axe-head; his hair was black and oiled; she saw his jaw glistening from too close a shave. His eyelashes were longer and softer than her own, his eyes like black fur. She smiled, approving him.

As he smiled back she squeezed his arm into the soft of her side. 'More than average, Morri. Why, just feel this arm!'

'Ah,' he said, and halted. He grinned, rather sheepishly. 'Feel that, Glenys.' He guided her hand to his biceps, flexing slowly and powerfully, till her fingers were clipped between his fore and upper arm. 'Try and get away, uh?'

But with admiration and a squeal she failed. He dilated with mastery and pride and moved his shoulders happily inside his coat. 'What a strong arm!' she praised, and moved gently and as it were by accident, so that the arm was behind her back and then crooked about her waist. As they walked on, up the sunken road, her head was against his shoulder, and his nostrils snuffed the dry exciting smell of her hair and the fox stole. Soon they were past the quarry, and without a word said left the road and leaned for a while on the fence that led to Bryn-Eithin. Below them, swung in an arc, they could see the lights of three villages, and linking these the road and railway spattered with red and yellow. Down in the valley bottom were the smudged lamps of the Red Vein collieries, those in the sidings winking and blinking as the trucks were shunted into long clanking lines. All this din of wheels and brakes and line-points came to them thin and silvered across a hillside of gorse and fern, as much a part of the place as the yelp of a dog from Bryn-Eithin or an owl hooting from the Penllwyn wood. Over against them, in the next valley, the Court Mawr steelworks troubled the dark, and suddenly they saw a vast red surging behind the clouds as fire died upwards from the jaws of the ovens. As the darkness thickened again, 'Look,' she said, and pointed to the way they had come, the unlit tunnel of the sunken road.

'What, Glenys?'

'It's horrid!' She turned quickly to face the trembling sky over Court Mawr. 'All that dark—and the quiet—and the things there may be in it——'

But to him the dark was friendly. 'You wouldn't do underground, Glenys.'

'No,' she said grimly. 'I wouldn't.' She pressed against him.

He fell silent, for a moment oppressed by things he couldn't understand. This down she had on the valley, which seemed so good to him——. But there, she was different—that was the fine thing about her. He drew her to him, holding her clumsily, his hands moving irresolutely over her back as though afraid of crushing her.

'I'm glad I met you, Morri. I couldn't have stuck it out here after Cardiff if I hadn't.' She pulled at his lapel. 'It's the one thing I'm sorry about, going——'

'To-night, Glenys?'

'I've got to. I must catch the twelve-ten down. You know how it is.'

He broke in. 'I've brought it, Glenys.'

'I'm terribly ashamed, Morri, taking it. It's awful for a girl to have to do. And if dad knew——'

'He don't have to. Nobody don't.'

'You're a lovely boy, Morri.'

'That's all right, Glenys. You'd better——' He released her, fumbled in his pocket for his wallet. There was a thin sheaf of notes in it, held by elastic, which he handed over without counting.

'I'll pay it back, every penny. And the other.'

'That's all right,' he said again, dry-mouthed, watching her put it safe in her handbag. 'Glad I had it, Glenys.'

'As soon as I saw you I knew you were the real man around here. There was something as soon as I set eyes on you. I knew.'

'No,' he muttered, 'I'm not much really. Haulier, you know. Not a bad job, mind—still——'

She began to tell him how fine he was, how generous, and again how strong. Her stole, heavy with scent, brushed his underjaw, and with it he could smell the untamed animal odour of the fur itself. 'I've got to go, Morri—you can see that—with dad the way he is. He doesn't understand me. He never has. No one ever did about here. I know how they talk. They think it wicked for a girl to look nice and want something better than around here.' She checked on her mistake, but he had noticed nothing. 'He'd kill me if he knew I'd taken money from a man—from you, Morri. You won't tell, will you?'

'No,' he said, 'no.'

'And you'll come down and see me?'

'Regular, Glenys—often as I can.'

'Any time you want to, Morri. If you don't forget me. You may, Morri. These other girls about here'—her voice changed, began to throb through him, '—you must be awful with them, I'm sure, a boy like you. Aren't you?'

He was torn between truth and vanity. 'It's you, Glenys.' he blurted, 'it's you are the one.' And he spoke truth. Her looks, her clothes, her maturity struck at something in him deeper than vanity. She was music to him, and singing, and poetry.

She took his face in her hands and kissed him. 'Nice Morri!' But her mind was still full of the money he had given her. 'I'll be on my feet in a couple of months, easy. I'll have a nice little flat, I expect. Nothing'll ever be too good for you with me, Morri.' Her thin fingers stroked his hair. 'You're a real man, Morri—the only one around here. You're different—anyone can see that.'

'Glenys,' he said, 'Glenys!'

His voice, his face, his hands were to her pages read and known. Centred in her brain was the icy spiral of calculation, but this did not stop her growing excited, confused, sentimental.

'Glenys!' he cried hoarsely.

'No, dear,' she whispered, trying to break from him. 'Please, Morri!' Then her nails tore his wrist with the violence of fire. 'Morri, you mustn't!'

'Why not, Glenys? Damn it all——'

'Because you lent me the money? Let me go, will you!' She struggled from him, her handbag falling to the ground. 'I didn't think you'd do a thing like that. If I've been nice to you it wasn't because of the money.' He bent, humiliated and tormented, but she was before him, straightening again, making show to unclip her bag. 'You'd better take it back, if that's the way you feel about me.'

'No,' he said ashamedly, 'I wouldn't take it. Glenys—don't be angry. I didn't mean anything, honest I didn't.' He drew her to him again, patted her shoulder, abasing himself, yet with it all feeling cheated and desperate. 'Don't be angry, there's a girl. I didn't mean anything, honest now.' She was so weak compared with him, her bones like pipestems under the silky flesh, that his desire suddenly melted into compassion. 'So small,' he said, 'so little, mun. I donno my own strength. I'd do anything for you, Glenys, honest I would.'

'And I'd do anything for you, Morri, so long as you didn't think it was because of the money. You're the dearest boy I ever met. Hold me again, Morri. Hold me closer! And kiss me, to show——' But he was glum, baffled, half-hearted, his arms were slack and heavy. She pressed her lips to his, at first acting a part, but soon taking fire from his brute strength. 'If it wasn't that you thought it because of the money,' she prompted. 'Please say it, Morri.'

The thought troubled him. Had it been the money?

'Please say it, Morri.'

'It wasn't the money,' he said, and hid his face in her hair.

'Because I'd be common then, wouldn't I? If you're a nice girl, it's very hard——but I should have known with you, Morri.' Honour satisfied, her handbag safe, she encouraged his caresses; above them the sky trembled and glowed, and he saw the white of her skin flush with rose. Something in her expression shocked him even in the flood-tide of passion, but she spoke. 'Look, Morri, you see—I'll do anything to make you happy!'

It was a little after eleven when he reached home. His brother was not yet off the afternoon shift. His aunt, who looked after the two of them, had set his supper alongside his brother's under a clean teacloth, and was still darning by the fire. She was a dry-tongued, cold-faced collier's widow. He was slightly afraid of her. But to-night he greeted her off-hand, for after all her day was over, then wetted the tea from the kettle on the hob, and sat to table. Straightway the black-and-white kitten by his aunt's side came over to claw at his leg, and he lifted her up. 'Goh,' he breathed, 'like little toy bones!' He could feel them no thicker than pipestems under the silky fur. At the thought his eyes glowed, and his aunt, watching, saw his lips move.

'Been drinkin'?' she asked sharply.

'No.'

She twitched at her wool. 'Been mashin' then?' The edging of contempt offended him, but he wasn't braced for anger. Instead, his eyes lit up again under their long black lashes. 'And who's the lucky lady?' she asked. His silence irritated her. 'Or is it a secret? P'raps I could make a guess.' Ostentatiously he yawned, but she struck off a name on her little finger. 'It wouldn't be Gwen Vaughan now, would it?'

'Her?' He smoothed his thighs, good-humouredly. 'Chair-legs!'

'No, no, it wouldn't be Gwen—and of course she's sweet on that Thomas boy. Now would it be Mildred Lewis, I wonder?'

He yawned again. 'She's waiting for the whistle, I don't doubt.'

'Ay, but is it your whistle, Morri?' She was a cunning woman who made her approaches by indirection. She now struck down a third finger. 'Or it might be Mrs. Colonel James's daughter from the Mansion who's waiting for the whistle. P'raps you went for a ride to-night in the Colonel's Rolls Royce, was it, Morri?'

'Ah, cut it out!'

'No, somehow I don't think it was Miss Colonel James. Then there's—' her voice cut like glass, '—it wouldn't be that fly piece of Hugh Bowen's, I suppose?'

'No harm in s'posin'.'

'You fool, Morri!'

'Think so?' Again his eyes glowed, his hands opened and clenched and then lay open.

'What sort of good is she to you—a piece like that? All high heels and a bit of fur round her neck—and scent! Her old man out of work these ten years and more—I'd like to know where she gets things from.'

'Then why the hell don't you ask her?' he flashed.

'I don't have to.' He looked up, startled. 'There've been trade over that counter since Eve's day. And there's no need for language.'

For a moment he looked like flying into a rage. Instead: 'What's a hell or two among friends?' he said roughly, and flung his collar and tie to the sideboard behind him. He felt clawings at his trouser leg, and was relieved to be able to swing the kitten up to his shoulder. *Mm-mm-mmrr-mmrr-mmrr*, she went, and bit gingerly at his ear. Her fragility moved him to an ecstasy of strength and protection. As her fur brushed his underjaw and he could smell the queer animal smell, he breathed hard; his eyes smouldered. They know, he thought, they know the ones they like; they know the real men.

'Old enough to be your mother,' said his aunt.

He jumped up, shouting. 'For Christ's sake will you keep your tongue off her!' She stood up to brazen it out, but for the first time in her life was afraid of him. 'You've got your old man's temper,' she said slowly; 'and look what that done for him. I thought you had more sense.' She sat down again, began to put away her darning. His hands unclenched, his jaws slackened. 'All right,' he said unsteadily. 'All right then. Only shut your mouth.'

His aunt was nodding her disgust when they heard the scrape of boots on the bailey and the double stroke of the latch. His brother Mog came in, black-faced, red-lipped, and with whitey rings under his eyes. He was a brisk-moving man, and just now his coaldust lent him the lugubrious mask of a nigger minstrel. He dropped his cap inside the fireguard. 'Ay, ay,' he said cheerfully.

'I'm off to bed,' said his aunt. 'Everything's ready on the table.'

'Okeydoke.'

At the passage she turned, defiantly. 'And you might try to put some sense into this brother of yours.'

Mog grimaced. 'Uh-uh?' He started to eat, and supped tea noisily. He was six years older than his brother. 'Whass the fuss?'

'Nothing,' said Morri. He picked up the kitten. It might as well come out this way as any other. 'She been on to me, the old fool——'

'Oi, oi!' Mog was shocked.

'Gabbling. Been on to me 'bout girls. As though I'd give a

brass tack for any girl 'bout here.' His tongue ran inevitably to
the one name. 'Talking about Glenys Bowen—you know.'

Mog stopped chewing, his mouth overfull. 'You haven't——'

He stroked the kitten. He could feel rage rising in him again.
By god, they had only to say——

'I'm askin' you!'

'No,' he said sullenly. Something in Mog's tone made him
strengthen the lie. 'Catch me!'

Mog reached for his mug. 'Okeydoke.'

'Anyhow—why?'

'Heard to-night from whassisname up Top Row—Dai Jinkins
—that's him—she've took best part of ten quid from that butty
of his—that left-handed feller, whassisname.'

His hard fingers closed like gates around the kitten. She
squealed and her claws ripped his wrist. 'More fool you,' said
Mog, as Morri watched a pinhead of blood fill the deep end of
each scratch. Under the scratches he saw other abrasions and one
long pale weal running back to his cuff. Well——

'And thass not all. Poor flamer!' Mog's nigger minstrel eyes
rolled and then rested on the big black Bible on the sideboard.
'She's the Scarlet Woman on the White Horse, and the Sixth
Plague that plagued Egypt. Boyo, she's the Fire that Burns.'

'Meaning?'

His lips were nearing the scratches when Mog's answer sickened
him. He drew his wrist away. 'So you been lucky, Morri.' 'Ay,'
he said after a moment, 'I been lucky.'

Mog stared over his shoulder. 'Sure?'

'I said, didn't I!'

'Okeydoke, da iawn!' He watched Mog untie his thongs and
shake the grit from under his knees. So this has happened to me,
he was thinking; no one can do anything for me, and to-night
she'll go to Cardiff and that'll be the end. He saw Mog glance
at him again, uneasily, and hated his brother. He was glad when
he went upstairs for his bath. For a while he sat on, looking at his
wrist. When at last he knew what he must do it was a quarter to
twelve. She would be catching the train the next station up: he
would join her at the Red Vein halt. He didn't move till he felt the
kitten clawing at his leg.

When Mog came downstairs after bathing he found the room empty and the door ajar. He was worried, but closed the door, sat down, and lit a fag-end. He was at the end of his smoke when he noticed the kitten under the table. He picked her up, but she was dead. Blood and froth were about her mouth and nostrils, her bones yielded everywhere under his hands.

'Morri?' he whispered. 'For Christ's sake, Morri!'

He hurried to the door and stood listening, watching. He could hear the waggons being shunted into the Red Vein sidings, and the sky filled with blood as they fed the ovens at Court Mawr. 'Where are you, our kid?'

He tugged on his boots and was crossing the bailey when he heard the twelve-ten for Cardiff pull out of the halt. Soon it passed him, slithering on the down gradient. It whistled, one long shrill blast, and slid into the Penllwyn tunnel.

The whistle hung on the air like a shriek. 'Oh, Morri,' he cried softly, 'where are you? Where are you, our kid?'

Ora Pro Boscis

For Sir Rhodri Plas Mawr it was the best of Friday mornings. Not because the sun was shining and the wind blowing, not because Bessi the Blaen had the evening before littered four healthy puppies, not even because he owned all he saw. He caressed his vast nose and said 'Ah!' He was happy and excited both, like a dog rolling on a dead mouse. It was court day.

He'd show 'em! By jumping george, he'd show 'em! Lot of thieves picking over his land, huh. The rabbits they'd got away with would load a gambo, and the birds—his face lost its smile—his lovely birds—it was worse than murder. His lovely shiny-breasted birds tied up in sacks, and all to pack a poacher's belly. 'Worse than murder!' he grunted.

'Yessir,' said the maid, clearing his breakfast tray.

His mouth opened, but he shut it again without a word. In the shadow of Sir Rhodri's nose it looked like a lead mine under Snowdon. Not that the nose was uncomely. For a man twice his size it would be perfection. It had line and rhythm and character, and when he blew it it had tone. And though ashamed of it as a lad, as a man he was not dissatisfied. It marked him out in a crowd, gave folk something to remember him by, and he thought it patrician. Not a collier's nose, he used to tell himself, and others; not a grocer's nose, and they didn't grow that way on dustmen or duns. A virile organ, he had been assured.

'Well?' he asked the girl.

'Mr. Bevan is downstairs to see you, sir.'

'Couldn't you say so at once? Tell him fifteen minutes.' He wanted a word with Bevan. Right enough to point out that his place on the bench was best left empty—after all, he hadn't sat a dozen times in as many years, just now and again when for the look of the thing he paid a visit to Plas Mawr—and justice was justice, neither for rent nor rape, quite right. But Bevan's hints that he'd better stay away altogether—.He blew his nose hard, and those below remembered the Last Trump.

'Morning, Bevan.'

'Morning, Sir Rhodri.' A poor little squit of a fellow, Bevan, no more to him than a row of spring cabbage.

'Sorry to keep you waiting. Lovely morning, Bevan. And a great occasion.'

'As you say, Sir Rhodri.'

'I hope the Bench will make this a lesson to the whole neighbourhood. This—what's the chap's name?'

'Thomas Thomas.'

'Thomas Thomas—ah!'

'They call him Tomos Tynypwll round here,' said Bevan. 'I doubt if there's many know his right name. And some call him Tom Bugle.'

'Musical, is he? A real taffy, eh?' And Sir Rhodri recited:

Tomos was a Welshman, Tomos was a thief,
Tomos came to my house and stole better than a leg of beef, blast
  him!

He laughed and rubbed his hands together. 'Well, so long as they get it right on the charge sheet, eh?—Thomas Thomas or Tomos Tynypwll, no odds. He needs a lesson, Bevan, and all these pinchers and poachers. We must be firm with this bugler who bugles my birds.'

He was disappointed that the agent, usually so sharp, missed his joke. 'We'll be that all right. We'd better not show too fierce, though. Just let the law take its course, Sir Rhodri.'

'Who said anything else? Justice, that's what we want. That's what we'll get.' Sir Rhodri warmed up. 'If I was a vindictive sort of chap I'd be sitting on the bench this morning, not among the public. But I've always been a man to uphold the constitution and appearances. In my position, Bevan, I must set an example. These labour chaps, you know——.'

Bevan agreed this was very handsome of Sir Rhodri. 'And since you feel that way about it, Sir Rhodri, I really believe it might be better——'

'Well?'

'To be frank, Sir Rhodri, that if you decided to stay away even from the body of the court——'

Sir Rhodri shook his nose, and the rest of his head swung with it. 'Nonsense, Bevan! Damned nonsense! My rabbits, aren't they? And my birds. Come now, Bevan: fair play's a jewel, as they say. If I haven't a right to be present, who the devil has?'

Bevan admitted his right. 'But I still think it might be better. I wish you would, Sir Rhodri.'

'Now look here, Bevan——' Sir Rhodri grew red and hot, like a hollow radish. 'I don't know what's going on behind my back with some of you.' He waved Bevan's mouth shut. 'First there's you, pretending to save me trouble; then there's that fat-lugged sergeant telling me I needn't bother to be present; then there's old Powey; and now there's you again. I'm a patient man, but I'm getting angry. Know the word, Bevan? Angry— See!'

Bevan saw and said he saw, but that didn't save him now. Sir Rhodri rolled him out like a dollop of dough, north-south and east by west, and when at last he thumped him back to shape it was only to a rough likeness. '*See*, Bevan?'

'I can only say I acted for the best.'

'All right then.'

'And I think you'll be sorry, Sir Rhodri.'

'You'll be sorry unless you shut up,' said Sir Rhodri, shoving his snout forward.

Yet the thought stuck with him as he drove the two of them a mile and a half to town. Sorry, indeed. Tomos Tynypwll might be sorry and anyone else he gave the rough end of his tongue to, but he, Sir Rhodri, the big shot around here—why, he owned the place. He'd show 'em!

Yet when he met the local justices behind the court-room they lacked hwyl. No question of it, they were sick as dogs to see him. Not even sherry brought them together—Bristol Milk at fourteen bob a bottle. And it was galling the way they stared at his nose when they thought he wasn't looking. It wasn't as though they'd never set eyes on it before. And that chap Bevan—the look on his face. Pious. Smug. Bit of a martyr. Sir Rhodri was becoming most uncomfortable. Perhaps they thought he meant to bully them, give justice a squeeze, like an orange, like a—chrrm! Like a parlourmaid, he was going to say, but that was levity. He sought to cleanse their hearts of doubt. He cared less than a tick's elbow for the rabbits, he assured them, never touched the things, no fat on their ribs, but a principle was at stake. Property. Ah, property! Where should we be without it?

Where would you be without it? thought the magistrates, for a moment forgetting his nose.

Time to get a move on, thank heaven! Sir Rhodri, to show his high-mindedness, did not take the seat reserved for him, but sat like an ordinary chap on an ordinary form. His appearance was bound to make a stir, but he thought the public rather pleased than resentful that he had shown up. Bit of feudal feeling left still, thank God, despite the bolshies. Not that he saw anything to grin about.

The preliminaries were quickly over. 'Call Thomas Thomas.'

The crowd (it was now he noticed what a big crowd it was) rustled, hummed, and sat back. Two johnnies in mufflers sitting in front turned to stare at the great man, but this was one of the penalties of greatness and he looked through them.

'Thomas Thomas!'

Tomos Tynypwll went into the dock, and Sir Rhodri gaped.

He was dressed in corduroy trousers, yorked under the knees, a green velveteen waistcoat of his granddad's time, a red and white neckerchief, and a railwayman's jacket. He was bland as a blown-up pig's bladder, yet gay as a gander in May. He looked the sort of chap who'd take dandelions to a harvest home and touch the parson for a pint on the strength of it. There was a happy murmuring along the wooden seats, and Sir Rhodri wasn't sure whether he had gone blue, grey, or cheese-green. The height and build, the shape of the sconce—and that nose! Doubting there were two such in Wales, he foolishly felt for his own.

Tomos greeted a friend in court, one of the mufflered johnnies, and was sternly reproved, whereat he ducked his head, and his case was begun. For a time Sir Rhodri heard nothing of it: disbelief, humiliation, and rage beat about his skull. Not that this mattered much: he knew the evidence pretty well. Jenkins the keeper and Police Constable Ponty Jones would testify that they had seen the defendant on enclosed land at a suspicious time, that they had given unsuccessful chase, that two newly-dead rabbits had been found in a shed at the defendant's home. The case was cast-iron and stone-doddle. A ticket for Botany Bay in the old days.

He was thinking: How little we know our fathers!

'Then how do you account for the two rabbits found in your shed?' he heard Gracegirdle ask from the bench.

'Thass easy.' Tomos hoicked his thumb at the keeper. 'He put um there.'

Gracegirdle did his imitation of Silvanus Williams of Pontygwyndy, K.C. 'Quite so, Thomas Thomas. You have proof of this—er—allegation?' But Tomos was muttering at Jenkins the keeper, and he had to repeat the question, without irony this time.

'Proof? Three bags full, mun. There's a feller—he told this feller he'd put rabbits in my shed one day, Jinkins did.'

'Why, you flamer!' cried Jenkins, but was roughly silenced. 'Order in court,' said Tomos reproachfully.

'One moment, Thomas Thomas. Who told whom, and what?' Tomos goggled at him. 'I mean, who told someone else about putting rabbits in your shed. This is an extremely serious allegation—charge—I hope you realize that?'

'Seven years hard,' said Tomos. 'For Jinkins, your worship.'

Gracegirdle waved this away. 'Please, Mr. Thomas. You say the keeper told someone he would put rabbits in your shed. Very well—whom did he tell?'

'My sister Blodwen's oldest girl's young man's uncle, your worship.'

'Your sister Blodwen's youngest——'

'Oldest, your worship!'

The Clerk whispered in Gracegirdle's ear. 'Yes, yes, I was coming to that. Can you produce this—er—distant witness, Mr. Thomas? This distant relative, I might almost call him.'

Tomos winked at the men in mufflers who squirmed till their corduroys purred like cats. 'On'y in a wooden box, your worship. He's wedi pobi, gone aloft, drawed his wages.' He raised his hand. 'As the hymn says——'

'Never mind what the hymn says! This is a court of law, sir, not a harvest home!' Tomos was heard to mutter something about the singing at Beulah. It was at this point that Sir Rhodri allowed his eye to be caught by the man on the stand. Smiling, Tomos stroked his nose. Sir Rhodri looked away.

'I'm trying—' began Gracegirdle, then altered his sentence. 'I'm trying to help you.' He smothered Tomos's attempt to thank him. 'What was the name of this witness you mention as deceased? As dead!' he bellowed, before the defendant's eyebrows got half way to the ceiling.

'I called him Davy,' Tomos admitted. He pointed to the men in mufflers. 'These boys knew him well, poor feller.'

'So you called him Davy?' Gracegirdle was doing Silvanus Williams again, but Plas Mawr is a long way from Pontygwyndy. 'And what did your sister Blodwen's oldest daughter's young man call him, pray?' He snatched the word from Tomos's mouth. 'Besides uncle, I mean?'

'He called him Flannel Belly, your worship.'

'I must warn you——'

''Cos he used to wear a bellyband from September till May, your worship.'

There was tittering in court. 'Quite a long bellyband,' said Gracegirdle, to fetch the laugh over to his side of the hedge. The Clerk was whispering. 'Yes, yes, I was coming to that. This Davy Flannel—was it he or the keeper who told you about the rabbits?' The Clerk whispered again. 'I know, I know. This Davy, then, told you, and Jenkins told him—so you say.' Tomos nodded. 'Now what precisely did he say? The exact words, please!'

'He told him he'd put rabbits in my shed.'

'But my good fellow—the exact words! He didn't use the third person, I imagine?'

'No,' said Tomos. Gracegirdle felt he was getting near the bone at last. 'There wasn't no third person.' People were putting their hands over their mouths, shuffling on their seats. 'Except me.'

The magistrate dropped to second gear. 'I mean, did the speaker say, for example, "I intend to put rabbits in the shed of Tomos Tynypwll"?'

'No.' Sir Rhodri saw Gracegirdle thanking God for a mono-syllable. 'He didn't mention you at all. Jinkins may be the last of the litter, your worship, but he's not such a pig as to bring the Bench into it.'

The keeper struggled to his feet, but Ponty pressed him down again. As for Gracegirdle, he looked both hot and faint, but saved his face by threatening to clear the court. 'Silence! I must have silence!' He felt everyone was laughing at him, but how the devil could he do other than he was doing? And the Clerk was whispering in his ear. 'I know,' he snapped. 'I was coming to that.' He looked sideways at his fellow magistrates, and didn't like what he saw of Mrs. Evans the Farm.

'Now, Tomos,' he began quietly, 'I've given you a lot of rope, and I shan't give you any more. You understand? I want a straight answer to a straight question. You were seen inside the Plas grounds on the night in question. Do you deny that after the evidence we have heard?'

'Not guilty,' said Tomos, after some thought.

'Yes or no, do you deny it?'

'Deny what?' Tomos smiled at a friend in court, and was fiercely rebuked. 'No,' he said.

'You don't deny it?'

'I mean No, I wasn't there.'

Gracegirdle was breathing very hard now. 'You have heard two independent witnesses testify they saw you there, yet you deny it.' He almost pleaded with the scallywag before him. 'I want to help you. Have you an alibi?'

Tomos's face cleared. 'No,' he said gratefully, 'but I gets backache awful in wet weather.'

There was laughter in court and Tomos looked well pleased. Sir Rhodri coughed four or five times, blew his horn, and kept his big red face in his big white handkerchief as long as he decently could. If only the joke wasn't partly on him! So thinking, he frowned unconvincingly at the mufflers, who nudged each other and stared him out. 'Another interruption and I'll clear the court,' snarled Gracegirdle. Then: Justice, he thought finely, justice and Hywel Dda, let me do justice. 'I meant,' he said, 'have you anyone to testify that you were in some other place at nine-thirty Tuesday night the twenty-third of June?' He thought it best to repeat his question, so that this big-nosed imbecile could take it in. And

Lord, he prayed, give me strength this day! But Tomos was so long a-pondering that he had to ask it a third time, sharply.

'Mistaken identity,' said Tomos then.

'You know what that means?'

'Someone 'bout here the spit image of me, your worship.' He winked at the mufflered johnnies. 'Like Mrs. Davies the Deri's new baby the spit image of Jinkins.'

No wonder Grace Gracegirdle lost his temper. 'You—you,' he began, while the horrified Clerk rushed to his side. 'Who the devil could be mistaken for you, you—you——'

It was Tomos's moment. One of the mufflered johnnies made a noise like a hen, Gracegirdle clapped his hand to his forehead, and Sir Rhodri felt his stomach turn its toes out, as the defendant turned at leisure towards the crowded seats. For a half-second he stood nodding, and then took his nose between fingers and thumb. 'As it might be Sir Rhodri himself, your worship,' he said respectfully, but loudly.

The hen became a crazy farmyard, then laughter enveloped the room. This was what they'd been waiting for, the dole-drawers, the mouchers, the rabbit-snatchers—to see old Privilege up at the Plas with a stoat on the end of his nozzle. Uncollared colliers hooted at royalties, blackcoats at dividends, even the godly had their snigger. There was comment so crapulous from the mufflered johnnies that, on the bench, Mrs. Evans' bonnet shot the length of its elastic. The uproar grew, the gavel rapped noiselessly through it, Gracegirdle was on his feet and shaking his fist at Tomos, whose hand, as it kept to his nose, extended its fingers in an old-fashioned and unmistakably derisive way towards him. Then officers began to clear the court, and Sir Rhodri, though they passed him by, went outside too. Well, he'd been made to look a fine fool. Sooner he cleared out of the place the better. But he couldn't clear out of the story—he knew that. They'd be telling of noses in a hundred years around Plas Mawr. He glowered after his agent, but Bevan was keeping out of harm's way. He scribbled a note on a sheet of paper and handed it to a constable.

He was still there, in the little hall, when Bevan came up behind him. 'Case dismissed, Sir Rhodri,' he said nervously.

'I want to see that chap Tomos!'

Bevan fluttered his wings. 'D'you think it wise, Sir Rhodri?' 'Who are you to judge?'

They had not far to go to find him. He was mouching down the corridor with the mufflered johnnies. 'Hey, you!' But Sir Rhodri's summons struck even himself as the wrong one. 'Mr. Thomas, could I have a word with you?' 'Go ahead, you,' said Tomos graciously. Sir Rhodri groped for words.

'I've always fancied one of they cigars,' said Tomos, eyeing Sir Rhodri's waistcoat pocket. 'And these boys here.'

Sir Rhodri lived up to his nose. 'Here, take the lot.' They were pleased, and said so. They've got me on a string, he thought, but had lost his vexation. After all, if the old dad—'There's just one question, Mr. Thomas, if these gentlemen would perhaps be good enough to drink my health over the way there—' He nodded for Bevan to go with them. 'Just one question, Mr. Thomas, if you don't mind.'

'Not at all. Ask you, boyo. Got a match?'

Sir Rhodri handed over a boxful. 'Keep them. What I wanted to ask, Mr. Thomas—you wouldn't remember, perhaps, but did your mother ever go to work up at the Plas?'

He saw something in his brother's eyes he couldn't put a name to. He felt pretty shabby, did Sir Rhodri then. 'No, not my mam. But my dad was always about the house. That would be before you were born, I fancy.' He smiled and blew smoke all over the place, including Sir Rhodri. 'Biggest nose in Wales, my old dad.'

Sir Rhodri dropped his bowler.

All We Like Sheep

A man and his dog were working sheep on the hillside behind Siloh. This was a famous place for sheepdog trials, a dry rough-tufted terrain on a big bald mountain between two coal valleys. From where he stood he could look east and west to two black and glittering rivers, smudged with tip-strewn villages and steamy pit-heads, and beyond these to the ferny flanks of the next rows of hills. It was a still afternoon, and curtains of smoke clung to the chimney pots so far beneath him, hazing the long jerky chains of houses. To the north a progression of humps and ravines carried him fifteen miles to the claws of the Beacons, and south he saw all the valleys of western Monmouthshire crawl like veins on an old man's hands to the coast plain and steely strip of estuary. There was a time when he had farmed Brynllan, near the valley bottom, but that was a long time ago. He now kept sheep and a few milkers on the crofting at Brynhir. His name was Cadno.

He was a tall clean-shaven man of seventy, with a perverse and bitter face, though now he looked pleased enough, even excited. He spoke mildly to his dog, a sly upland mongrel whose tongue streamed scarlet from his blackish jaws, but the dog, though he stirred his tail and wriggled, kept his distance. This was their relationship: obedience and just treatment—neither asked for more. For a long time back Cadno had been content here on the mountain; something in the unyielding land dowelled with his own temper. Stooping, he picked up a jag of stone, worn at the base but with a wounding edge still. He nodded several times. He was like that stone, he knew it. The dog watched him, warily.

In another half an hour he would be on the other side of Siloh wall, at a funeral. Gwion Lewis's funeral. They had been great friends once, Gwion and he. It was proper he should go to his funeral. Though whether Gwion would have gone to his—he dropped the stone—ay, he'd have gone, only too true! But he hadn't lasted, had Gwion; he had no rocky core to him. The old man looked around. The emptiness, the cold, the winds and the barrenness would have broken him. A weakling at heart— you could tell it by his wish to be brought home to Capel Siloh. All that money too——

He had decided to join the funeral on the hillside. He chuckled maliciously. It would be a surprise for some.

All We, like Sheep! A pity Gwion couldn't know——. He spoke again to the dog, his voice edged, so that the brute flattened his tall ears and fawned briefly before coming to heel. In one place the cemetery wall had slid outwards and the gap been plugged with armfuls of gorse, but these too had recently been dragged aside and there was nothing now to stop man or sheep from walking in among the graves. Almost immediately inside the gap he came upon Gwion's open grave with a coffer of fresh-turned earth beside it. Stepping closer, he stared into it, his lips projecting a little, his eyes hollowing under pressure of his brows. He nodded, as he had nodded at the stone, with a solid yet humorous satisfaction. So this would be the last of Gwion! Apart—his eyes changed, subtly, unpleasantly—apart from his story. He saw Gwion at that moment as he had seen him fifty years ago: short and thickset, with a wedge-shaped head and brief blunt nose, and those black and pool-like woman's eyes under the blue-black sweeping eyebrows. A great one after the girls he'd been, with those eyes of his, a great one for courting— he grunted—a great one for not getting caught. They were the musician in him, too—those eyes—not only the sweet singer, but they showed his feeling for music, his passion for lovely sound, his dream of power. What a conductor he would have made! All the great names, he'd have beaten them all had he lasted. Suddenly it seemed to the old man standing by the grave that the days of their youth had been all song and happiness, with choirs in every village and orchestras the length of each valley. He began to shake with rage. 'You know, God!' he cried menacingly; 'You know!' The hair rose on the dog's neck, his eyes widened with surprise.

But he must be going. He kicked once, clumsily, at the heaped-up earth and watched a few handfuls trickle into the grave, then he crossed the graveyard, past the chapel, went through the gate and so downhill. In a few minutes he could see the funeral climbing towards him, so he stepped in to the hedge, the dog obsequious behind him, and as the hearse went by removed his hat with a gallant flowing gesture. Everyone seemed surprised to see him. As though he'd be anywhere else that day for twenty pounds! He contorted his mouth to hide a grin, and seemed to those watching to struggle with a deep and painful emotion. But just as the last of the walkers reached him the procession squeaked to a halt. The road was now too steep and rough for wheels, and from here they must carry. Six strong men (he knew the story), a guinea for each of them, would carry old Gwion to the chapel, where the minister (he grinned again, hiding his jaws with his hat—three guineas left for *him*) would laud to high heaven a man he'd never known but who had religion enough to leave a bequest to Siloh. As though God cared a rap for their coloured glass and gewgaws! It was all vanity.

Gwion's brother-in-law had got down from the first coach. As chief mourner he was fat with self-importance; unction oozed from him like the richness of good sage cheese; he stood to gain a tidy penny and was filled with a vague and well-controlled benevolence. In view of them all he advanced on Cadno, like a plump and splayfoot pigeon approaching a hawk, his hand outstretched, his mouth wet. 'It's the heart, friend,' he cried for all to hear. 'We feel it *here*.' He tapped his left breast. 'It was good of you to come, Cadno! It was *good* of you.' For some of his words he appeared to plunge into a bog of emphasis and pull them sucking forth. He turned his face to the hearse, from which the coffin was being hauled. 'He would have *appreciated* it, Cadno. After all these years—poor Gwion! You were such friends—*su-uch* friends!'

Cadno nodded, his eyes searching the past. 'It's all vanity,' he said roughly. 'We learn that much.' Disquieted, the brother-in-law moved away, still smiling with his skin. Several of the mourners greeted Cadno, one or two offered a handshake which he accepted brusquely. They needn't expect honey and wine from him. Yet they had been on his side at the beginning of the trouble: summer friends and sunshine neighbours, all of them. He started to walk uphill behind the coffin, watching the brother-in-law at the minister's ear, telling the tale no doubt, the furtive glance behind. Was he telling the truth—how Gwion had robbed him, stolen his sheep? Or twisting it all to Gwion's side? He felt hard as a stone towards them all. Ay, Gwion boy, they were against you then who now come lickspittling along behind; urging him to make a court case of it, groaning at a sheepstealer's wickedness. To think of it was to marvel how soon trust turned to treachery, friendship to hate. How soon folk forgot and forgave. But not he, Cadno! He was hard—ay, he gloried in it. Like a rock to friend or foe—and Gwion chose to trick him over the sheep, steal from him. The dismissal of his case in court had hurt him at first, but it made no difference in the end. Everyone knew the truth, knew Gwion a thief. He had bided his time; his chance, he knew, would come.

All We, like Sheep! He nodded sardonically at the coffin. The hand of God made manifest. At the green gate he spoke to his dog who slipped away to the grass verge. Gwion boy! God and Cadno had been too much for him. It was Gwion himself, three months before the trouble, who made the choice. Truly the Lord foresaw and guided all. Taking his seat at the back of the chapel he thought with approval of the sure and cruel humour of God.

Cadno reflected. For two wretched sheep! He had been less hard in those days. If Gwion's need was so great he would have given him the sheep. At least (he forced himself to the truth) he would have given him credit. He could have asked, anyway.

The hymn was finished, the minister was into his address. Cadno shut his ears to it. He shut his eyes too, that he might not see the quirking curiosity directed his way, and was carried back to the old brick concert hall that night forty-odd years ago, to the packed benches, the solid arch of the choir, the harmonium to the left, the violins and double bass, to Gwion's lifted shoulders, his weaving arms. To Handel's *Messiah*. Gwion's choice! Ay, ay, there were grand singers in the valley those days, nothing like them now. But they sang badly that night. Did they know? At least, did they suspect? 'Worthy is the Lamb'—a ticklish chorus for a sheep-stealer to conduct; 'He shall feed His flock like a shepherd'—even the dullest would sense it, surely; 'Behold the Lamb of God'—and 'All we like sheep are gone astray.' He remembered and thrilled to the dangerous exhilaration of those waiting hours. He guessed God Himself must have smiled and wagged His great head at so deadly a stratagem. For when they reached 'All we like sheep' from scattered seats in the building came a tremulous, mocking 'baa-aa!' He could still see Gwion's frightened start, the droop of his baton, could hear the 'sh-sh-sh' of the shocked audience, the voices of those brave enough to sing on; but that devilish baa-ing was too much for them, they blundered into silence, shuffled their feet, rustled their copies, turned gaping to their neighbour. And all the time the bleating continued, 'baa-aa, baa-aa,' till Gwion after one feeble gesture to his choir hurried from the rostrum. A week later he had left the valley.

Opening his eyes, Cadno smiled sourly. That was forty-odd years ago. He could admit it now: if Gwion had lost, so had he. Cadno Brynllan to Cadno Brynhir, that was the measure of his loss. Those fields by the river, the gay friesians with their dripping teats, the fat soft sheep—for the stony uplands, the three Welsh blacks, the springy sweet-fleshed ewes. No matter! He looked at the mourners, naming them to himself. Ay, the same ones, bitch-driven by their women, the ones who'd set against him for taking that justice the law denied. In a year he had lost his milk round, odd things happened at market, he had bad luck too. They began to say he was mean: why couldn't he let a couple of sheep be missing without all that vindictiveness? What if the poor man did steal them? You had only to think of Jacob and Laban and the half-peeled rods to know that kind of thing had always gone on, in the most respectable families too. And they said that to interrupt the *Messiah* was sacrilege, the bleating a blasphemy. Little they knew of the God they so freely flattered and cajoled, that grim Ironist who had taken His laugh at Cadno too!—Not that Cadno held this against Him. They understood each other very well, God and Cadno.

He heard the minister speak of forgiveness. The greater the offence, thus he heard him, the more merit in forgiveness. What after all was man's forgiveness compared with the Infinite Mercy of God? Cadno bent his head, lest he be seen to smile. Infinite Mercy a sheeptod! Justice not Mercy was what God had promised. They were deceiving themselves fatally, these apostles of Mercy, these milk-thinners, these shortweight counter-jumpers, these Dai Smallcoals from the pits. Had they forgotten that dismal horde who departed past the left hand of the Almighty into the Everlasting Pit? *Everlasting*—that was the strong word. Not for a day, a year, not even an age—but for ever! That was God's way. That was Cadno's way. These people before him, they were afraid of the Book. Afraid to know that hard and subtle God Cadno had found on the mountain. He heard, as he expected to hear, the preacher speak of Gwion's life after he left the valley, how he had toiled and moiled and prospered in his chosen field of endeavour, and how, when his immortal part took wing for heaven, his clay sought confusion in the clay of his fathers. But the preacher said nothing of Cadno forced to leave the honeyed lands of Brynllan: all Gwion, Gwion, Gwion, you'd think he was a saint, a cherub, a deacon in Siloh. But God is not mocked, thought Cadno.

He was glad when they were on their way to the open grave. The dog had been watching for him through the gate. Some signal no one else saw—he slipped inside, his nose to Cadno's knee. Cadno felt a moment at hand he had waited for almost a lifetime. He watched with relish the smooth lowering of the coffin, and it was then he flicked lightly at the dog's head. He was away through the gap in a flash.

The brother-in-law approached him, holding the minister's arm. 'In the *heart*, friend,' he said; 'it's *there* we feel it. Forget and forgive'—he raised his podgy hands—'forgive and forget. We are all members of a *Whole*, Cadno.'

Cadno sneered: 'You mean, a Pit.'

The minister flinched, one or two changed feet among them, and the brother-in-law dropped his hands. He was hurt; he had behaved so well; he would have protested; but at that moment two terrified sheep burst through the gap in the wall, a sly and furious mongrel at their heels. The first swerved under the feet of the mourners, scattering them, the second fell into the grave and its hoofs beat a frantic tattoo on the coffin lid. 'Baa-aa,' they cried, 'baa-aa!'

The mourners surged and stammered, growled then grew still. But Cadno, his face taut, had turned from them to seek approval skywards. Suddenly they saw his jaws loosen in a smug and ugly grin.

'All We, like Sheep!' he cried, in a great prophet-voice.

And knowing their deed blest, man and dog turned for the gap and the farm at Brynhir.

A Man after God's Own Heart

I came to the pub just as I was feeling too fagged to go any further. The Seven Maidens—did you ever hear a nicer name for a pub? It lies about eight miles the other side of Pensarn, and it's worth the walk. Clean. Fresh sawdust, fresh beer, tobacco smoke not yet stale—it had all the mellow sustenance that makes clean pubs and clean stables such lovely nosefuls for thoughtful men. Mind, it's very lonely around there. If you dropped dead on the road, you'd not get the pennies on your eyes for a week or more. But the Seven Maidens is the hub of a six or seven mile wheel, and of an evening by paths, green roads, and hedgerows, its customers come to their decent pleasure.

I booked a room there for the night, and took it easy for a while, and vaselined my feet, and knocked a sprig down with the round handle of the poker in my room. It was about eight o'clock when I went downstairs: blinds drawn, paraffin lamp alight, good fire going, the haze of fine fellowship blue-grey to the ceiling. There were four or five farmy sort of men around the skittle board at the one end, and perhaps three or four others away from them playing darts and arguing about the score. In Welsh, of course, so I gave them good night in the old tongue and went to the fireside.

But for one man I had it to myself. I nodded to him as I sat down, and made the usual remark about a good fire. However —and here the story really starts—he just fixed his eyes on mine, then dropped them, and said nothing.

'Have a drink?' I asked him, and at that he looked up. The landlord fetched it, looking more than a shade interested, I thought. A rusty, genteel-gone-shabby sort of fellow, my new acquaintance was, dressed in a darkish suit, very much worn, and a cheap felt hat on the bench near him. A dog-without-a-tail look

about him. Unmistakably no countryman. 'Your health,' said I,
and took a swig—after all I *had* been walking and was still
thirsty—whereon he nodded and swigged too. We were properly
introduced, I thought. But not quite. It must have been five
minutes before he opened his mouth. 'King David,' he said. Just
that. In English.

'King David,' I repeated.

'King David,' said he, and looked into his pint. 'A man after
God's own heart.'

'That's right,' I agreed. 'He was.'

I felt sure it was the first time in a long while for anyone to
agree with him about King David.

'You think that?' he asked.

'I do. He was a man after God's own heart. We are told so.'

'Yes,' he said. 'We are.'

We fell silent.

'You think that?' he asked suddenly. 'In spite of everything?
That he was *that*?'

'I do,' I said again. 'The Good Book tells us so.'

He nodded, and I nodded. I drank, and so did he. We warmed
one to the other, and after we had drunk some more I persuaded
him to shift over to the empty parlour. I thought at the time that
everybody there, landlord, wife, and customers, behind their
elaborate ignoring of us were keen enough to know what was
going on, but there were no questions, not a hint even, before
I left next day. He smoked a lot of cigarettes, I remember. Mine,
all of them. But I got his story out of him.

His name was Reedy. He was born in Cardiff, near the Hayes.
His father was a watchmaker, and he became a watchmaker himself. I gathered that Reedy the elder left him a twofold inheritance:
a dwindling trade and a more than wholesome fear of God and the
Devil. He was at pains to tell me he had always been a chapelgoer
and for many years a steward, and I could imagine him very well
with his eyes fixed always on the works of a watch or on the
preacher for the day. Physically he wasn't much of it: medium
height, no particular colouring, narrowish, yet not displeasing.
After the old man died he lived all on his own, except for a

woman who came in three times a week to clean through. At first there was a bare living, but once he found himself dipping into his bit of capital he knew he had to make a change or go under, so at last he advertised for a married couple to take the rooms over his shop. Eight shillings a week would make all the difference, and he had it worked out that he could have his dinner with them and maybe get the shop scrubbed out as part of the bargain—though when it came to the push, he hadn't the nerve to ask this last. Within a week he got his couple, a Mr. and Mrs. Evans. At this time Reedy was forty-six. The Evanses were in the early thirties. The husband was a porter for a firm somewhere near, and, on Reedy's showing, a decent, hard-working man.

Mrs. Evans?—It took him just over a month to fall in love with her.

I am sure I wasn't the first he told this story to. I am sure I shan't be the last. At times evidently it gets too much for him, and tell he must.

Soon he could think of nothing but Polly Evans all day long, usually with the deepest misery—so much so that when she ironed his collars he hated putting them on and soiling them. He remained a chapelgoer, but was losing his grip fast. He had a conscience that was always nagging him, but this too made no difference. During the tenth week he went upstairs one day when Evans was out, knocked at their living-room door, and she let him in. For a time they sat talking, but he started to make those absurd answers of a man whose mind is elsewhere, till after a bit she asked him if he felt bad, and out it came. He babbled and cried and fell at her feet and kissed her shoes, and when she forced him to stand up he clung to her frantically, feeling that if he let go the world would fall away from under him and he go down into the echoing emptiness of hell. When she didn't push him away, he was unbearably happy and unhappy at the same time. He was as near fifty as forty, remember. And he asked her to go away with him.

Naturally she refused, and he was honest enough to tell me how relieved he was when she answered No. But it couldn't rest there. After what he had done he was ashamed to pass the time of day with Evans. He was afraid of him, too, but Polly evidently knew when to keep her mouth shut. It was a fortnight later before there was a development. Evans had been put on some late job that kept him out till twelve each night, and now Reedy, resolved to put all to hazard, called Polly into the shop after closing time. Once again he fell on his knees before her, begging her to take pity on him or he'd throw himself into the dock and end it all.

I hold no brief for Reedy. I hold no brief for Polly. Her decision, and their intended action, are none of my business. But this is where we come to King David, if only indirectly. For at this moment God came between him and Polly.

So he said. There are other explanations. But the fact is that he did not—could not—touch Polly, who must have been very puzzled by it all. But she did not get annoyed, or feel slighted, or persuade herself she had been made to look a fool. She took life as it came—and she was a good sort. And dullish.

With this, things took a new turn. First and least important, he found business better for the next few weeks. A reward for virtue, maybe. I say least important, because he was past caring about the business now. He had a mind above watches and his pew might just as well have stayed empty on Sundays. God had come between this man and woman, but He could not prevent him thinking of her with an intolerable desire. Day in, day out, it racked him now, and there was always this Presence between them. His health was poorer. He lost much sleep. How Polly acted during those weeks he did not tell me, but I imagine her as eating heartily and singing as she worked, and from time to time shaking her head over the daftness of men. 'But not with a married woman,' he told me, with a quite painful sincerity despite his inconsistency. 'There was something held me back from that. Not common adultery. But if only she was free!'

If only she were free! For a time the idea was just a feebly unpleasant rankling way back of his mind, and then one day it bit into him like a ferret into a rat's brain, with a dry and bitter crunching. For a time he was thinking how convenient it would be if Evans fell ill or if the chances of his employment brought him to a painless, instantaneous end. Lifting crates and dodging among trucks—the thing was not impossible. I think he would have regarded this as a lifting of the ban, a sign that he could go straight ahead and marry the widow. Anyhow, the suggestions were in the air if the Almighty cared to adopt them. But Evans was healthy and took good care of himself, and so it was that Reedy's brain spawned strange and frightening speculations.

Then everything moved very fast. Evans, as I said, was working nights. Polly had gone to the second house of a variety show, probably at short notice, for her husband could have known nothing of it. Reedy was indoors alone. He sat there brooding and pitying himself till at last he felt he must get out for a walk or go crazy. So he locked up and maundered miserably the length of the embankment, feeling lower and lower, and looking at the shining water and the not-so-shining mud, until he set off for home again. He told me, but I don't believe him, that a Voice inside urged him to go back. Anyhow, voice or no voice, he got back to find Reedy's burning like a pot of fat.

You will have noticed that Reedy had a turn for melodrama; and now, while the brigade did its best and the neighbours crowded so spectacular a fireside, he tells me he wept.

Then Evans arrived. He saw him running from a van that had given him a lift, and as though it had to be, Evans saw him too. I didn't get much of a picture of Evans from Reedy: it was all Polly when it wasn't himself. 'Where is she?' he cried. 'Inside,' sobbed Reedy, and Evans, poor devil, rushed for the house and was inside before the firemen could catch him. They found him at the head of the stairs, later. He had tried to hide his face at the end. Death had not been merciful. But dreadfully thorough.

'It was Providence,' said Reedy. 'Right or wrong, it was Providence.' In a way it was. Certainly the situation was changed. Polly was free. He tried not to think of it like that until a respectful period had gone by, but he couldn't very well help himself. I think he suffered remorse, but not so long as he made out— decidedly not longer than the respectful period. He harped on that Voice, rather. Sending him back just then, in time for Evans. I did not hint that there might be voices other than the One that had warned him off Polly.

At the end of the respectful period he asked her to marry him, and she agreed. By this time he had a job assembling watches at a mass manufactory, and she was back at the cinema where she had worked when single. They could not altogether avoid publicity, but chose a registry office for the ceremony. 'I couldn't have faced out a big do,' he confessed. There was a honeymoon at Bournemouth. One more sentence and an explanation tell everything. The marriage was never consummated. God, he explained, still stood between them.

They had to part, need I say? There must be a clean sweep, and for that he must leave Cardiff. According to him, he gave her more than half of all he had, and then he moved about a bit before settling outside Pensarn. He kept a little general shop there, and next day I had a look at it from outside, but I did not see him anywhere. I had been thinking about Evans too, and frankly, I did not wish to see him. He was lost to the world there, and that was what he wanted.

Of course, he was only in part King David. They both sent Uriah to his death in the forefront of the battle, that they might enjoy the man's wife. The resemblance ends there, except that they both had to pay heavily. God's curse was on them both, Reedy explained many times. But he had one comfort with it all.

King David was his stand-by. He thought, you see, that there was hope for him who got nothing from his sin, and that unpremeditated, if he who begat Solomon on Bathsheba was yet a man after God's own heart.

A White Birthday

With their next stride towards the cliff-edge they would lose sight
of the hills behind. These, under snow, rose in long soft surges,
blued with shadow, their loaded crests seeming at that last
moment of balance when they must slide into the troughs of the
valleys. Westward the sea was stiffened to a board, and lay brown
and flat to the indrawn horizon. Everywhere a leaden sky weighed
upon land and water.

They were an oldish man and a young, squat under dark cloth
caps, with sacks worn shawl-like over their shoulders, and other
sacks roped about their legs. They carried long poles, and the
neck of a medicine-bottle with a teat-end stood up from the
younger man's pocket. Floundering down between humps and
pillows of the buried gorse bushes, they were now in a wide bay
of snow, with white headlands enclosing their vision to left and
right. A gull went wailing over their heads, its black feet retracted
under the shining tail feathers. A raven croaked from the cliff
face.

'That'll be her,' said the younger man excitedly. 'If that
raven——'

'Damn all sheep!' said the other morosely, thinking of
the maddeningly stupid creatures they had dug out that day,
thinking too of the cracking muscles of his thighs and calves,
thinking not less of the folly of looking for lambs on the cliff-
face.

'I got to,' said the younger, his jaw tensing. 'I got reasons.'

'To look after yourself,' grumbled the other. He had pushed
his way to the front, probing cautiously with his pole, and
grunting as much with satisfaction as annoyance as its end struck
hard ground. The cliffs were beginning to come into view, and
they were surprised, almost shocked, to find them black and

brown as ever, with long sashes of snow along the ledges. They had not believed that anything save the sea could be other than white in so white a world. A path down the cliff was discernible by its deeper line of snow, but after a few yards it bent to the left, to where they felt sure the ewe was. The raven croaked again. 'She's in trouble,' said the younger man. 'P'raps she's cast or lambing.'

'P'raps she's dead and they are picking her,' said the older. His tone suggested that would be no bad solution of their problem. He pulled at the peak of his cap, bit up with blue and hollow scags of teeth into the straggle of his moustache. 'If I thought it was worth it, I'd go down myself.'

'You're too old, anyway.' A grimace robbed the words of their brutality. 'And it's my ewe.'

'And it's your kid's being born up at the house, p'raps this minute.'

'I'll bring it him back for a present. Give me the sack.'

The older man loosed a knot unwillingly. 'It's too much to risk.' He groped for words to express what was for him a thought unknown. 'I reckon we ought to leave her.'

Tying the sacks over his shoulders the other shook his head. 'You leave a lambing ewe? When was that? Besides, she's mine, isn't she?'

Thereafter they said nothing. The oldish man stayed on the cliff-top, his weight against his pole, and up to his boot-tops in snow. The younger went slowly down, prodding ahead at the path. It was not as though there were any choice for him. For one thing, it was his sheep, this was his first winter on his own holding, and it was no time to be losing lambs when you were starting a family. He had learned thrift the hard way. For another, his fathers had tended sheep for hundreds, perhaps thousands of years: the sheep was not only his, it was part of him. All day long he had been fighting the unmalignant but unslacking hostility of nature, and was in no mood to be beaten. And last, the lying-in of his wife with her first child was part of the compulsion that sent him down the cliff. The least part, as he recognized; he would be doing this in any case, as the old man above had always done it. He went very carefully, jabbing at the rock, testing each foothold before giving it his full weight. Only a fool, he told himself, had the right never to be afraid.

Where the path bent left the snow was little more than ankle-deep. It was there he heard the ewe bleat. He went slowly forward to the next narrow turn and found the snow wool-smooth and waist-high. 'I don't like it,' he whispered, and sat down and slit the one sack in two and tied the halves firmly over his boots. The ewe bleated again, suddenly frantic, and the raven croaked a little nearer him. 'Ga-art there!' he called, but quietly. He had the feeling he would be himself the one most frightened by an uproar on the cliff-face.

Slowly he drove and tested with the pole. When he had made each short stride he crunched down firmly to a balance before thrusting again. His left side was tight to the striated black rock, there was an overhang of soft snow just above his head, it seemed to him that his right shoulder was in line with the eighty-foot drop to the scum of foam at the water's edge. 'You dull daft fool,' he muttered forward at the platform where he would find the ewe. 'In the whole world you had to come here!' The words dismayed him with awareness of the space and silence around him. If I fall, he thought, if I fall now——. He shut his eyes, gripped at the rock.

Then he was on the platform. Thirty feet ahead the ewe was lying on her back in snow scarlet and yellow from blood and her waters. She jerked her head and was making frightened kicks with her four legs. A couple of yards away two ravens had torn out the eyes and paunch of her new-dropped lamb. They looked at the man with a horrid waggishness, dribbling their beaks through the purple guts. When the ewe grew too weak to shake her head they would start on her too, ripping at the eyes and mouth, the defenceless soft belly. 'You sods,' he snarled, 'you filthy sods!' fumbling on the ground for a missile, but before he could throw anything they flapped lazily and insolently away. He kicked what was left of the lamb from the platform and turned to the ewe, to feel her over. 'Just to make it easy!' he said angrily. There was a second lamb to be born.

'Get over,' he mumbled, 'damn you, get over!' and pulled her gently on to her side. She at once restarted labour, and he sat

back out of her sight, hoping she would deliver quickly despite
her fright and exhaustion. After a while she came to her feet,
trembling, but seemed rather to fall down again than re-settle
to work. Her eyes were set in a yellow glare, she cried out
piteously, and he went back to feel along the belly, pressing for
the lamb's head. 'I don't know,' he complained, 'I'm damned if
I know where it is with you. Come on, you dull soft stupid sow
of a thing—what are you keeping it for?' He could see the
shudders begin in her throat and throb back the whole length of
her, her agony flowed into his leg in ripples. All her muscles
were tightening and then slipping loose, but the lamb refused
to present. He saw half-a-dozen black-backed gulls swing down
to the twin's corpse beneath him. 'Look,' he said to the ewe, 'd'you
want them to get you too? Then for Christ's sake, get on with
it!' At once her straining began anew; he saw her flex and buckle
with pain; then she went slack, there was a dreadful sigh from
her, her head rested, and for a moment he thought she had died.

He straightened his back, frowning, and felt snowflakes on
his face. He was certain the ewe had ceased to work and, unless
he interfered, would die with the lamb inside her. Well, he would
try for it. If only the old man were here—he would know what to
do. If I kill her, he thought—and then: what odds? She'll die
anyway. He rolled back his sleeves, felt for a small black bottle
in his waistcoat pocket, and the air reeked as he rubbed lysol into
his hand. But he was still dissatisfied, and after a guilty glance
upwards reached for his vaseline tin and worked gouts of the
grease between his fingers and backwards to his wrist. Then with
his right knee hard to the crunching snow he groped gently but
purposefully into her after the lamb. The primal heat and wet
startled him after the cold of the air, he felt her walls expand and
contract with tides of life and pain; for a moment his hand
slithered helplessly, then his middle fingers were over the breech
and his thumb seemed sucked in against the legs. Slowly he
started to push the breech back and coax the hind legs down. He
felt suddenly sick with worry whether he should not rather have
tried to turn the lamb's head and front legs towards the passage.
The ewe groaned and strained as she felt the movement inside
her, power came back into her muscles, and she began to work

with him. The hind legs began to present, and swiftly but cautiously he pulled against the ewe's heaving. Now, he thought, now! His hand moved in an arc, and the tiny body moved with it, so that the lamb's backbone was rolling underneath and the belly came uppermost. For a moment only he had need to fear it was pressing on its own life-cord, and then it was clear of the mother and lying red and sticky on the snow. He picked it up, marvelling as never before at the beauty of the tight-rolled gummy curls of fine wool patterning its sides and back. It appeared not to be breathing, so he scooped the mucus out of its mouth and nostrils, rubbed it with a piece of sacking, smacked it sharply on the buttocks, blew into the throat to start respiration, and with that the nostrils fluttered and the lungs dilated. 'Go on,' he said triumphantly to the prostrate ewe, 'see to him yourself. I'm no damned nursemaid for you, am I?' He licked the cold flecks of snow from around his mouth as the ewe began to lick her lamb, cleaned his hand and wrist, spat and spat again to rid himself of the hot fœtal smell in nose and throat.

Bending down to tidy her up, he marvelled at the strength and resilience of the ewe. 'Good girl,' he said approvingly, 'good girl then.' He would have spent more time over her but for the thickening snow. Soon he took the lamb from her and wrapped it in the sack which had been over his shoulders. She bleated anxiously when he offered her the sack to smell and started off along the ledge. He could hear her scraping along behind him and had time at the first bad corner to wonder what would happen if she nosed him in the back of the knees. Then he was at the second corner and could see the old man resting on his pole above him. He had been joined by an unshaven young labourer in a khaki overcoat. This was his brother-in-law. 'I near killed the ewe,' he told them, apologetic under the old man's inquiring eye. 'You better have a look at her.'

'It's a son,' said the brother-in-law. 'Just as I come home from work. I hurried over. And Jinny's fine.'

'A son. And Jinny!' His face contorted, and he turned hurriedly away from them. 'Hell,' he groaned, re-living the birth of the lamb; 'hell, oh hell!' The other two, embarrassed, knelt over the sheep, the old man feeling and muttering. 'Give me the tittybottle,' he grunted presently. 'We'll catch you up.' The husband handed it over without speaking, and began to scuffle up the slope. Near the skyline they saw him turn and wave shame-facedly.

'He was crying,' said the brother-in-law.

'Better cry when they are born than when they are hung,' said the old man grumpily. The faintest whiff of sugared whisky came from the medicine-bottle. 'Not if it was to wet your wicked lips in hell!' he snapped upwards. He knew sheep: there was little he would need telling about what had happened on the rock platform. 'This pair'll do fine. But you'll have to carry the ewe when we come to the drifts.' He scowled into the descending snow, and eased the lamb into the crook of his arm, sack and all. 'You here for the night?'

Their tracks were well marked by this time. The man in khaki went ahead, flattening them further. The old man followed, wiry and deft. Two out of three, he was thinking; it might have been worse. His lips moved good-humouredly as he heard the black-backed gulls launch outwards from the scavenged cliff with angry, greedy cries. Unexpectedly, he chuckled.

Behind him the ewe, sniffing and baa-ing, her nose pointed at the sack, climbed wearily but determinedly up to the crest.

Four in a Valley

They had been lying on the haystack for an hour outside time. He lay now, his face against her bare shoulder, as much asleep as awake, feeling the soft heat welling from the hay, from the girl's damp skin, from the yellow air that trembled so lightly round them. The haystack was in the eastern corner of the cleaned field, the hedges behind them of elm and hazel, and near their heads a golden sprawl of honeysuckle went through and over the contorted arms of a blackthorn. Its perfume saturated their nostrils like sweet wine. There were tall beeches breaking the hedge-line to the right, and lower down, where the field met the river, a pale-green copse with a blood-ring of foxgloves encircling it. Across the river the ground soon began to rise through steep fields, now emerald with after-growth, then through the dark fern belt, and so into upland grazing pocked with rock and tree-stumps. The sun glistened a narrow hand-breadth over the hill-top, and the first shadows stumbled black as water into the valley bottom.

The girl moved a little, caressing the man's hair. She could feel sweat between his face and her shoulder, the scratch and tingle of his day's beard. She looked down anxiously. He was a man in the middle twenties, thin-featured, with black wavy hair, his skin tanned and glowing. He was wearing shabby suède shoes, worn flannel trousers, and a khaki shirt. The shirt neck was open, and his jacket lay beside him. Across it had been thrown a green silk muffler covered with bright yellow greyhounds.

'Tom,' she said quietly, 'Tom?'

He heard her but made no answer. He breathed the half-sigh of a sleeper, moved his lips soundlessly, and pressed his cheek down to her breast. The girl too sighed.

He had been courting her for less than six months, and for a third of that time they had been lovers. She thought back confusedly, to days and evenings and the baffling hours of dark, troubled that it could be this way. She had been on her guard against him from the beginning: he had a bad name, and they said none of the Kemys lot were ever any good. There was his father, a fairday cockerel still; the quiet dim mother; the sister who cleared out of the county. She shook her head, her lips tightening. She would know one way or the other before she left him to-night.

He lay still, his face set. Behind the shut eyes he grew wide awake, thinking. He had felt her sigh, and knew what she was planning to ask him. He thought of himself with a disinterested clarity, as though his case were someone else's, thought of the girl at once sensuously and impersonally. To-night, he guessed, would be the end.

He was extraordinarily aware of his surroundings. He could feel as well as hear a tight sustained creeping in the hay, as the dry shafts and beads of grass were rubbed together and compressed under their weight. In the red warmth of his eyelids he could see the tremble of elm leaves in the infrequent pulsation of air from across the valley. There were birds everywhere, the sharp *weep-wink* of chaffinches within a few yards of them, the chittering of hedge-sparrows, and far down the field the fluting of a blackbird, full, pure, and passionless. He could hear the scrape of her finger-nails on his scalp, the intake of air into her lungs, its gentle expulsion. He smiled without his face showing it, smiled behind his eyes, deep in the brain.

The angle of heat on his face told him that the sun had dropped nearer the hill. Under his right cheek he felt the pucker and moistness of her skin, and the rounding like a pillow for his mouth and jaw.

The gold ring on the third finger of his right hand was locked painfully under the knuckle. Rings! His thoughts caught on that. They had their uses. He'd worn his the night the Lledrod boys rushed the Christmas dance; there was a split cheek-bone in Lledrod to-day for them to remember it by. That was the first night he saw her home. No arm round her waist, not even a kiss. Who would have dreamt——

He grew taut. The blackbird had stopped singing. And then, while his last note seemed to echo and throb in silence, all the other birds grew silent too. Into their silence he read their fear. He opened his eyes and sat up, screwing at his ring.

'Tom,' she said, and put her hand to the red patch made by his cheek.

He tilted his head, chopping with his hand for quiet. Hurriedly and as it were guiltily she thrust her arms into the sleeves of her dress. But he was gesturing away her fright. 'No,' he said, 'not that. Somewhere though——'

'What? Who?'

But he was kneeling now, tight-strung as a wire, his hand shielding his eyes. 'Listen,' he told her.

'Oh, why did you frighten me? I can't hear anything.'

'That's it,' he said. 'You can't. Nor me. Everything's gone still—and why? Ah!'

He had watched a black trail of jackdaws into the copse. Then, high above them, he saw a great brown bird glide across the valley, a winged spirit of lazy and disdainful power. 'That's him,' he said. 'No, her. I knew it. I heard the difference. They know what's good for them, those others. They shut up pretty quick.'

'Then you were awake,' she said reproachfully. 'And I wanted you to talk and answer.'

He laughed round into her face. 'Anybody'd want to stay put with you, Dil. What a girl!'

But she pulled his hand away from her neck. 'No, Tom, we've got to stop all this and talk. I've got to know, Tom.'

'Know what?' he asked. 'You know all you want to know. I've told you, haven't I?

'You've told me what?' she asked, a little bitterly.

'Told you—well, how I feel about you. Told you you're the one for me. Told you how I reckon I fell for you, hard. You've got to be fair. I have now, haven't I?'

While he said all this, in short jerky sentences, he was following with shaded eyes the brown bird as it hung and glided and hung again over the opposite hill-side. The shallower level of his mind sufficed him for all he had to say; what was really present to thought and sensation was the buzzard in its arrogance and poise, and all the tiny creatures of earth now hiding from its eye. For not only were the hedgerows dumb and wary, but around the fields he knew how the rabbits had lolloped to their burrows and lay now with their eyes winking at the sunlit tunnel ends; the water-rats along the river's edge had plunged stealthily to their holes, and the long-tailed field-mice had withdrawn their quivering snouts under a branch, a leaf, or hidden them in the shadow of a grass tuft—each and every one of these certain that the fierce round eye was open for him alone. But his awareness of this pattern of frightened life was untouched by sentiment or sympathy. That was the way of it. That was how it was.

'That's something and nothing,' she retorted. 'I want you to listen, Tom—now!'

'I am listening.' But he pointed upwards. 'You don't see this every day, Dil.' A second buzzard was driving across the valley, wheeling before the hill-side, and with a majestic wing-stroke soaring across the sun. It was the male bird. Soon it joined its mate, and the two superb creatures began to plane in vast arcs over the valley's amphitheatre. The sun's ball was now exactly balanced on the hill-top, and from time to time each bird would disappear into the pale blaze and emerge jet-black and smaller, till the eye recovered its discrimination of size and colour.

'If you won't listen——'

'I've said! I'm listening. I've got my ears open. I can't open them any wider.'

The colour heightened in her cheeks.

'Well?' he asked.

She spoke nervously but with dignity. 'It's about when we are to be married, Tom.'

'Married?' he repeated, almost absently. 'Well now, that's easier asked than answered, Dil.' His eyes were bright and hard; she felt them slip like lizards from her face. 'It's awkward,' he went on. 'It's not as though I'm not as keen as you, Dil—you know how I feel—I've been giving it a lot of thought, one way and another.'

She made as though to speak, but instead sat watching him. As his head turned gently, now sideways, now forwards, she found herself drawn to watch what he was watching. The she-bird was swinging in huge irregular loops within the confines of the hills. For a time the male would keep lazily with her, but now he began to vary his courtship by taking in a higher, wider circumference, from which he would ever and again glide smoothly to her rear. As he re-mounted, he came to take an increasingly sharp angle of flight, so that soon he was rising into the grey-blue vault of sky. His glides grew correspondingly steeper, but still aimed into the heart of the valley. Then she gasped and gripped her knees. The buzzard had climbed higher than ever, for a moment he hung motionless, his wings and tail stiff, and then he was falling like a stone towards the point where his mate's nonchalant soaring would bring them into collision. His speed increased; no longer a falling stone, he was a spear hurtling from the blue. The female, without a beat of her wings, sailed untroubledly towards annihilation, but in the last impossible fraction of time, when it seemed that the outstretched beak must already be piercing her, he drove sideways, like a plate turning, and passed swiftly under her. Again he mounted, though less high, and again dived his death-dive at her; again and again his wings spread flat and slashed the air beside and under her. Unflurried, she pursued her powerful, easy course. Their strength and certainty in that pure and translucent playground endowed them with a divine, unfeeling splendour.

'You said you'd been thinking a lot.'

He looked at her, smiling, ruthless, and clear-headed. 'That makes a man think,' he said, gesturing towards the sky. 'I'd like to be like that hawk, I would.'

'In a way, you are.'

This pleased him. He seemed all openness and affability, but she had seen his eyes narrow, the creasing of his forehead. 'Hawks,' he said slyly, 'they've never been before no parson. Look, Dil,' he continued, 'you know how things are with me. Why rush it? Isn't it fine as it is?'

'Fine.' Her tone was raised, between statement and question, but he was satisfied to take it for agreement. He stretched out beside her, put his hand on the round of her calf. 'Then why spoil it?' He began to stroke her, hoping to excite her, make her forget, or at least postpone, whatever she had in mind to say, but she sat still and unmoved. 'What catch am I?' he asked her. 'Haven't even a job to go to.'

'I have.'

'That's different, Dil. Things a chap can't do.' He grimaced. 'You know how it is.' He rolled over on to his back, his arms reaching up for her. 'Come on, Dil.'

'No,' she said, and could hear the primness in her voice. 'I've got to know. And I've got to know now.'

'God, Dil, what a funny girl you are. Haven't I told you?' He drove his shoulders into the hay. 'Come on, Dil.'

She shifted away from his hands. 'Not again. Not until I know.'

With that he sat up coolly. 'All right, if that's the way you want it.' He watched the buzzards sinking into the valley. 'Only make up your mind. And don't blame me afterwards.' Try as he would, he couldn't spare more than half his attention for what he was saying; it was like the recitation of an old worn lesson. 'But I won't be fooled about with, Dil. There's as good as you tried that, and it didn't come off.'

She flinched. She would have spoken, but he cut away her words. 'We can pack it in when you like. There's nothing on my conscience, and nothing on your mind. I take my fun, but I know what I'm doing—always.'

'No,' she said then, 'there's nothing on my mind. And I think you do know what you are doing. I know now, too.'

He grinned, barefaced. 'Then we are back where we started. No hard feelings, Dil?'

She looked past him. The sun had sunk with a succession of little pauses behind the hill, the air was cooler, and everything shone clean and soft in the evening light. The buzzards had dropped almost to the valley bottom, their curving backs yellow-brown against the green hill-side. Twice the she-bird skimmed the front of a thicket of fir, the third time there was a short dull report, she appeared to be blown upwards in air, and then drifted like a rag to the ground. 'Oh,' she cried. 'Oh!'—that anything so strong and beautiful should be broken and made ugly. 'What is it? What happened?' The male bird beat upwards with frantic wing-strokes till he was clear of the hill-top. 'Dead as a stone,' she heard her companion mutter, his voice edged with jealousy. 'That'll be old Harris.' He pulled on his jacket, began to knot his muffler. 'I'm going down there. Okay with you?' But he rose to his feet only to stand stockstill. 'Look,' he said. 'Watch this.' The buzzard had begun to descend into the valley. No, no, she wanted to cry to him, fly away, oh, please, please fly away! For my sake, please! Several times he checked and swept uneasily sideways to recover height, but always he was drawn to the object of his terrible fidelity. His flight was losing its smoothness and power; he began to drop in short ragged stages towards the brown body below him. 'Don't,' she cried, 'please don't!' She saw the eye along the barrel, felt the tightening finger, heard the dull explosion. The buzzard made a rending effort to pull away, then an untidiness was blown through his wings, his strength left him, and he fell crumpling to earth.

'The damn fool! If he didn't ask for it.'

Her throat was too full for her to answer. He watched her, knowing nothing of the rage and pity within her. 'Well,' he said briskly, 'time to be off.'

'Don't let me keep you.'

He read only repartee into her words. He laughed aloud and slapped his leg. 'You're a one—and I mean it. I'll go, don't worry.' A tremendous and ingrained vanity made him add: 'Unless you'd like it to stay the way it is?' He lifted his eyebrows at her. 'No? Ah well, can't say I blame you.' Going down the ladder, his head and shoulders still visible, he gave her a brusque, humorous salute from over the right eye. 'I'll be seeing you.'

'You,' she said, 'a hawk!' She began to shake.

He had a skin thick beyond her piercing, and was not ill-content to be his own man again. She heard him whistling un-concernedly as he slipped through the hedge and made for the river shallows. What a fool I've been, she thought; oh, what a fool I've been.

She cried a little, and then some wry appreciation made her smile. She looked down. A rabbit had frisked to the dampening grass, she saw a branch move as a rat slipped through the hedge where the man had slipped before. Jackdaws began to scold and jabber from the copse, there were nervous twitterings filling out to song, and suddenly the blackbird threw a long cool note in front of her.

Their troubles, it seemed, were over. It was wisdom, surely, not to exaggerate her own. So thinking, she touched at her eyes and smoothed her dress, and after one rueful glance about her, set foot to the creaking rungs of the ladder. But, standing in the field—'A hawk,' she whispered, 'a hawk!' She would have said more, as much to the world as to herself, but she saw the dew glossing her shoes and instead went hurrying homewards under the dusk-sanded sky—a sky she had never known so still, so rich, and yet so unbearably empty.

The Brute Creation

This was the field. The white tents, the four hundred yards of grass, the hurdles and the pens flashed at his eyes, the flags and the bright dresses of the women. The first dogs had already gone out. He was suddenly sober, a shepherd with a job to do. He knew that most of his fellow competitors disliked him, and that some of them feared him, but to be feared was honey on his tongue. He knew, too, how they hoped to see everything go wrong for him this afternoon: he wouldn't trust those scabs down the field not to loose a tough one when his turn came. They said it was the run of the game, the sheep a man had to work; he growled to think how often he got bad ones. Some of these farmers, squat, basin-bellied, fat-legged, he'd like to see them on the mountain. That's where you showed whether you could handle sheep, not on a green handkerchief like this.

He was a red-headed one from the farmstead up under the Black Rocks. A scurfy, thin-soiled place with the whole mountain for a sheep-run. Sometimes he had a woman up there, but never for long; they could stand neither the place nor its tenant. The tall, black rocks rose up behind the cottage like a claw; the mountain sprawled away thereafter in bog and stream and the rush-ridden grass of the grazing grounds. Lonely—too lonely for everyone save him—too lonely sometimes for him. That was when he would come down to the town and haggle with some sly or trampled creature to come up for a week, a fortnight—no one had ever stayed longer than that. And they all left him the same way: they waited till he was far out on the mountain after sheep and then fled downwards, from home field to path, from path to mountain road, and so to where the lower farms spotted the slopes round Isa'ndre. Fled, they would say, as if the devil were behind them, a devil with big hands and red hair.

He lumbered his way to the stewards' table. There were thirty or forty dogs entered for the different classes, the air quivered with their excitement. Their merits and failings were as well known here as those of their masters, and even more discussed. He saw men eyeing his black-and-white bitch as she moved close behind him. 'Novice?' asked one of the Isa'ndre shepherds, jerking his thumb. 'Novice!' he sneered, and then, savagely: 'Open! The Cup!'

The Cup! That tall white silver thing on his shelf for a year, his name on it for ever. A wide smile covered his face and he looked down at the bitch. 'You better,' he said. 'You better, see!' Her tail went tighter over her haunches, her eyes seemed to lose focus.

They were ticking his name off at the stewards' table. They were looking down at the bitch, a fine-drawn, thin-faced youngster. 'You ought to have entered her for the Novice. It's not fair to a young 'un.' 'She's going to win,' he told them, grinning. 'She better!'

He was walking away, swinging his stick. Behind him they shook their heads, shrugged, went on with their business. He grew restive and arrogant among men who seemed always to be moving away from him. Crike, he'd show them.

And then he was out at the shepherd's post, and far down the field they were loosing the three sheep which he and his bitch must move by long invisible strings, so that his will was her wish, her wish their law. A movement of his fingers sent her out to the right on a loping run which brought her well behind the three sheep. She sank instantly, but rose at his whistle and came forward flying her tail and worked them swiftly through the first hurdle. No one of them attempted to break as she ran them down towards the shepherd, turned them neatly round to his right, and then at a wave of his stick fetched them down past his left hand and so away to the second hurdle. They were now running too fast, and he whistled her to a stalking pace while the hurdle was still seventy yards away. The sheep halted, their heads up, and at the whistle the bitch proceeded with short flanking runs which headed them into the gap.

The shepherd was now five separate beings, and yet those

five integrated so that they were one. He was the shepherd, he was the bitch, he was the three sheep together and severally: he could hardly distinguish between them as aspects of himself. The sheep had been turned across the field towards the hurdle in front of the spectators' benches at a moment when a string of children ran madly towards a stall selling drinks and ice-cream. As they faced the benches, the shepherd could feel alarm and irresolution grow in the sheep. The bitch felt it, too, and showed by a short, furious spurt that she was worried. Her worry moved simultaneously within the shepherd's mind.

The bitch steadied on his whistle, crouched, rose again, and raced out to fetch a straggler back. At once a second sheep broke away on the other side. By the time she had them once more in a group her anxiety was apparent to every shepherd on the field. They broke again and it looked as though they would pass round the hurdle, but a fierce whistle helped her cut them off. The pattern renewed itself: yet again the sheep faced the hurdle and the fluttering benches behind, yet again the bitch sank in their rear. The time was going by, she had lost the benefit of her quick work at the beginning and the shepherd brought her once more to her feet. She raced to their right, but grew confused on his signals and sank at the wrong time, letting a sheep escape. The crowd began to laugh, for she seemed little better than a fool to them now. She collected the sheep for the last time, but they at once strung out across the face of the hurdle, and at the shepherd's furious whistle she openly cringed and began to creep away from the sheep. Hoots of laughter and miaowings pursued her across the field; only the shepherds were silent.

The red-headed man turned from the post, his face like murder. The time-keeper's whistle had blown to clear the field, and at his own whistle the bitch came slowly to within thirty yards of him. Nearer she would not approach. 'That bitch,' said the steward who had spoken to him before, 'you want to go quiet with her. She'll make or break after this.' The red-headed man hardly looked at him, but gripped his stick and made for the gate.

First he went to eat food and then began a round of the back streets, the spit-and-sawdust bars where the legginged touts and copers drank, and where the policemen walked in twos. When he entered a pub he moved ponderously, swinging his weight from side to side like a friesian bull, and he had a bull's eyes, gleaming, reddish, ill-tempered. At the Hart he pushed across the counter a corked medicine bottle. "Fill this! All whisky. No water." He slid his ten shilling note into a spill of beer, grinning into the landlord's cloudy face.

Behind him, wherever he walked, slunk the bitch. She was hungry and thirsty, but too terrified even to lap water. From time to time he stopped and looked at her; he had no need to threaten; her bones had softened inside her. He could wait for the reckoning; delay would add to the pleasure. And the more he drank the blacker-hearted he grew. She'd make him look a fool before them all—all right, they'd see.

Later in the evening he went down to the woollen mills where before now he had found someone hardened or needy enough to accompany him back to the Rocks. He avoided the women who knew him, and struck into a bargain with someone he had not seen there before, a woman in the early thirties with an old, used face, dressed in country black. 'Come back to my place,' she wheedled. 'We can talk there. P'raps I will, p'raps I won't. We can settle it after.' They were both smiling, his face cunning, brutal, hers set in a mirthless coquetry. 'All right,' he said thickly, his hands opening and shutting. 'Where?'

They were walking down a dingy, low-fronted street. 'There's a dog following us,' she said.

He began to curse the bitch, his luck, everything that had happened that day. 'Eh,' she said, 'you don't want to take it that bad. She looks frightened.' She patted her knee, clicked her tongue to call the bitch to her, but the creature stayed at the same distance, sitting and shivering.

'Leave her,' he growled. 'She'll follow. She better!'

The bitch turned away at his tone, but when they went on to the woman's room she trailed them behind, like a lost soul. Hours later when the woman slid from the bed and went to the window overlooking the street the bitch was still there, outside the house, lying uneasily at the edge of the shadow. Behind her the red-headed man stretched and groaned in his sleep and she looked round at him, his huge lardlike shoulders, the thick neck and hairy hands. 'Swine,' she whispered, 'filthy swine!' Moonlight fell through the window with a pale green radiance, so that she could stare down the swollen whiteness of her body to her spread feet and the greasy fringe of the mat on the floor. 'Great God,' she whispered, 'Great God in heaven above!' She went quietly to the cupboard in the corner and hunted through her food-shelf till she found a piece of meat and a cake crust. She was back at the window with these when he sat up and asked what she was doing.

'The dog's outside,' she said, afraid of him. 'I was giving it food.'

'She don't eat tonight,' he told her. 'Nor p'raps tomorrow.' He leaned back against the bed-head, savouring her fear of him. 'I'm a bad 'un to cross. She got to learn it.'

'P'raps I got to learn it too, up at your place.' She reached for her raincoat and pulled it over her. The action, the covering her nakedness, gave her resolution. 'You can get dressed and clear out, and the sooner the better.'

He shook his head. 'I don't take orders. Not from muck like you, I don't.'

'I'm muck,' she said bitterly. 'Christ knows, but I'm too good for you at that. I'm wise to you, anyway, and I'm not coming.'

He closed his fist. 'I got a mind——' he began, but she had opened the door and stood half on the landing, staring in at him. 'Don't try anything,' she said. 'If I call, I got friends.'

'You!' he jeered. 'Friends!' But he got slowly out of bed and dragged on his clothes, swaying with exhaustion and drink. 'Muck like you,' he said, tying his laces. 'Friends!' He coughed and hawked with his heavy laughter.

Warily she watched him out of the room, backing away from the head of the stairs. He began to clump his way down, his boots hammering the boards, making all the row he could in that listening house. Then he was through the door with a shattering slam. She went back to the moon-filled window and looked into the street. For a half-minute she saw him leaning against the wall below her, then he began to walk away. The bitch emerged from shadow and, disregarding her low whistle, slunk after him.

The night air, cool and clean, drew him briskly forward. His head felt loose and large, but his legs moved steadily, his weight back on his heels, so that his progress rang and echoed between the houses. He felt he could walk a hundred miles. A brief good-humour filled him. Hadn't he been too clever for everyone? That landlord! He rumbled with beer and satisfaction. The woman he'd had—he swallowed appreciatively. If only he'd had a fair deal in the Field!

His good humour was gone. He looked round for the bitch. That woman. The judges. That blasted landlord scowling at him. Crike, he'd take it out of someone before he was through.

The houses had changed to hedges. There was no pavement, nor now a strake of dusty grass to walk on. The ring died out of the road; his boots were beginning to drag. He struck angrily at an ash branch which had missed the hedger's bill. If only it were that woman, the judges, the landlord—he thrashed it till the branch hung torn and a faint bitter odour of greenery tinged the air. He turned and called to the bitch but she kept her distance, her haunches tight, her head hanging forward.

It was then he heard the clopping of a horse, the scrape of wheel rims, and saw away behind the bitch the yellow blob of a headlamp. He went into the middle of the road, stood waiting with his stick raised.

'You, is it? said the man in the trap. The words were uncordial, the voice unfriendly. 'All right, get in. I'll take you to the usual place. That your bitch behind there?'

He was a compact, dried-out man nearing sixty, spry with gaiters, side-whiskers, and a hard hat, a big farmer from higher up the valley. He was a great one with the chapel and the local bench, and the red-headed man at once despised him and stood in awe of him, for he was the kind who could put the police on to you. The kind who would, too, if you touched his pride or pocket.

'She won't come,' he said sullenly.

'Not the first time to-day she made a fool of you,' said the farmer coolly. 'All right, if she won't ride I reckon she can run.'

He drove the mare smartly, as though she were before judges in a ring. The hedgerows were dipping past them, the mare's hooves tapped sleep into the red-headed man's brain. First his head rolled sideways and then he was canted on to the floor, groaning with discomfort, the sourness of drink rising into his mouth and nose. He was thinking, or dreaming, of the woman in her room when the shaking of the trap became so intolerable that he must open his eyes and struggle up. But the trap was stationary, and it was the farmer kicking hard at his feet to wake him. 'We are there. I was just going to tip you off.' He snaked the whiplash out sideways, gathered it neatly back to the handle. 'This bitch of yours now——'.

'Where is she?'

He pointed with the whip to where she lay gasping thirty yards down the road. 'I'll take her off your hands as a favour.'

For a moment the other couldn't take this in; he stood staring at his hands as though they should contain something. Then, 'Not for sale,' he said abruptly.

'I'm not talking about a sale.' His hard little eyes stared into the red-headed man while he reached for a wallet with a wide rubber band round it, opened it and drew out a note. 'Still, I'll make it legal.'

'Legal, hell,' said the red-headed man. He leaned so heavily on the back of the trap that the mare pawed uneasily. 'She's worth five, ten pounds. What's this? A scabby ten bob!'

'Take it,' said the farmer. 'I'm doing you a favour.'

'Favour, hell. I'll see you stuffed first!' He leaned forward into the trap, closed his fist. 'I got a mind——'

The man in the trap had made his decision. Instantly his whip cracked and the mare bounded forward so sharply that the red-headed man fell floundering on to the road. He came on to all fours, cursing and threatening, but the trap was disappearing round the next bend before his hand could close on a stone. 'Chapel bastard!' he swore, and turned to the bitch. This was her fault. Everything that had happened today was her fault. He'd see that she paid. 'Come here, damn you!' he called.

Suddenly he thought of the whisky in his pocket. The medicine bottle was undamaged and he took a long, noisy suck at it. Whisky was a whip, he told himself, and began to lurch up the mountain road.

But tired! After three hundred yards on the steep road he felt that till to-night he had not known what tiredness was. His legs were moving against rather than with his will. Only the pattern of resentment shaping in his mind drove him on. All the faces of the day, he saw them staring at him, landlords, stewards, judges, the woman who'd thrown him out—he ought to have smashed his fist into their grinning mugs. He'd been too soft, he'd let them outsmart him. To-morrow he'd go back and find them, his fist like this, see, smash them all. Smash, smash, smash!

His head swayed with thought. The bitch was the cause of it. Well, that was something he could take care of to-night. When he came to the path, to the peat stream, there'd be a pool big enough. He turned to look at her. 'Come here then, little 'un,' he said, wheedling and hoarse. 'Come to the old man.' Exulting in his stratagem, he began to coax her forward with soft words and endearments. Once she moved so much as a foot she was lost; she was powerless against the god she recognized in him, helpless against her craving for kindness after so horrible a day. 'Well then,' he said at last, stroking her head and slipping the leash on to her collar, shoving her frantic tongue from his face. 'We shan't be long now.'

Crike, but he was tired. 'I'm drunk,' he said aloud, and she wagged her tail with joy. 'Owl drunk. Where's the whisky? Crike, but I'm drunk!'

This was it! He must find a stone, a big stone. There it was, shining in the water, black with a glitter on it, just under the surface. Careful, he said, careful now. He heard a curious slapping sound and was puzzled what it could be. It was the bitch drinking. 'That's right,' he grinned. 'Plenty of water.'

He slipped the leash because it wasn't long enough for him to hold the bitch and reach the stone. But she wouldn't run away. She was ingratiating herself with him, frisking her tail, fawning and slobbering.

'Crike!' he said vexedly. There was a bright ringing weight in his head from where he had been stooping. And dimly he was aware that this was no real pool, just a couple of inches of water over pebbles, and they moving treacherously under his feet.

He shouldn't have stooped. He reeled as he straightened up, and saw a blinding moon flash from the heavens. His heels shot from under him, and he fell face down into the water. Still the great moon flashed and pealed, only it was all about his head now. He must get his head up out of the moon. It blinded and deafened him. He heaved with his back, thrust with his great hands, for a moment his mouth gasped air.

From the bank the bitch watched his play with increasing excitement and delight. She was barely a year old. She dabbled the water with her forefeet, whined and then yapped her pleasure. She wanted to join in the game. Emboldened now and dizzy with joy that the black of the day was behind her, she leapt for his arching back, and stood proudly with her two paws on his shoulders. She could feel him moving in muscle and lung, and she tried ecstatically to lick his face. But always her muzzle was repelled by the water; so she retreated to the bank and sat for a while wagging her tail in expectation that he would play with her again.

The shadows had shifted a broad handbreadth when she paddled out to him a second time and sniffed at the back of his head. Soon her paws were once more on his shoulders, for long seconds she sniffed and whimpered. Then the hair rose along her backbone, the muzzle pointed, and briefly she moaned in her throat before her long and lonely howl went tingling to the moon.

The Still Waters

'Let us now praise famous men, and our fathers that begat us.'
It is a serious, almost a divine, call; but here in Llanvihangel we
prefer a revised version: 'And the womenfolk that bare us.' We
judge it more prudent, for one thing—we better know what we
are about—and for another, here in Llanvihangel we are of the
matriarchy. Our men are nothing, or at best but male spiders who
exist to breed and be devoured. Nor shall we ever mend: in every
generation the spear yields to the distaff. To-day is as bad as
yesterday, and to-morrow will be worse.

And first of to-day. Whoever approaches Llanvihangel from
the Henllys side will have seen that hump of black barns under
the shoulder of the Foel. A remarkable old woman lived there
for close on seventy years, her name Lisa Owen. She had two
husbands in her time, but the first gave her no children, and the
second only a son. She frightened me terribly when a boy. I can
see her now, a gaunt woman, with a green-and-black checked
bodice, rough black skirt, and always a long black apron. Her
hair was white and very thin, so that you could see the grey skin
of her head through it, her nails were broken and her hands like
hooks; she carried out of doors a tapering ash stick, and all my
memory is of her cutting at the dog with it, or scattering the
fowls, or whacking the rumps of the cows, or threatening her son
Dafydd. Once only I felt it. I had been sent to Frongog with
fourpence for eggs. I knocked at the door, but there was no
answer, and I walked across the yard to the barn. Suddenly I
could hear someone getting a hiding—not a good healthy hiding
like the kind my mother gave me, with plenty of roaring and
dodging, but a purposeful and unescapable hiding, with the
slashes of a stick and sobbing and gasps. It went to my legs, the

fright of it. I couldn't move. I saw a farm dog go half on his belly round the pigsty—he was well out of it, for the time being. Then Lisa Owen came out of the barn, with her stick in her hand. 'It's the devil's work,' she cried in English. 'O Cythraul Diawl!' Then she saw me. 'Well?' she asked. I was dumb as a door-knob. 'Well?' she asked again, and her voice cracked like a branch. 'Well?' But my terror was a bait to her, and she struck sharply at my legs. 'Devil take the boy! Are they all bad?' A cruel stroke dulled my left thigh, and then without a sound I was running, running, running from the gaunt woman and her black farm and the boy who'd been thrashed in the shed.

With such a mother, the boy Dafydd must grow up crooked or daft. And daft he was. The kindlier use of the term. 'A bit twp' was the Llanvihangel phrase. 'He's all right, Dafydd Owen—just a bit twp.' You could tell this by the people he touched his hat to: the minister at Beulah (holiness), the auctioneer (authority), and myself. He touched his hat as a cowed dog grovels, with a sly placatory roll of the eye. His '*Owbe's* were offered with a high-pitched nervous affability.

It was a good-bad day for him when the Angel at length prised Lisa Owen's hands off her holdings under the Foel. Good, because he was free of one tyrant; bad, because he was freed for another.

I saw his wife in Newport yesterday. With her children, of course. Three children—none of them Dafydd's. But by her former husband. Oh, *most* respectable. Those of us born between Rhymney and Wye will hardly need a description of Mari Owen; there are so many in her image. A woman within a year or two of forty, dark but not black, a slight wave to her hair, which is drawn back from her ears into a tight coil on the nape of her neck. Her eyes are dark brown, the lashes long, the glance slanting smoothly from your own. Her skin is white and healthy, the lower lip full and sensual, the upper a shade too thin for ease of mind. Not a tall woman, her body strong from work but with an agreeable roundness. How often have I studied such women in my native Gwent—the fool spider meditating his ruin! That smile which says "Rush on disaster, for disaster is sweet'—how well I know it. And how I feel its power. That voice which rides on words like a wave of the summer sea—it will call to my bones when we of to-day are with the bones of yesterday.

I ask: What chance had Dafydd Owen, a bit twp he was, when such a woman wove a web for him? A widow too. Three kids to call him dad. What chance for me, perhaps, without my schooling? Let us now praise famous men, and our daddas that sent us to college.

The names of Sarah and Maldwyn Price will fall flat on ears beyond Monmouthshire. Even there they fall flat on most. Let us, to the honour of Llanvihangel and the glory of its womenfolk, conjure them from the silence of two centuries. So limited a fame is Maldwyn's for hanging that he may well ask himself whether it was worth it. What Sarah his sister asks herself now it is hardly for me to inquire.

You will seek in vain for Maldwyn in *The Annals of Roguery* or *The Tyburn Chronicle*. He is not even to be found in so unfastidious a repository as *The Complete Newgate Calendar*. For he was a novice, obscure—and Welsh. But the Machen Collection preserves an abstract of his trial in an italic-sprinkled folio, between the sentence of transportation for shoplifting on Elen Jones and that of branding and transportation on Edmund Jackson, Esq. This seems to be the only time Maldwyn rubbed shoulders with a gentleman (or do I strain the significance of that *Esq.*?).

I could wish to quote. The day is the seventeenth of December, the year 1759, the place Monmouth town.

Mr. Justice Fenton: The matter needs no dragging out. Put in the deposition of George Price.

This George Price, I interrupt to say, was Sarah Price's husband and brother-in-law of Maldwyn Price. The similarity of name was therefore, in a sense, fortuitous.

Clerk: If it pleases your lordship, the deposition was not properly witnessed.
Mr. Justice Fenton: That point is not yet established. Put in the deposition.

Clerk: The deposition of George Price, farrier, of Llanvi-hangel in the County of Monmouthshire: Being now in prospect of death and desirous of a clear conscience, I throw myself on the justice of my Country and the mercy of Almighty God, etc., etc. Till fourteen months ago I was a farrier at Llanvihangel, but in the month of September I so burned my hand and arm that I have never since had their use and could not follow my trade. On that account my wife and three children have been subject to great poverty, and sometime to that extent we were the twenty-four hours with nothing to eat. My brother-in-law Maldwyn Price helped us as he could, but he is a simple-minded man and subject to fits, and so is but rarely in employment. It was in the month of June this year I opened to him a project that we might waylay a traveller on the South Wales road and so find food for my family. He was much upset by this, and talked strongly against it, but my wife (his sister) urged it as strongly, and brought in the children that their want might plead with him, and at last he consented. He has always been a good uncle to my children. It was on Tuesday the fourteenth of August that we went towards dusk to a point on the South Wales road where three oak trees grow from one root. Here we waited, till a man on horseback came towards us, and him we robbed of three shillings and some pence. But I have said that my brother-in-law is simple-minded and subject to fits, and to our great misfortune he fell straightway on the road and did not recover himself for the best part of an hour. I was now frightened, fearing he would be searched out and known, and therefore, after we had delivered the money to my wife Sarah, I judged it best that we leave Llanvihangel for a while. We thereupon went north to the Beacons and had work of a kind on farms and gentlemen's houses. But one night, at Tre'rddol, we heard men at the door asking after us, and with that fled into the hills. There was a chase, and we were parted, and I have not seen my brother-in-law since. But I hear he is in custody, and now make this deposition that I did both originate and carry out this robbery with which he is jointly charged, and that he was at all times against it. He is a good man, but simple-minded.

Mr. Justice Fenton: Pray conclude the deposition.

The Clerk now brought evidence that George Price had died of an injury to his back when he fell into a ravine during his flight. Mr. Justice Fenton expressed himself pithily on a good riddance, and the case was taken further. It is all very matter-of-fact in that eighteenth century judicial English, and we must imagine for ourselves the plight of Maldwyn Price, alone, desperate, and hunted through the Beacons. Like other simple creatures he had the homing instinct. Where else should he turn save to his sister? Probably he went by mountain tracks along the bleak highlands towards Nant-y-Bwlch, turning in alarm from the coal workings below Tredegar, and so south and east to the known river and the gentler hills that look to the Channel. He was seen north of Llanvihangel, 'very wild and exhausted', by a tinker who, however, kept his mouth shut till his information was of no value. There was a reward of five pounds on his head by this time, but our tinker was maybe outside the law himself and unable to draw blood money. And now let Sarah Price take up the tale.

Sarah Price: It was after dusk of Tuesday, the seventeenth September. I was with my children in the house when someone knocked at the door. I called out: *Who is there?* and my brother answered. I was unwilling to let him in, but was afraid for my children and so gave him shelter.

Mr. Justice Fenton: How long was he with you thereafter?

Sarah Price: For five days, until he was taken by the officers.

Mr. Justice Fenton: You deny on oath that you were a party to this robbery?

Sarah Price: I do. My actions have proved it.

A brisk answer. To know what these actions were, let us turn to the evidence of Humphrey Jenkins, who made the arrest.

Humphrey Jenkins: Acting on information laid I went on the morning of Monday, the twenty-third September, to the house of George and Sarah Price. The door was opened by Sarah Price. We found Maldwyn Price between a piece of boarding and the water-butt. He cried a good deal when we led him off, and asked in God's name that he be permitted to speak with his sister and kiss her children, but this I had no power to allow. He was straightway committed to gaol, where he continued to cry after his sister for that day and the night that followed. Since hearing that his sister laid information against him, he has been very low.

How foolish of Maldwyn Price to be so very low. But there, we have heard he was simple-minded, a bit twp—like Dafydd Owen. And subject to fits. It was Mr Justice Fenton alone of surgeons who now took his cure in hand, a quick and bitter cure. If it was so bitter after all. For, to look on the bright side: this is no world for the simple-minded, and was there any other way he could have found five pounds towards the succour of his nephew and nieces? At three shillings and some pence a time it would have taken him thirty highway robberies to collect such a sum, and he simply hadn't the talent for it. Perhaps this weighed with Sarah his sister. Besides, we have a duty to the law.

But let us return to Mari Owen in Newport, with her children. Let us return to her with a sense of history. For how natural it is to think of Sarah and Mari together, of Maldwyn Price and Dafydd Owen. What chance, we have asked, for Dafydd when Mari came a-courting? He had been ruled so long he was glad to be ruled again—and this one was warm and kind, honey and milk were under her tongue, and her head upon her was like Carmel. They were married very quietly, as befitted a widow, and for a month the sun stood still in heaven. Then one bright morning, before the dust could dim Dafydd's wedding bowler, Mari marched her husband to the recruiting station at Newport Drill Hall. She did the talking, while Dafydd nodded and grinned and said 'All right too!' in his high-pitched affable way, and before they turned for home he was a '39 enlistment in the Welsh Rifles. We have a duty to our country, and Dafydd, though he hadn't fussed much before, was now in line to do his. He was killed in the covering action at Arras in '40—no medals, no mentions, just another Daio gone to Catraeth with the dawn—and Frongog is now Mari's, and will be her children's in their turn. A good provider, this Mari Owen—like Sarah Price before her. Nor should we forget Dafydd's pension: Mari didn't—she was in Newport about that yesterday.

There are times, let me admit it, when I fear I am hard on these women of ours. Lisa Owen, for instance—it's a fine old proverb (it may even be scripture): Spare the rod and spoil the child. And Sarah Price—we can't hide that her brother *was* a highwayman. In old wives' wisdom: The quiet ones are always the worst. As for Mari—I have said that she made Dafydd happy for a month. We might perhaps count this as two, for to end as we began, with Ecclesiasticus: 'Blessed is the man that hath a virtuous wife, for the number of his days shall be double.'

Their Bonds are Loosed
from Above

And Jael went out to meet Sisera, and said unto him, Turn in, my lord, turn in to me; fear not. And when he had turned in unto her, into the tent, she covered him with a mantle.

And he said unto her, Give me, I pray thee, a little water to drink, for I am thirsty. And she opened a bottle of milk, and gave him drink, and covered him.

Then Jael Heber's wife took a nail of the tent, and took an hammer in her hand, and went softly unto him, and smote the nail into his temples, and fastened it into the ground: for he was fast asleep and weary. So he died.

Blessed above women shall Jael the wife of Heber the Kenite be, blessed shall she be above women in the tent.

You wouldn't think there was anything in the fourth and fifth chapters of Judges to give a woman named Manod a bad turn, and she living in a fine house next door to a Methodist chapel. But that's where you'd be wrong. It gave her a turn all right. One Monday morning.

The house was in Eglwys Street, and its name was Brynhyfryd. You never saw a nicer house of its kind, with a coloured glass panel in the front door, a piano, and a big oak dresser from Flintshire blue as the sky with willow-pattern china, and on the window table in the parlour a well-dusted Bible with gold clasps. You never saw a nicer widow either, of her kind: clean and respectable, threepence in the plate every Sunday, and none of your fly ones dangling a line for anything in navy trousers. A widow who kept to herself, and could keep to herself, for what with the insurance on Manod, deceased, she had more than her leg to fill an old stocking with. He was a peculiar fellow, that Manod—you never knew quite where you were with him. He had ways. And what a soaker! It couldn't last, everyone knew that—after. Here to-day and gone to-morrow, and a last big bottle of brandy gone with him. Well, here's our wreath. It wasn't as though we didn't warn him.

No one in Eglwys Street will forget Sunday the 24th. Three hundred planes over, the wireless said. They rough-ploughed the city and sowed it with glass. No night for sleeping. The very dead shuddered in the ground.

Yet, like many another, Mrs. Manod came down that Monday morning with more curiosity and exhilaration than dread. Nothing had fallen too near, not a window was out at Brynhyfryd. Yet there was something different about the house, she felt it at once, something—she could not say. She lit a fire in the kitchen, had her breakfast. It was towards nine o'clock, as she drew back the curtains in the parlour, that she noticed the Bible open on the table in the window.

She would have shut it without thinking, and only later felt surprise, had she not noticed a number of ugly brown smudges on the right-hand page. This vexed her, for the Bible was a great treasure, and the less meddling with it the better. She bent forward to examine the smudges and could not help reading a few words. Among them were *nail* and *hammer*.

Mrs. Manod felt herself in the midst of a silence that stretched past earth to the tingling stars. Yet it was silence audible, vibrating on the ear like telephone wires on a mountain, in a high wind. She had, too, a sensation that everything save the Bible was receding from her on all sides, as though titanic springs had contracted outside our mortal dimension. But the Bible, its leaves humped up at her like two unbroken waves of the sea, displayed in glittering black letters the tale of Jael and Sisera, not word by word but verses, chapters, simultaneously. Then she grew aware of the pulsing of her blood, the jump of her heart. There was a smell from the smudges that sickened her.

But Mrs. Manod was a brave and strong-nerved woman. For some minutes, maybe, she stood gripping the table, then she took out her handkerchief, flicked at the smudges and their dusting of red earth, shut the Bible with a heavy slapping of leaves, pressed the gold studs home, and walked back to the kitchen.

Ten minutes later she re-entered the parlour. The Bible was

shut and flat, the window secure, everything was very tidy. She went back upstairs, put on her coat and hat, and went out, locking the door after her. The buses were running and she set about such shopping as she could.

Talk, talk, talk. Everybody talking—friends, strangers, even old enemies talking. She heard a woman—no one could help hearing her: 'Not a thing damaged, look, not a window, not a cup, not a blade of grass on the lawn. But the cuckoo in the cuckoo-clock, he started at eight this morning and went on cucking eight hundred and forty-four times. Our Harry counted him. Not even soot down the chimney, but that cuckoo he cucked eight hundred and forty-four times, like our Harry counted. "Spring in the air," I said to Harry, but "Spring a leak," said Harry to me. Something we've come to, I tell you!'

Mrs. Manod nodded, though the conversation was already racing past her. There was an explanation for everything, if only you could think of it. 'I had a book blown open on the table,' she said, loudly, to anyone who cared to listen. 'The window was shut, but the book was blown open. A big Bible, with gold clasps on it, blown open.' She said nothing about the smudges.

'That's right,' said the woman who had spoken first. 'Proper pagans, them Nazzies. They'd go for a Bible like St. Patrick for a snake. There's that cuckoo-clock of our Harry's—it cucked eight hundred and forty-four times, like I was telling this lady only this minute——'

'A big Bible, with gold clasps,' Mrs. Manod repeated. 'Blown wide open. The window was shut all the time.'

She was steady as a rock now, and stayed steady. In the afternoon she was asked to help with meals for the bombed-out, at the chapel next door, and was hard at work till nightfall. She was taking off her apron, fagged-out, when behind her a voice said: 'They hit the cemetery too. Mind, they aren't spreading the news up there.' There was a harsh laugh. 'Better them than us.' The first voice continued: 'One or two made a move last night who might have been expected to stay put for ever.' Someone else said 'Sh-sh-sh,' the talk ended feebly, as though they had noticed her and remembered Manod, deceased.

Inside her own door, Mrs. Manod hesitated and then went to

the parlour. The Bible was shut and flat, the curtains drawn, everything was very tidy. She thought once to look again at the smudges, but instead hurried upstairs, locking her door, forcing a chair-back under the knob for safety, fastening the windows. When after many hours she fell asleep, the night-light was left burning.

It was still burning when she awoke from nightmare. There was a bustling noise under her window, at the front door. She saw the clock on the chair at her bedside. Eight-fifteen. She rushed from bed, tore at the curtains, tore at the catch. 'Wait!' she cried to the milkman leaving her gate. 'Wait, I want to pay you!' 'But it was only——' 'No, wait!' she cried again. 'Don't go!' He looked up, groped for his book. 'Righto.' He began to whistle, a cheerful jiggy tune that helped her into her dressing-gown, to the switch on the landing. But no light came, and she had to pass the parlour door in the dark. 'It's not the money,' she said at the front door, blessed daylight flooding the passage. 'I had a bad night. I thought I heard something. I was afraid to go down. And I couldn't get a light—I wanted you to look. It's all dark from the black-out. I've been afraid, I think I must have been.' He was a big fat fellow, with a bloodhound's face and red hands, and put his book into his pocket. 'The electricity's off all through town,' he told her. 'It's the bombs.' He stepped past her, doubling his left fist into his right palm. 'For your sake and his, I hope he ain't here.' He looked back and saw the postman passing the gate. 'Oi! Might be a burglar in the house. Keep an eye on the front.' The postman was a small man, a local preacher, Mrs. Manod had heard him next door many a time. 'Then God have mercy on him, a sinner.' 'Amen,' said the milkman, nursing his fist.

But there was nothing there. The milkman went right through twice, pulling every curtain back, at Mrs. Manod's request looking into cupboards and wardrobes, and coming a bit red-faced from under the bed. 'Not a sign,' he said. 'Anything seem to be missing?'

'Not a thing, not a thing!'

'That's a bad lock,' said the milkman, in the scullery. 'You could think you'd locked that, and every other time it would have slipped right round to open again. Look.' He twisted. But

Mrs. Manod wanted to be on her own. She had her bag in her hand by this time. 'Not at all,' said the milkman, telling a shilling from a halfpenny by the feel of the rim. 'A pleasure. Any time at all!'

The postman was still there, frowning. 'If we can't help a fellow Christian without taking——' he began. 'But there, I can put it in the collection.'

The door closed behind them. Mrs. Manod stood for a moment holding her heart. Otherwise it would jump right out of her body. Then she pushed at the parlour door. The Bible was shut and clasped, the china shone, everything was very tidy.

The flat cover of the Bible was the loveliest sight she had ever seen. A fine broad cover of boards overlaid with black leather, blind-tooled, with a gold shield in the centre, the edges like yellow silk. And flat.

But was it quite flat? Was it? Or was there a ruffling of the gilt edge? a mere nail-breadth of white against the gold? And were these flattened crumbs of earth from the milkman's boots? O merciful Jesus, were they?

Mrs. Manod cupped her hands over her mouth. Then, resolutely, she crossed to the window table, unclasped the Bible, lifted it open. Again she had the sensation of a world speeding away from her through the tightening of titanic springs beyond any edge that thought could reach to; again there was envelopment by a strung silence through which hummed the tension of taut wires. The Bible had opened at Judges, at a page brown-stained and crumpled, and embedded in the twenty-first verse of the fourth chapter was a sharp, slender, headless nail.

Then Jael Heber's wife took a nail of the tent, and took an hammer in her hand, and went softly unto him, and smote the nail into his temples, and fastened it into the ground: for he was fast asleep and weary. So he died.

Mrs. Manod stood there by the table for a very long time. She could feel the heavy gush of blood from her heart, and even the damp and chill that slowly crept upwards from her feet; but she had no power of motion, nor any means of purposeful thought. There was horror all around her, but it could not break in one bound through the stupefaction which blanketed her reason. She was roused at last by a growing awareness of a smell so foul she could not endure it, and went blunderingly to the kitchen, where she was sick.

For a long time afterwards she sat by the kitchen fire, watching the orange flame clamber through the sticks and coal. She rubbed her hands together, thrust her shins almost against the bars, and once she got up hurriedly to lock the door leading to the passage. She was piecing things together. She had never lacked nerve, had Mrs. Manod. There had been a time, indeed, at a crisis of her life, when she had shown a hardly credible courage and strength. She was thinking back to it, now.

An hour later and she had joined a small group of women outside the cemetery gates. These were locked, and a well-spoken, patient official was assuring one caller after another that there had been a slight disturbance, it was true, that no one could be allowed inside just for the present, but that everything was in hand and by to-morrow he didn't doubt, etc., etc. There was no need for distress: the authorities would take care of everything with promptitude, efficiency, and reverence. But Mrs. Manod wasn't satisfied. In Eglwys Street lived an employee of the parks and cemeteries authority, who looked none too easy when she knocked at his door after tea. Well, all he could say was—his words added up to nothing. What part of the cemetery? Well there, Mrs. Manod, you really must excuse him from answering a question like that. He hedged, raised his hands, shook his head, but Mrs. Manod got her answer from his wife's pitying yet gloating eyes. All would be as it was to-morrow, though. She startled him at that, grabbing his arm. To-morrow? He was certain? He'd swear it on the Bible.

'There's a woman for you,' he told his wife, when Mrs. Manod had gone. 'There's devotion! And all for a chap as killed himself with a bottle of brandy. Paralatic, as the saying goes. He was a rum sort of chap, too, something about him, you never quite knew where you'd got him or not.' He put his feet inside the fender. 'I'll smack him down good and hard to-morrow, too true I will.' He told his wife stories that made her back crawl. 'It's a secret, mind. Not a word! I'll have that bottle of beer now, Emmie, I think.'

Mrs. Manod had a busy evening. First she cleaned the parlour. The bits of earth she threw into the kitchen fire, remarking their colour; the carpet had a good stiff brushing; the nail (it was rather like a very long gramophone needle) she put into an envelope in her pocket; the Bible was shut and dusted. When she had finished, everything was very tidy. She also took the bolt from the coal-house door and rescrewed it in the scullery, and she saw to the catches of all the windows. It pays to be careful of one's bit of property. And she felt better when she was doing something.

Before she could go to bed the raid of the 26th started. It lasted till long after midnight. There were explosions between her and the cemetery at which she smiled grimly. In time, bombs fell nearer Eglwys Street and the doors and windows rattled in their frames. This worried her, and from worry she came near panic. If they were blown in what was to stop anyone—she had almost said *anything*—entering? She thrust sticks into the kitchen fire, threw on more coal, lit a second night-light. In a quiet fraction of time she heard the crackle of her slates as shrapnel fell. Surely no one would be tempted from cover on a night like this? A mobile gun had run to the end of the street; it began firing raggedly, so that the house shuddered, her saucepans jingled, and the toasting-fork alongside the chimney fell frighteningly into the steel fender. This dreadful gun, punctuating the uproar, was worst of all to bear. Her bowels leapt at its crack and whine; she waited through its silence in agony.

Suddenly, terror drove out terror. The din was at its worst when she saw the knob of the scullery door turn. She got stiffly to her feet, her head jerking forward. The knob was twisted sharply, then furiously, but the bolt held. For a moment it rested, then turned slowly and powerfully left, right, left, right, but the bolt was heavy and the screws long, and nothing happened. It rested again: the knob itself like a tiny round baffled face. Mrs. Manod grinned. She'd always been too clever for him. Too clever for everyone.

She was still grinning at the knob when there came a knocking at the front door. She stopped then, her eyes going from scullery to hall-passage. The knocking came again, more loudly. She wavered. It might be *him*, but it might be a warden, a fire-fighter, a gunner, a first-aid worker. Carrying a night-light she went swiftly upstairs to her own front room, saw that there were matches handy, blew out the light, and opened her window an inch or two. 'Who's there?' She strained her eyes downwards. Over most of the street there was a pale blue light pronged with orange and red, but the chapel fell blackly across Brynhyfryd. 'Who's there?'

The gun at the corner sent all other noise rocketing outward. It was in her heart to slam the window, draw the curtains and have light, but instead she pushed it up further and leaned her shoulders out. 'Answer!' she cried. 'Who's there?' An unspeakable savour of corruption reached her nostrils. 'Go back,' she cried; 'Go back where you belong!' She began to laugh. 'The door is locked, and you can't get in. I've always been too clever for you.'

Knock, knock, knock. 'Go back,' she shouted; 'Go back where I put you. You've only got to-night. And the door's locked and bolted.' She screamed with laughter.

Then Mrs. Manod saw a sight few may see and live. Huge fountains of fire spouted from the railway station to Eglwys Street, each with a roar that shook her head like a doll's. The hollow air sucked her forward, the window sprayed like hail into the street, stunned and bleeding she saw where the dark had been a tattered human figure beating at the knocker below. She fell back into the bedroom as the house opposite reared like a huge red horse; there was a thudding followed by a lurch, and then a long grinding and crackling. The floor, she found, had tilted under her. Through a hole in the wall opposite she could see flames blowing like washing in a wind, and as she huddled herself together the corner of her room slid out into the roadway. Two thoughts came to her mind. The first—and she had never been more serious—was: Well, the government will have to pay for this! The second was: Nothing in the street below could survive that explosion. She nodded to herself. Nothing.

She must move, though. There were flames behind her, she could tell, as well as over the street. She got to her feet, painfully. She had never lacked nerve, had Mrs. Manod.

But at the head of the splintered stairs she stopped, and for all the fire around her her blood grew cold and slow as ice. Something was coming upstairs to her, something on all fours, tattered and scorched, with great labour and application. 'Don't!' she cried. 'O merciful Jesus, don't!' It didn't raise its head at her outcry, but slowly dragged its knee one step higher. At each movement it appeared to overcome some more than mortal dislocation. And past the clean and acrid smells of smoke and red destruction there came the odour of its decay.

Yet its slowness was deceptive. How quickly it came near! She ran back to the bedroom, but the door was out of plumb, she couldn't fasten it, and hurried panting to where the wall fell to the street. But the flames—she could not face them. Through all the uproar of the night she heard a rubbing and shuffling at the door and saw it open. What entered was shrouded in charred linen, but part of the head was exposed, and part of the arms. Her jaw yammered like a dog's at the foul bone, the blue-black of rottenness, the horror of the skull. It turned in her direction at once, moving on wrists and knees, the fingers hooked ahead, purposeful and informed. The nail! The nail! She snatched the envelope from her pocket, flung it between the hands. It stopped, the fingers groped and found. Thank god! she thought, thank god! It would leave her now.

The left knee crept forward, the left hand thrust for her foot. For the first time it lifted its face, and Mrs. Manod threw herself shrieking into the street.

Mortal time had almost ceased for Mrs. Manod. She had but one flicker of sight and thought to come. When her eyes opened it was to see something like a filthy whitish caterpillar crawling head-first down the broken brickwork towards her.

They were as good as their word at the cemetery. Everything was very tidy there the next day. But the man from Eglwys Street swore an oath. 'Where's this one been?' he asked. His companion thought for a second. 'Hell and back, by the look of him.' The man from Eglwys Street bent and considered. 'By god!' he said.

He went away, but soon returned. Manod, deceased, was giving him something to think about. 'Leave him be a while, that's the orders. His wife was killed last night. She'd have given him the apples of her eyes, that woman would. I wish I had one like her.' He bent his back again. 'See that?' He scraped with his fingernail where you or I wouldn't. 'Stuck in the side of his head. You could still play the Dead March in *Saul* with it.'

'What are we leaving him for?' grumbled the other. 'Adding to our work!'

'That woman pined for him,' said the man from Eglwys Street. 'Only last night she was asking and bothering. Before she got hers. They can be buried together now, in the one grave. Dear, dear, I think that nice,' said the man from Eglwys Street.

The Green Island

I

There was a man lying on the headland over Ffald-y-Brenin. His name was Merrill. He had been there for more than an hour, sometimes smoking, sometimes shifting his weight from elbow to shoulders, till the wild things had grown used to him. For a time a tawny-yellow hare sat sideways on to him, his long dark ears stiff as pitcher handles, his eye an unlidded jewel. High up against the blue a hawk was watching. Black and distant though he was, he looked filled with a compressed and savage energy. He had seen the hare, but saw the man too, and was afraid to stoop. Once only a lark began to rise, a short and struggling flight in the sun's eye; then, as though touched by the hawk's shadow, he checked his song, fluttered in a spiral, and fell like a stone to the ground. The man sat up, twisting his head towards the lark's point of impact. When he straightened, the hare had gone.

Winter had clung hard to the Welsh hills, spring was short and bitter, but now in the last days of May sunshine fell like cloth-of-gold over the western seaboard. Where he lay his heels sconched the last short salt-bleached violets, there were cowslips half-opened, and he saw the blue shield of the sea across a flame of gorse. Near the cliff wall the bushes had been clamped to earth by heavy winds from the south-west; their branches were tentacles of grey and gold, the spikes gripping at the stub grass. Further back, where Merrill was lying, the clumps were less compact, they grew higher, with strong flowery arms curved upwards like the fronds of ferns. When he sat up he could see to the north, between these spiky arms, the far-off outlines of mountains, sharp jags and rounded moels. Fronting him, out in the Bay, was Ynys Las, the Green Island. It lay a couple of miles offshore, its eastern cliffs groined with shadows as the sun moved down sky. It had the look of a fragment broken from the mainland, and the local story, he knew, rested on this: how king Bleddri had flung a gobbet of his country after another king, Maredudd, who was sailing for Ireland with his, Bleddri's, wife. It had missed, of course. 'They always miss', he said, getting to his feet. 'Always.' The thought pleased him and he repeated it as he brushed himself down. He shaded his eyes with his hand, staring westwards. 'Cunning', he said. 'Or they think they are.'

He looked at his watch, then turned and walked slowly away from the headland. It was a country of low hills and wooded cwms, and from where he stood he could mark the writhing valleys of two rivers. In slow gradation the height of land changed from green to cyclamen and rose, and so faded into the purple masses of the watershed. Here and there he could see a farm building, long, low, and white-washed. There was a drift of sheep across a near-by field, and from a farm away to the left, but hidden, he heard a dog barking excitedly.

At a step he was out of sight of the sea. A sheeptrack wound down in front of him; he took this, in one place pushing breast-high through gorse and the soft white arms of bramble. At the bottom of the slope he trod a line of stones across a quag, turned right up a gulley hanging with crab-shaped honeysuckle buds, and so came to a ridge which gave him a view of the long southern arm of the Bay. He was looking into the sun, a million light-pricks shot from the water into his eyelids, he shook his head.

'Cunning', he said again, and laughed less pleasantly. 'Or fools. Or we are.'

His train of thought lasted him over the ridgeway and down till he fell in with a cart-track leading to the sea. Soon he was among trees, oak with a feathering of ash, and infrequently the brilliance of young beech. All save those in the bottom were sidespilled by the wind, and where the tree-line ended in scrub and fern were less than twenty feet high. Their roots were enormous and exposed. It was as though they had cast out anchors, and these were dragging through a green surf.

He heard the brook before he saw it. It was on his left, running strongly in a gulch, and as he came to the end of the trees it swung right in a curve, and he crossed it by a low stone bridge. In a minute or two he would be at Ffald-y-Brenin.

Unease made him stop here and light a cigarette. He drew on
it without enjoyment, even without taste. 'What of it?' he said
suddenly, and louder than he had intended. The narrow valley
burst on to the Bay with blue violence; the Green Island lay
basking like a seal. His arms reached out for it with a trembling
passion. His jaw jutted, and he nodded fierce approval of the
ideas farrowing in his mind. His mouth had dried so quickly that
when he caught at his cigarette a sliver of rice-paper stuck to his
lower lip. Then he dropped his arms. He had the feeling oil had
run over all his limbs.

Flinging down his cigarette, he followed the brook to the
house and workshop at Ffald-y-Brenin. These were under the
one long roof, and fronted the Bay. The brook was imprisoned
in a green-flagged channel for its last twenty yards, with a drop-
gate to control its flow. Thence it ran to the black wheel which
drove the saws and lathes, and after a tumble of ten or twelve
feet went in wide transparent runnels through the shingle to the
sea. He heard the soft roar of a saw as he came towards the workshop door, but after a moment's hesitation went on to the house.
A board on the wall outside said: DAFYDD ABSALOM,
TURNIWR, and underneath, obviously an afterthought, was
written in chalk: *Wood Turner*. As he read, two dogs ran out of the
house to welcome him, one with a huge ugly bucket-head, the
other a crossbred sheepdog in whelp. They pawed at him and
barked till—'Shut it!' shouted a voice from the workshop, when
they dropped at once to four feet, their eyes rolled, and bucket-
head went off round the corner of the house.

So he saw me come past, he thought, pushing at the house door.
Well, he would.

Mrs. Absalom was laying their tea. 'Oh', she said, 'it's you, Mr.
Merrill?' 'Yes', he said, 'it's me.'

'Well now—the men always come home for their eats, don't
they?'

'They come home for everything they can't get elsewhere.' He
spoke his sentence carefully, watching her the while.

She moved warily to the door. 'Dafydd!' she called. Merrill
smiled ungraciously. But he didn't take his eyes from Mrs
Absalom framed in the doorway, with the glitter behind her.

'Where's Mrs. Merrill?'

'She's been resting. I knocked at the door a few minutes ago, and she'll soon be down. Ah, there's a busy man that Dafydd's been', she went on. 'Finishing the spoons for the day after to-morrow—and there's the Wise Man's to go to to-morrow night. No time, no time at all!' She looked over her shoulder. 'What are you staring at?'

'You', he said bluntly. 'And you know it.'

Her lips moved soundlessly. 'Staring's rude, Mr. Merrill.'

He looked slowly the length of her body. 'And thinking's ruder, Mrs. Absalom.'

'We must control our thoughts. Everybody knows that. It's in the Bible. And why should you stare at me?'

'I'll tell you.' Her full lips parted, she patted her smooth black hair. He would have moved towards her, but—'Here's Dafydd', she said calmly. 'Beat off the mess', she cried to her husband. 'Here's Mr. Merrill back.'

He heard Absalom clouting the wood-dust from his clothes before coming indoors. Then Mrs. Absalom brushed past him, smiling her sly smile, to wet the tea on the hob. 'Tea was always such a meal up at the Hall', she said mincingly. 'All the things silver, and the lovely cups and saucers. Dear me now, weren't those the days!' Briskly she untied her check apron, smoothed her hips, patted her hair again. 'I wonder if Mrs. Merrill . . .'

Her husband came quietly in. He nodded briefly when he saw Merrill, who was by the passage door. 'I'll just go up', he was saying, when he heard a door open and close and his wife on the stairs. 'No, I needn't.' He stood waiting for her to enter, moved solicitously, and was annoyed by the swift downward flash of Mrs. Absalom's eyes.

'Did you sleep?'

'No—but I rested.' She turned to the Absaloms. 'This is really the quietest place in the world.'

'It is not bad', said Absalom, halting on each word.

'For sleeping in', his wife added tartly.

Absalom seemed in one of his moods, the sulkiness of his face imposing silence on others as well as himself. His face was swarthy, with a coarse glow of health along the cheekbones, the eyes black and slanting, the mouth red and hard. Some unresolved queerness of personality marked him as with a scar. When as to-day he came straight to table from the workshop, grey or ruddy sawdust fine as flour might be seen in the whorls of his ears, in the wrinkles under his eyes, and even threaded on his lashes. His hands were dusty as a miller's. A spot of oil had fallen against his index finger: he saw his wife's eyes on it and ostentatiously took out a red handkerchief and wiped it away.

'You are very busy, Mr. Absalom?'

He nodded, hesitated, was driven to words. He had determined on resentment against his wife when Mrs. Merrill's question came placidly in. 'Unless I've been wasting my time.' He was groping in his pocket. 'On this, say.' He laughed unexpectedly, showing an unpleasant scum of dust at the corners of his mouth. 'If you ever saw better than that up at the Hall', he challenged Mrs. Absalom and sat back watching them all. He had placed on the tablecloth a small rimless bowl of a simple but beautiful shape, dull green and veined all over, with some of the pattern running to the greener shades of blue. 'Oh, may I touch? May I touch?' cried Mrs. Merrill. Absalom's face ridged with a smile, yet as though against his will. 'Now, Mr. Merrill', he said rapidly, 'you are a college-trained man.' He pointed to the bowl between Mrs. Merrill's long white fingers. 'What is it?'

Merrill took it from his wife. It was hard, heavy, cold as stone. He tapped it with the ball of his finger. It must be wood, yet this was like tapping a pebble.

'Would it be malachy?' asked Absalom, thrusting his head forward.

'Malachite?'

'Dafydd always gets mixed on those big words', said Mrs. Absalom.

'It's all the same thing. Is it?'

'I don't know.'

'Ah', said Absalom, turning to his audience, 'then there's things after all even a college-trained man don't know.'

'A great many', Merrill agreed, wondering what idea of a college Absalom carried in mind. 'It's wood, of course.'

'The colour?' cried Absalom excitely.

He shook his head.

'The weight? The coldness? The grain—go on, look at the grain!'

To Merrill his triumph and mystery were overdone. He looked at the two women and realized with a shock that while Mrs. Absalom regarded her husband's excitement with a cynical humour, his own wife was watching him, Merrill, with a withdrawn but real mockery. 'You tell us', he said roughly.

'Whatever it is, Mr. Absalom', said his wife, 'it is very, very beautiful.'

Absalom's nod had to do for thanks. 'I thought a clever man like Mr. Merrill would know it was oak', he said, with what struck Merrill as unpleasant deference. His gesture overrode their surprise. 'Ffald-y-Brenin oak.' He took the bowl from Merrill, turned it gently in his hands, and went on to explain how three years ago, fearing it might have gone rotten, he had removed the block from under the mill wheel. 'My grand-dad's dad put it there, they tell me.' The block had proved hard and heavy as a rock, but the green of moss and slime and perhaps some mineral quality of the water had dyed it to the heart, and from this heart he had turned his bowl on the pole lathe. 'No doubt, I should have been making spoons for the Abermaid porridge-eaters', he admitted belligerently.

'Is it for sale?' asked Merrill.

Absalom was staring down the table, and seemed to be thinking hard. 'Not for sale', he replied shortly.

'That's foolish talk', said Mrs. Absalom. She pronounced the word 'fullish' always. 'What are things for if not to sell?'

But Mrs. Merrill was shaking her head. 'I can understand that so well, Mr. Absalom.'

He smiled at her, his eyes half-closed. 'Besides, I can show it at the Eisteddfod. This will make the Abercych men mad, I tell you. All over Wales I shall get a first with this.' He held the bowl to his ear as though it were a seashell full of music.

'But you can make another', Merrill persisted.

'Can I?'

'From the rest of the block—of course you can.'

'If you think it so easy . . .'

'It wouldn't be, for me. It should be, for you.'

Absalom spoke pointedly to Mrs. Merrill. 'It's because the wood is unnatural. It cracks on the lathe, or it cracks in the drying. This was the third for me to try.' He passed the green bowl back to her. 'This one may crack yet. Things are very different often from what they seem. And if it cracks who'd want it? No one would keep a flawed thing, would they?'

'It isn't flawed, is it?' Mrs. Absalom asked sharply. 'So why a lot of old talk?'

'Why indeed?' Absalom had moved towards the door. The meal was over. Merrill took out his pipe, Mrs. Absalom had reached for her apron. 'I'll help you clear', said Mrs. Merrill. Merrill saw how she stood tired and pallid in the shadow near the passage. We are made as we are made, he thought, watching her; and wondered whether he had been fatuous or profound. 'If you don't mind—' said Mrs. Absalom, bright and arch, with her Hall-parlour good manners. She moved past him with the tray. 'Clean as you go— that was always the rule, and such a good one, isn't it?'

He stood in the doorway, staring across the shingle and pebbles and the water's dark edge. Ripples were rising a hundred yards out, on a sandbank, but flattened as they reached deeper water. Then once more they crumpled upwards, crawling in with hardly any increase of height, till near the shore they curled into radiant feathers, hesitated and fell over with quiet nudgings into the hissing shingle. All was silent in the workshop, but the crossbred bitch sat against the wide door. Behind him he heard the women talking as they washed up, and presently they came out to join him, for a minute as they said, before Mrs. Merrill went upstairs to remake her bed.

'Would you like to go for a walk?' he asked his wife. 'Not too far, just around the beach.'

She shook her head. 'Later I might. But I'm going to watch Mr. Absalom. He is going to make me a special spoon. But not a sweetheart's spoon.' Beside her Mrs. Absalom glowed with a svelte good health; the sun which lost itself in the soft brown hair of the one woman glittered on the twin raven wings of the other. 'What lovely hair you have', said Mrs. Merrill at that moment. 'And how it gleams in the sun!' Mrs. Absalom turned, her red lips parting. 'And how warm the sun is,' Mrs. Merrill continued. She looked at her husband. 'And how sad it should grow cool and dim and then dark.'

Merrill frowned, disregarding the commonplace, but not so Mrs. Absalom. 'Only for the night', she replied cheerfully. 'And then it comes again.' For a moment she rested her hands on her hips, the very image of sly and jocund womanhood. 'That's the one thing about the country', she concluded, 'it makes you moody between whiles.'

Absalom was coming out of the workshop. The bitch fell in at his heel, grey-flanked and brindled down the spine and tail. She was far gone, her bag heavy, the teats like huge red teeth under her. Her tail swept slowly and unceasingly.

'Ask him again for the green bowl', Mrs. Absalom told Merrill. 'He will sell when he thinks it over.'

Absalom's teeth flashed. 'I am going to make your spoon', he called, all good humour. 'It will be something to watch, I can tell you.'

'I'll leave the bed till later. I'm coming! And you', Mrs. Merrill told her husband. 'We must all see.'

But Mrs. Absalom was shaking her head. 'Not me. I had my spoon a long time ago.' Her glance passed through Merrill's as she turned back in and they went off to the workshop door.

Absalom was waiting for them there. It was a small square room he had to work in, without any windows, but with a door almost the width of the front wall. Inside there was room for two lathes, one the old-fashioned pole lathe, the other driven by the wheel. There was a pleasant mustiness in the air there. Just inside the door stood an untrimmed chopping block, on which lay a short-hafted, heavy-headed axe. Merrill felt its edge as Absalom fetched three glowing rounds of cherry wood for them to sit on. He and his wife were opposite each other; Absalom had set himself to face the light.

'It is quite easy really', said Absalom. At the same time he smiled rather cunningly. 'What you call a snip.'

'When you know how!'

'When you know how. Now watch me, Mrs. Merrill, and

afterwards'—he dropped his eyes—'you shall make one for your husband.'

With a fast snaky motion he snatched an oblong of sycamore from the lathe-bed behind him. It went over to his left hand, slid and was gripped, and his right caught up the axe close to the head, his index-finger lying along the blade. Without any pause he had begun to chop. *Chuck-chuck-chuck* went the axe: each stroke fell a half-inch above its predecessor till the block bristled like a cock's comb, and then a last and heavier blow prised the whole cut away. *Chuck-chuck-chuck*—against his will Merrill grew interested. He raised his eyebrows at his wife. A shape was already emerging, the handle and the block where the bowl-end would be. So far Absalom had not appeared to give a thought to his work's end, but now for the first time he paused and let the whole thing lie on his palm. Then three savage strokes seemed to his watchers to ruin the whole block: the wood was rapidly reversed in his grip and a hasty feathering began anew along the handle and shoulders. He's showing off, thought Merrill; serves him right if he makes a mess of it—as he must. The spoon spun once more as in a conjuring trick, the axe hacked and gouged: as though in an instant the hollow of the bowl grew visible. Without a word Absalom set the axe down and reached for a thick-backed straight-bladed knife. Splints and shavings came whittling off the handle, again the shoulders were fiercely attacked, a dozen times Merrill could have cried, 'No, no, another cut will spoil it!' But a dozen times the cut was made till the shoulders carried a short spiky frill of splittings. *Crit, crit*, they were clear once more, clean and shapely. Absalom now caught from the lathe-bed a knife whose blade was first bent completely over parallel to the tang and then the bend contorted to a sideslipped S. With this he began to scoop at the bowl with that same apparent recklessness, the S-blade passing after each stroke within an inch of his naked wrist. 'Like to try?' he asked Merrill, grinning.

He picked up a spokeshave. 'A snip', he said again. This was pure conceit and showmanship. His elbow and forearm hugged his side, the fulcrum for his flashing wrist; the spokeshave moved at a fantastic speed with a backhand motion; the sycamore peeled away in curls and tendrils. 'When you know how.'

Again he gouged at the bowl hollow till it seemed he would break through the thin wood. 'We must make this very special'.

The handle was now long and slender, with a spatulate tip; he had achieved an exquisitely simple angle at its junction with the bowl. By a lucky accident, maybe, the grain of the wood followed the shape of the bowl, wavy yellow lines on white.

'Not bad', said Absalom complacently. 'Now when we . . .' He went over to the lathe, followed by Mrs. Merrill. 'It will be very plain', he told her. 'I never decorate. I am like my dad—all for line.' He reached once more for his knife, pleased as a child with Mrs. Merrill's praise.

Merrill went outside. All for line! He thought of Mrs. Absalom. Back at the house he found her folding linen on the kitchen table. 'I have seen the ninth wonder', he said drily. 'It was a very pretty spoon.'

'If Dafydd put his mind to it then it was', she agreed. 'I don't say he is better than the Henllan turner or those at Abercych, but he is as good.'

'Is he really?' He stood looking through the window. 'You are not going to Abermaid with Dafydd on Thursday?'

'I am not thinking to.'

'I'm going out to the Island.'

'You have quite a fancy for the Ynys, haven't you?'

'So you'll be able to come', he went on calmly.

She shook her head, smiling. 'I'd be afraid, Mr. Merrill, if I was on that island.' She spoke more slowly. 'I don't like being afraid.'

'Afraid of what?'

But she only smiled at him.

'Of me?'

'And why should I be afraid of you?'

'Of Dafydd then, if he knew you'd gone.' He persisted. 'Go on, say—would you?'

'I might be. Or again I mightn't. Anyway it's all a lot of fullishness we are talking. Why don't you go back to the workshop?'

'Because I'd rather stay with you.'

She had moved into the doorway as earlier in the day. 'I wonder why, Mr. Merrill?'

'Oh no, you don't! I know you pretty well by this time', he told her. He saw how she was watching him through narrow eyes. 'And you must know me too', he added harshly. 'Or you think you do. And if you do, it saves me a lot of words.'

She took him up quickly on that. 'Then there's no more to say, is there, Mr. Merrill?'

'Except that you'll come to the Island. I wouldn't eat you, you know.'

'I am not afraid of being eaten', she replied, with a slow and tantalizing smile. 'No, I am afraid of something quite different to that. Seasickness perhaps.'

'There are precautions', he assured her.

'Are there now? I wouldn't know. But the best thing is not to cross the water, surely?'

He knew the pleasure this kind of talk gave her, these hints and veilings and indirections. For hers, he knew, was the twofold sensuality of mind and body that kept with her to the last minute of each day.

'And when will Mrs. Merrill be coming back?' she asked him.

'Tuesday. And you know.'

'You will be quite the bachelor, I can see. And all fancy-free, I shouldn't wonder.' He thought wrily of his own hypocrisy in condemning her bad taste, momentarily saw himself mean and ugly. 'Quite a bachelor', he repeated, 'and fancy-free. And so— the Island.'

'It's very pretty, I must say', she said, shading her eyes. 'But goodness, I shouldn't like anyone to throw the Green Island after me, Mr. Merrill.'

'There's no danger. And they always miss.'

She laughed aloud and stepped out on to the doorstep. At once the bitch, greedy for affection, waddled over from the workshop door. Mrs. Absalom began to sing 'Watching the Wheat', her light and tender voice like a shaft of the yellowing sun. 'I'm going to the shop again', he said at the end of her verse. She only nodded, her hand falling to the bitch's head. Behind him the song restarted, at once piercing and pathetic, the lyric melancholy of young love. Damn her! he thought. If it pleases her to play clever!

Inside the workshop door Absalom and Mrs. Merrill were examining the pole lathe. The spoon, he judged, was finished. 'Look', she cried, 'oh look! Isn't it wonderful?' 'I've seen it before', he answered but covered his ungraciousness with a smile and by crossing to the lathe. He rubbed his fingers along the ash pole, testing its spring. 'The clever people in the Museum down at Cardiff they tell me', said Absalom, 'this pole lathe would be thousands of years old—ones like it, I mean. Would that be right now, d'you think?' He didn't expect an answer. 'I sometimes think when I'm turning in here that I'll be the last man in Wales to use it in the way of trade. And that's a hard mouthful to chew on. I'm the only man of my age at it now.' He began to speak bitterly. 'It's all your shoddy stuff now. Well, I've never done it and I never will.' He rolled back some sacks in the corner, so that they could see spoons, bowls, egg-cups, butter-scoops and cream skimmers, all simple and elegant. 'That's yew', he was saying. 'There's a good wood for you.' He named sycamore, burr oak, yew again, and holly. 'And you'd never guess that— it's plum.' Objects turned with a peculiar swift stealthiness in his broad hairy hands. 'And here's a good one!' They all laughed. '*Llwy gam*.' This was a hobgoblin kind of spoon, with a huge bowl, thick round stem, and then a ridiculously disproportionate flattened end piece, all the parts fighting away from each other on a flowing double bend. 'Not quite your usual thing', said Merrill, turning it over in his hands, and then: 'Yes, I see it!'—for centrally through all its grotesque curves there flowed the fine bold line he had come to look for as Absalom's sign manual. 'I like it. Can I have it? And don't be afraid to put the price up.'

'*Llwy gam*—the crooked spoon.' Absalom raised his head. 'All right, it's yours. But watch your chin when you eat your porridge.'

'But why should you be the last to use the old lathe, Mr. Absalom? Is it so very hard?' Mrs. Merrill asked concernedly.

'It's all done in a hurry to-day. They can't be bothered.' His 'they' swung with his arm out from Ffald-y-Brenin, through Wales and the wide world.

'Then you must teach your son perhaps', she said, 'to use it after you.'

His vivid tricky face lost all expression. 'Yes', he said, and abruptly: 'Well, I must be getting on with my work.' It was blunt, direct dismissal.

'What you said about a son', Merrill told his wife as they walked down the shingle. 'He didn't like it, did he?'

'He would like children, that's why. And he knows he will never have them.' She spoke with complete calm. 'Mrs. Absalom will see to that.'

'Come, come—that's not for you to decide', he bantered.

'No, for her. And she has decided. She will be as barren as myself.'

He stopped convulsively. 'Look', he said, 'we settled . . .'

'I said that only by way of statement. If I can face it, you can.' He shrugged his shoulders. 'I've been wondering whether you'd be as pleased after all if I didn't come back on Tuesday. It's for so short a time. The journey is so long.'

'Why *pleased*? Is that the right word?'

'It was probably the wrong one.'

'It's for you to say. I'd want you to do what you wish—though that's not always so simple, I admit. Think it over, could we?' He hesitated. 'I'll come back with you on Thursday, if you like.' But he was thinking how stupid he was to say anything of the kind. As though anything could be solved by going back or unwinding the ribbon-pathways they had come. Not even pity—pity could solve nothing. He fell back on his earlier phrase: We are made as we are made—as though that explained or excused anything. 'Would you like me to?'

She shook her head. 'No, don't come. I'd rather not. Perhaps we'll both have time to think. For we'd better think.' But he looked stubbornly out to sea. 'Is it to stay as it has been?'

'It's what we said. It's no one's fault. It's happened, that's all. Anything I can do—anything I can give you . . .'

'I want nothing from you except what you seem unable to give.'

'Haven't we had this out before?' he asked angrily. 'It changed, it all changed. I didn't want it to.'

'And I didn't want it to. But it means I'll leave you.' He kept silence. 'We can't go on living a sham.'

'Why not? The whole world's a sham, God knows!'

'I am, I know', she said quietly.

'I didn't mean that. You know I didn't mean that!'

'No?' she said. She shivered.

The breeze was freshening with the turn of the tide, and the waves were louder as, their height increased, they poised, revolved compactly, and then flushed out over the beach. And at the moment when the grey-green waters halted before their immemorial recession, the earth too stood hushed and all its creatures noiseless. Not a bird was singing.

Merrill made as though to speak, but checked himself, and it was in silence they walked back to the Absaloms' house.

2

They were walking up to Cornel Ofan where the Wise Man lived. 'Why Cornel Ofan?' Merrill asked. 'Why Terror Corner?'

Absalom halted and pointed. They had come up through the anchored oaks of Ffald-y-Brenin, the King's Fold, and were on the cart-track over Felindre land. High up and half-right and facing them was the Wise Man's house. 'You'll see the road at the back', he explained. The hill was humped like a burial mound, rounded and soft with scrub and pigfern, but on its near side a buttress of rock crept its whole length, grey among green. The house squatted seaward of the buttress, its windows flashing like spectacles in the sunlight. 'You'll see the view too, from the top', Absalom went on to Mrs. Merrill. He was wearing a navy-blue suit which vulgarized him. 'They say he lives high up where he covers all the roadways and paths, so that he can see everybody who comes. Then he slips indoors into a little place behind the ingle, and hides. But the caller comes indoors and tells Mrs. Wise Man all about it, and there he is listening all the time. Then he comes swanking in and won't even let you start to talk.' Mrs. Absalom began to imitate a deep male voice. '"No, don't tell me, little one", he says; "You don't have to tell the Wise Man. Your little cow has a bad tail—I know it; the Pembroke black. Take home this ointment in the brown box, and bite her tail to the bone in the middle of the bad. Then spread the ointment thick as homemade jam, and tie the tail up in a paper bag from the Farmers' Co-op; and in four days if it isn't as clean as a leaf come to me for more ointment. Oh, and don't forget the two shillings, will you, little one? Even a Wise Man must live."'

They went on, half-jesting, to tell more of the Wise Man's remedies. To cure a burn, hold it in front of the fire—the heat would draw the burn out. To a bad cut apply a slice of home-cured fat bacon. He cured dogs of distemper by making a fold in the skin over the backbone, threading a cord through, and tying both ends in a fancy bow.

'So your Wise Man is a fake?' Merrill said.

The Absaloms shook their heads, shocked. No, he was very much the Wise Man. There were tricks to every trade. Apologetically, Absalom explained how he owed the Wise Man his life. He had had shingles when a boy, and the ends had almost met across his chest, and when the ends met (every fool knew this), you died. He grew excited and waved his arms as he described how the doctor from Dolau gave him up, and then the doctor from Pant, and at last the great Doctor Jones of Abermaid. And then his father had carried him in the dark, through a terrible storm, along this very track to the Wise Man, who plastered him from neck to navel, from nape to napkin-end, with hot mutton-fat and let it congeal into a life-jacket, and gave him to drink of the juice of the fleshy green herb which grows in wall-cracks at Cornel Ofan. He could take the evil eye off man or beast, but no one had openly accused him of putting one on; and he alone in the county could cure rotten bone by the old forgotten shepherd's maggot-cure. As the Absaloms grew more eager to defend and praise the Wise Man, Merrill wondered whether they were not a little afraid of him.

The shadows were stretching themselves when they reached Cornel Ofan. But first they went thirty yards past the house to the top of the hill, to admire how strategically the Wise Man had placed himself. And here the Merrills saw one reason for the name of the house, for the backside of the hill had been gashed by a stone quarry which ran right back to the mountain road: this approached it head on and then turned terrifyingly away without so much as a wire fence by way of protection. 'Wild Wales', commented Merrill. 'Nice at night time.' Long elliptical banks, invisible from the valley, showed that the house stood within an ancient hill fort. The view ran out on three sides over the same country of wood and hill and cwm Merrill had admired from the headland over Ffald-y-Brenin, but the mountains of the north had swung into fresh focus. They were livid as a bruise and their outlines hard. Ynys Las looked flatter from here, and with the yellow ball of the sun behind it its nearer cliffs were the colour and texture of soot. Broad streams of light trembled in the water at its either side, their lemon brightness coarsening to steel-grey and the steel-grey to mackerel as they spread from the sun. 'What a throw!' said Merrill, thinking of King Bleddri. His thoughts shifted to Mrs. Absalom standing by his side, and he smiled. She too was smiling, and he exulted to think she might smile for the same reason. What smooth black glossy hair she had, drawn back from her forehead and ears and rolled like a shell on the nape of her neck. Her throat was white and full. He thought of the flesh milky under the dark blue dress.

'Shall we go in?' asked Absalom.

Turning, they saw that the Wise Man had come out to welcome them. 'He's not going to hear us talk first then?' Merrill whispered to Mrs. Absalom, but loud enough for them all to hear. 'Some things he knows without talking', said Absalom.

The Wise Man looked half-prophet, half-charlatan. He was tall and heavy shouldered, with a massive head and thin white hair. His features were blunt and fleshy except for his nose which was bony and curved in the roman way and poked forward like a big beak. He gave Merrill the impression he did his listening with this aggressive nose, from the way he had of lifting his head in two or three short jerks when he was spoken to. This same trick gave him an air of extraordinary deliberation. He wore a well-kept suit of old-fashioned cut, with wide lapels and squarish trouser-legs, a soft linen collar and spotted tie over his flannel shirt, and his boots had lumpy polished toecaps crissed with little cuts. He was clearly on his dignity with guests he did not know, and after one Welsh sentence of greeting to the Absaloms stood waiting for the Merrills to be introduced to him.

'I have heard so much about you', said Mrs. Merrill, and this

seemed to please him. 'They talk, they talk', said the old man.
'You have not had those old shingles again?' he asked Absalom.
In the Merrills' faces he read knowledge of the wondrous cure
and nodded his satisfaction.

'*Fy nghartre bach i*', he said, opening the gate, and then solemnly
in translation: 'My little home, my dears.'

Merrill wasn't sure whether his manner held more of magni-
ficence or absurdity, but found it worth watching.

They were shown into the small parlour. This like its owner
was a showpiece. The walls were covered with a thick shiny
yellow paper mellowed rather than sullied with age, but the
ceiling was white-washed boards. On the floor was a bright red
turkey carpet. There were half-a-dozen pictures, two of them
enlarged and coloured portraits of an elderly couple whom he
judged to be the Wise Man's father and mother. Hung where they
could hardly be seen till the lamp was lit were likenesses of St.
John, with a huge quill pen, and a bearded St. Matthew with a bull
peering over his shoulder. There was a red mahogany table in the
middle of the floor, and a harmonium with rosewood panels
against the wall farthest from the fireplace.

Including the Wise Man there were already four people present.
His wife was a shrunken woman of seventy, who wore an
exquisite lace apron to honour her guests. Her fingers were worn
with work, she had bright keen peasant eyes, but she was to
surprise Merrill and charm his wife by a delicate formality in all
she did and said. Next was a draper from Abermaid, twelve miles
away; he had important business with the Wise Man, and had left
his Austin Seven at the entrance to a field. He came naturally and
volubly into the conversation with explanations why he hadn't
brought her past the quarry. 'Over you go', he told them dramatic-
ally; 'Bump you go once, and still there you are. Bump you go
twice, and still there you are—only not so much of you. Bump
you go three times, and then—Where arru?' He roared with
laughter. 'Collishon—therru are!' he cried. ''Sploshon—where
arru? 'Sploshon you have there—not a quarry at all. Oh dear
dear annwyl!'

'Explosion?' This was the other guest, his life's story written
in his face and hands. 'I could tell you about explosions too.'

'And you shall', promised the Wise Man. 'Mr. Thomas here', he explained gravely, 'is a great one for reciting, and after supper he shall recite "The Explosion".' Mr. Thomas nodded several times, his undamaged eye rested on Merrill as though to say: I will too—and what a treat! 'After supper', continued the Wise Man, 'anyone who will may show his craft.'

Merrill saw Mrs. Absalom smile. He turned his head, with the feeling someone was watching him.

'A difference between craft and crafty', Absalom was saying.

'My English is not good', said the draper. 'The old tongue I am at home in, the one the angels speak. Excuse me please, Mr. and Mrs. Merrill, our distinguished friends. But I say now they are damn scoundrels, those brothers. In fact, buggarrs.' The Wise Man held up his hand. But the draper was irrepressible, and perhaps the Wise Man didn't too strongly wish to repress him. 'Credit to all', he cried, 'and first, credit to the Wise Man of Cornel Ofan!' He turned confidentially to the Merrills. 'If I wanted to, I could tell you—oh such things!'

'You could, Mr. Meredith? Such as . . .'

'It is nothing', said the Wise Man.

'Indeed it is not nothing. Those brothers—but you know Abermaid, Mr. Merrill, do you not? You don't? Duw annwyl, Mr. Merrill sir, and you a college-trained man, I'm sure.' He appeared to lose his place but found it after a glance at the Wise Man. 'Those brothers I am talking about—I am a small shop, Mr. Merrill and Mrs. Merrill madam, in the drapery way of business, and I do very well until ten or twelve years ago, when those brothers who are also a small shop in the drapery way pay a *dyn hysbys*, a Wise Man as the English say, to put the evil eye on me. Consider now the change, Mr. Merrill sir. Where I had a hundred customers I now had fifty, and soon where I had fifty I had ten. The Workhouse yawned before me like the mouth of hell when the Fifth Angel sounded in Revelations and there arose a smoke out of the pit,—when I came to talk with the respected and reverend Mr. Joseph Jones, the Wise Man of Cornel Ofan.'

The Wise Man made a gesture of tolerance and modesty.

'And what did the respected and reverend Wise Man do?' He screwed his chair closer to Mrs. Merrill's. 'If only we knew the secrets of the ancient ages of the world, Mrs. Merrill madam—but we don't. It is the Wise Man of Cornel Ofan alone who knows those. No, no, Mr. Jones',—his voice dropped respectfully—'the truth is always the truth. There was the Witch of Endor for one, and she knew her left hand from her right or the Good Book is putting it on a bit; and there was Myrddin whom the English call Merlin for two—he was no softy till he was taken in by a bit of a frittery wench; and there is Mr. Jones here for a third—what a lovely man he is! He is better than the Witch of Endor as the male is superior to the female (with no offence to the ladies present, always excepted, as understood); he is wiser than Merlin, for no silly bit of a frittery wench ever put a pad of mist over *his* eyes; and in brief, he is exceeded in wisdom and fair dealing only by himself.'

The Wise Man rubbed his hand over the top of his head.

'For Mr. Jones', continued the draper, 'came to Abermaid and took off the evil eye, and where I had ten customers I once more had fifty, and the fifty became a hundred, and the hundred waxed even unto two hundred, and so I have lived in peace and prosperity as a good Calvinist ever since. Till a month ago, in fact, when those two buggarrs put it on again.' He laid his finger alongside his nose. 'But I have brought my troubles to Mr. Jones here. I could say a lot more . . .'

'You would be unwise to', interrupted the Wise Man.

'But I shall say nothing instead. There is a time to talk and a time to be silent. I will now be silent. In brief, I will only say . . .'

'Say nothing!'

There was an astonishing change in the Wise Man's voice. Mr. Meredith coughed and covered his mouth. 'Quite so', he agreed. 'I am when I wish of a silence to make the grave sound noisy. I have a call of nature. Excuse me, please.' He rose, bending his back as though completing a sale, and went into the garden.

'He is a good man that Mr. Meredith, but he talks too much', said the Wise Man. 'And all because I was once able—but there, most of it is nonsense.'

The draper returned to find them all drawn up to table. There was cold ham and salad and a green cheese which oozed yellow oil on to a paper doyley. And over the meal presided the Wise Man's wife, in the hand-worked apron she had had these fifty years, and with a gentle, prim courtesy. Mrs. Absalom was moved to a word of compliment. 'My dears', said the old lady, to her and Mrs. Merrill, 'if we have only a glass of water let us have it nice.' This was loudly approved by the draper, whose eyes were pricing all past his finger-ends, and by Mrs. Absalom; only the ex-collier looked baffled. Merrill felt the childishness in them all, couldn't help his sense of superiority. The Wise Man's love of flattery, the draper's eagerness to bestow it, Mrs. Jones's pride in her apron and silver teapot, Mrs. Absalom—he checked on Mrs. Absalom. They draw us, he thought, with single hairs, so deep she thinks herself and clever, but it's all in the flesh's red and white, our own incompleteness. Our own folly.

He caught the Wise Man's eye, bland and unrevealing, and turned to look out of the window. 'You can't see the Island from here then?' He hardly listened to the Wise Man speaking of the round of the hill, for Mrs. Absalom had turned too, to look over her shoulder. She seemed amused.

'He is very fond of the Island, Mr. Merrill is', said Absalom, as though exhibiting a child's cleverness. 'He is very fond indeed.'

'You call it the Green Island but it looked black to me', said Mr. Thomas. 'This Bleddri must have had a collier's hand with you. I could tell you of colliers too . . .'

'And you shall', promised the Wise Man. 'The explosion and the colliers—tell them you shall.' Silently Thomas laid his hands on the tablecloth. They were twisted and sprinkled with blue scars, and on the left hand two fingers ended at the first joint. He peered at them with his one eye, and without a word spoken the atmosphere changed. 'Mr Thomas', said the Wise Man gently, 'in his time has been in an explosion. He has composed a poem about it which he will recite to us later.'

And after supper he did. It was in all ways an astounding performance. The ex-collier began by taking off his coat. When he rolled up his sleeves they saw the hairy swelling right forearm and the blue fire-wasted strings of the left. His listeners had pressed back to the edges of the room, the reciter took his place fronting them. 'The Explosion', he announced quietly, and in the fraction of time his face altered—terribly. 'The Explosion', he said again.

His words were Welsh with snatches of mongrel English but his action and declamation so emphatic that the Merrills were never at a loss for their import. He began with a few humorous touches: Tal coming downstairs in the morning and drawing up the fire while the Missus got his breakfast and filled his tommy-box and jack. Then the walk to the pithead, greetings to friends, the cage, reaching the coalface. A word about the roof—No, no (this was the timberman, bass-voiced), the roof was all right. Tal looked at the flame of his lamp. Bit low, he didn't wonder. And now he was at work, balanced on his buttock, breaking out the coal. Once or twice he wiped sweat from his forehead and chest. He looked at his watch, told his butties the time, rested and reached for his food. Again the reciter's face altered: stupefaction, horror, despair masked him. He cowered down as the gallery rocked and roared in sheeted flame and blasted air, fell to his knees as the uprights snapped and the tough collars slewed and splintered, thrust up his broken hands against the world's shattered crust above him. O God, he panted, God of mercy, be with your children now! Merrill felt his heart bound and drop, his mouth was parched.

The uproar and destruction were past; and silence came crawling in, broken at first by the groan of timbers, the rattle of a stone from the quaking roof, little whispering rushes and compressions as the fall made solid the parting. Slowly men moved again, held up their lamps, blundered into speech, covered the faces of the dead. Time was there, and Silence, and the Dark. On his hunkers beside the fire he told how the lamps grew dim and died, and Blackness walled his eyes and stuffed his mouth, and his prayers grew dull and dead. In a sudden magic transition he spoke with sweetness of sky and sunshine in the living world, of birds singing free in air, of the women and old men at the pit-head. A minister prayed, a crowd sang, and with them they sang in Cornel Ofan, a hymn that sucked the blood from Merrill's heart. The reciter held up his hand, silenced them on a falling note— he had heard something. Tap, tap, tap, the rescue party were at work, sending their question through the rock. Is anyone alive there? Answer, if you live. With the point of his pick he answered on the wall; the men spoke in low voices. And always tap, tap,

tap, the blows of the crowbar ringing clearer till it rang into their heads. The tight crunching strokes of mandrils were heard in the fall, the hard slamming of a sledge. Men outside tore and battered, propped and lagged to make all safe; their nostril dilated like stallions'. Then the shaft of yellow light, the breaking of the wall, men stumbling or carried out, the loud cry of grief and rejoicing.

The audience at Cornel Ofan sat forward, sighing. But the artist was not quite done. Tal's meeting with his wife again, his embarrassment at any show of feeling, some dry joke that gave them the chance to laugh. Then solemnly he raised his right hand for the ending. All the lovely butties, men of Lôn-Isa and Top Row, where were they now? The young men, the bloods, the football players and sweethearts; the strong colliers with wives and children; the whiteheads with bent backs and furrowed faces, where were they? He called softly through his hollowed hands, naming men: Twm and Dai and Eben and Llewelyn, where are you, lovely boys? But alas and alas! There they must lie, in the sealed-off seam, and everlasting night enfold their flattened bodies. But their souls were with God, *yr Arglwydd Dduw*, on high.

The reciter reached hesitantly for his coat and put it on. He appeared dazed and asked for a glass of water. 'Our friend Mr. Thomas has earned better than water', said the Wise Man. 'I will fetch him beer. I am surprised', he added in magnificent compliment, 'that the sun still shines in heaven.'

'Ah,' said the draper sententiously 'We have been on the 'igh 'ights to-night. What a preacher you would have made, Mr. Thomas man from South Wales!'

'I'm sure I thought I was there', said Mrs. Absalom. She looked innocently about her, smiling. 'Dear me, it is much nicer to be here.'

The draper was watching the Wise Man pour out a bottle of beer. 'Perhaps if I too could have a glass of water?' he suggested humbly. 'With Mrs. Jones's permission, kindly.'

'But if I said the sun was shining in heaven', said the Wise Man, 'I was only just in time.' The corners of the room were brown and blurred, the far side of the valley softened from bright to gloomy green. 'A parting cup', said the draper, setting down his foam-draped glass. 'I must be back before dark, for the way to Abermaid is as the hard and narrow way to the New Jerusalem.' He began to hum 'I'm Ready for the Other Side', while the Wise Man brought him his hat and a carton of brown eggs. The Wise Man was to see him as far as his car; everyone could understand that there were some last weighty words of counsel to be received, for even before he brought his tune to an end the draper was wagging his head and winking with the importance of a man set apart from his Abermaid fellows. 'God', he said at going, 'is with us all times, and now I have Mr. Jones too. They shall need to grease their boots well, those brothers.'

All virtue seemed drained from Thomas still. He did no more than nod when the draper in farewell again assured him what a talent he had, and answered in a dull tired way when Absalom, suddenly all alive, began questioning him about his poultry run. The three women seemed naturally to fold together within the confine of their own affairs, and after a few minutes Merrill felt he could as well do without them all for a while as they apparently without him; with an excuse he went outside and took the road to the crest of the hill. He waited at the quarry edge and soon saw the Wise Man coming up towards him, his legs looking very short as he inclined his body to the slope. A brown bird hopped across the road and fell into space, startling Merrill.

'What was it?' he asked the old man. 'That bird—it was in the corner of my eye, moving.'

The Wise Man shook his head. 'How should I speak of what I did not see?' He jerked his arms in a vague but kindly gesture. 'You like Wales, Mr. Merrill? You like Ffald-y-Brenin?'

'If it were not so lonely.' He felt the ungraciousness of this as he said it.

The Wise Man pondered. 'Yet two are always company. And three notoriously a crowd.'

'And at Ffald-y-Brenin we are four—a multitude, a stranded ark.'

'So long as the animals go in two by two it makes no difference.' He chuckled as Merrill turned to stare him down. His eyes were not to be held. 'Do you have Wise Men in England, Mr. Merrill?'

'I have heard of Wise Women.'

'They are the deeper sex but not therefore the wisest. What do you think, Mr. Merrill—are they?'

'There are as many fools among them as among men, I expect.'

'As many fools . . .' He chuckled again, bending to look into Merrill's face. 'Very good, Mr. Merrill, I must say. And I expect a man like you thinks the number, the proportion as we say, pretty high too?'

'Pretty high.'

He nodded his satisfaction. 'As many as',—he began to count on his fingers—'as many as three out of four, would you say?'

Merrill knew some childish stratagem was being prepared against him. 'Or more', he granted, humouring him.

The Wise Man looked shocked. 'No, no, Mr. Merrill, we can't have more, can we?' His dignity was gone. With his antics and emphasis he was a whiteheaded buffoon. 'Not *four* out of four! Our company to-night, for example. Poor Mr. Meredith who has such faith in the *dyn hysbys*. I am sure you thought him a fool, Mr. Merrill, for I was watching you as he spoke.'

'I can't think . . .'

'An Englishman speaks!' cried the Wise Man with heavy humour. 'We may think folk fools but not say so behind their backs. I did not think you such a one for good form, Mr. Merrill. And rest assured—our friend would much prefer we discuss him and call him a fool than that we ignore him.' He almost wheedled. 'Let us have him as our first fool—please!'

'So long as he won't feel lonely', said Merrill as insultingly as he could.

'Never fear! Now there is our other friend, Mr. Thomas of Pengaer, one time collier of Senghenydd, Glam.' The Wise Man struck him off on a finger. 'He is a good one for the reciting, but what does that show? Only that he has a good memory.'

'So has a dog who sees the whip.'

The Wise Man threw up his hands. 'How true that is! He is our fool number two. Now let me think. You will understand, Mr. Merrill, that we do not discuss our guests, you and Mrs. Merrill who is so nice a lady though a little troubled to-night.' He had thrown the end of his sentence into the quarry before Merrill could turn on him. 'And would it not also be impolite to discuss

the Wise Man and his wife?—though you have your ideas about
me, I know it. Three out of four—and you thought a higher
figure. But that leaves only the Absaloms! Now shall we start
with Dafydd or his wife?'

'I think we'll change the subject and start for home!'

'There now.' The Wise Man walked along at his side. 'Mrs.
Absalom, well yes, but Dafydd—it would be a mistake to count
on that.' Again he dropped his eyes as Merrill turned angrily
towards him. 'I think I can hear the musical box in the house
there. It sounds very pretty in the night.'

Merrill heard it too, a tinkling as they drew near. Indoors they
found all the party listening to 'Dolly Grey' and watching with
attention the bright revolving cylinder.

'We have been talking of wisdom, Mr. Merrill and I', said the
Wise Man when it ended. 'But I don't know that we are much the
wiser.'

Merrill grimaced. 'I am sure we are not.' As he looked from
his wife to Mrs. Absalom he felt irritation and futility fill his
breast like physical pain. 'Are you tired?' he asked, seeing the
deeper lines of her face. And how had she shown she was unhappy? That old devil! With his talk of the Absaloms too.
'Wisdom', the old man was saying playfully, 'is according to her
name; she is not manifest unto many. That, Mrs. Merrill, as I
am sure you know is from the Bible.' She laughed, disclaiming
knowledge. 'It isn't such a bad old book after all', he assured her,
laughing.

'It isn't to be taken in vain', said Mrs. Jones reprovingly. She
was changing the cylinder in the blue and gold enamelled box.
'Listen!' She held up her finger, precise as a schoolmistress.
Again the cylinder began to revolve, music as of a tiny spinet
came enchantingly forth, and soon the melody had taken shape.
'Just a bird in a gilded cage.' Mrs Jones was obviously so proud
of her treasure, and the Wise Man though he affected superiority
so clearly gratified, that the sensation of their childishness came
to Merrill anew. Thomas's one eye glittered at the revolving
cylinder, a smile had lifted the grim corners of his mouth; the
Absaloms sat engrossed; his own wife, he thought wryly, might
be trusted to grace the occasion. The pretty box and its silvery

runnels of sound diffused a charming sentimentality among them all, and he surrendered to it himself. All that had been ugly in his thoughts was tinged with romantic feeling; his thrusting sensuality slackened to tenderness; he contemplated his wife with pity and sadness and Mrs. Absalom's bold profile without bitterness or desire.

The tune ended in a slurring of little bells. 'It's very', said the ex-collier, and groped for the right word; 'it's very *artistic*, Mrs. Jones.'

She shut the lid with a quiet, decisive click. The evening, it said, was over. Mrs. Merrill smiled. The peasant woman had made a great lady's gesture.

And soon, their farewells made, they were on their way to Ffald-y-Brenin. The moon was lifting somewhere behind the hill, filling the valley with a soft and misty light, and breaking the pattern of distances. The trees still kept their green, a black and woolly green, and the beech trunks when they reached the bottom were grey and dull instead of shining vellum. Absalom carried a lantern which he had not troubled to light and was in front with his wife, while the Merrills came behind with an occasional stumble. They spoke hardly at all until they came to the oak wood, whose darkness encouraged them to walk closer together, and here Absalom on his wife's direction lit the lantern. It gave Merrill the feeling that at every stride he must set his foot into the glowing orange pool; he had to shake his head to defeat its hypnotic influence. 'I can't walk behind it', his wife said suddenly. 'I feel, oh I'm terribly sorry, Mr. Absalom, I feel I'm going to fall forward into the light.' Absalom halted. 'There', he said cheerfully, 'that's better, isn't it?' He swung the lantern to his other hand, clumsily took Mrs. Merrill's arm. 'I'll lead, shall I?' Merrill had touched Mrs. Absalom's hand as they walked together. Without design he lurched sideways from a dried mud-furrow and bumped softly against her. At once his arm had sought her waist, his hand pressed the sliding hip, for three or four paces her weight fell against him. Then she was away from him, he had fallen behind, again he stumbled. 'Wait for me', he called to Absalom, as though he had been in the rear all the time. They halted. 'Almost there', said Absalom, swinging the lantern. He could see the efflorescence of the water through the interstices of the remaining trees. 'Right. I've caught up. I was day-dreaming.' He saw Mrs. Absalom's face quite expressionless but avoided looking at her. 'Dangerous thing to do', said Absalom. 'Better watch your step. Might come to harm. There!' he cried, and by pulling the lantern sharply up he douted it. They were clear of the wood.

Merrill took his wife's arm again as the brook splashed and bubbled alongside them. Ynys Las clung to the water like a cloud. The dogs had begun to bark their deep staccato volleys up the cwm; they heard a chain rattle. 'He's a good dog that Twm', said Absalom with satisfaction. Then: 'Shut it,' he shouted. 'It's me!' The dog fell quiet save for a couple of grunts as they passed the workshop, but the bitch went on whining her pleasure. 'Better have a look at her, I suppose', said Absalom, taking the key from under a shell on the window ledge. 'But she'll go a couple of days yet.'

They lit two lamps and the Merrills went on upstairs. But Merrill heard Absalom go outside and open the workshop door. He at once went back downstairs to find Mrs. Absalom standing by the passage door. She seemed in no way surprised to see him, in no way surprised when he walked to her and set his hands to her waist. Yet she shook her head. He set his hands to her breasts, but again she shook her head. But his arms went around her and he forced her head back, forced her to kiss him. The blood was flooding at his temples, his throat was full, he had the feeling he was drowning, losing himself in her. Then she pushed him off violently. Someone was passing the window. He not only felt, he heard his heart gush and pound in that endless second before the door opened and Absalom entered.

'So I'm not last then?' To the listeners his voice was dry and steady, he closed the door and shot the bolt.

'Yes you are', said his wife coolly, and patted her hair. She yawned.

Merrill began to climb the stairs. But an impulse he couldn't control made him turn again to look at Absalom. He had been watching him go, he could tell, but a black bar of shadow was across his eyes and nose, and his mouth was tight and hard. Nothing to be read there. 'Good-night', he said again.

'Good-night, Mr. Merrill.'

This was Mrs. Absalom, still yawning. Absalom's reply reached him later, when he was at the head of the stairs. 'Good-night', he said slowly.

3

Absalom and Mrs. Merrill were away by eight o'clock in the morning. A thin mist was over the sea, and things of the night seemed neither real nor to be remembered. 'It will be a blazer later,' Absalom guessed. He swung the handle of his rusted Ford. 'She'll come. If she don't break my arm first. Try her on the starter, Mr. Merrill.' The engine spat unevenly. 'Right. One more.' He made full contact, shattering the morning, then choked her down to an uneasy grumble.

Mrs. Merrill's farewells were already made. She was taking the front seat alongside Absalom. 'You'll get a cup of tea at Abermaid', her husband told her again, 'and lunch when you change at Maesheli. You'll be all right?'

'And Dafydd——' this was Mrs. Absalom. 'Look out for me by Felindre this evening. I might go up to Cornel Ofan. What time?'

Mrs. Merrill wondered at the odd quality of Absalom's smile as he bent to the dashboard. 'Half-past eight do?' The clutch went in brutally, the car ground for a moment and then jolted forward. 'And don't forget the *Cambrian News*!' Mrs. Absalom shouted, and ended almost on a scream. She turned to Merrill, beating her chest with her fist and choking. 'There never was a shout in me', she gasped. They saw the car lurch over the bridge, and here the big mongrel Twm who had been scuffling along almost between the front wheels felt his duty done and came bounding back to where they stood by the mill wheel. The bitch, jealous lest he distract attention from herself, twitched her ears and showed the white points of her teeth, and knowing the signs and knowing her temper he slunk past, nervousness and conciliation all over his jowl. They laughed together, the man and woman. 'She's a one, that Shan is', said Mrs. Absalom admiringly.

That was three hours ago. Since then the sun had dug his

fingers into the mist, combing it clear of the hillsides and the Ffald-y-Brenin oak forest. The shallow waves began to sparkle on the beach, the face of the sea came to glow with pink and rose and salmon, and high up against the blue sky a million globules of pearly light shimmered and danced before drying into pure translucent air. The high headland of Eryl Môr loomed baseless and unsubstantial, then hardened to the familiar brown cliff face protecting the cove from the north, and soon Ynys Las broke into view, a magic island in an old story, changing shape before one's incredulous eyes, from smudge to thin black reef, from reef to black bar, and from bar rearing and brightening till Merrill could see its upper limits burnt in a charcoal line against the intense air. The Island, the sapphire sea with its crystal pointing, these engrossed Merrill. He walked back to the house from the boat, his jacket on his arm, his neck bare. The strike of the sun, the wash of perfumed air from the sea exalted him; he flexed his fingers, marvelling at their suppleness and strength. Before him he saw two magpies beat from the near edge of the wood, the hen flying in a wide high curve towards Eryl Môr, the cockbird dipping and rising in gallant escort, the white horseshoe on his back and wings a glory in the morning. The hen broke her flight, the bird following her, and they flew twisting and courting till they fell below the skyline. 'Ha!' he cried, a fountain of joy bubbling within him.

There was no one in the living room but he could hear Mrs. Absalom moving about upstairs. 'Hello!' he shouted gaily.

It was like seeing her stop and listen. 'Hello', he called again. 'Come down. What are you doing up there?'

'It's what they say.' She appeared on the stairs. 'A woman's work is never done.'

'But it's a holiday to-day!'

'I don't know that I want a holiday', she said, with less assurance than usual. She was standing now on the bottom stair.

'You promised, remember?'

'Oh, no I didn't!' He held out his hand but she wouldn't take it. 'Besides, whatever would people think?'

'I didn't know Ynys Las was so crowded.'

'It wasn't the Ynys I was thinking of.'

'I tell you what', he said, dropping his coat. 'I'll carry you to the boat, and then you can say I made you. Look!'—and thrusting under her arms which tried to repel him he lifted her struggling into the air. 'No', she cried, 'no, no!' but he held her firm and started towards the door. 'Put me down, oh you must put me down!'

'When you promise!'

'All right then, I promise.' She was shaking with laughter when he set her down. 'Aren't we being awful, Mr. Merrill?'

Reluctantly he let her go. 'We'll want food. And something to drink. You'll get it?'

From the boat he saw her tying the mongrel to the workshop door, where he had choice of shade or sun. She set down water, threw three or four square biscuits inside. The bitch, her wallow too distended for her to lie with comfort, was yawning prodigiously and sitting back against the door. Momentarily the Wise Man, his own wife, the evening at Cornel Ofan blurred and buzzed in his head like a swarm of bluefly, so that he made slow brushing movements of his hands across his eyes to dispel them. No, he cried, No! This was a nutshell world this morning, its limits the round green hills behind the cwm, the face of the headland, the sea-line broken by the Green Island. Outside these limits nothing should exist till evening. His head grew clear. All was moving to its consummation.

'I can't think', said Mrs. Absalom when she came down to the boat, 'why you don't go to the Island without me, Mr. Merrill.'

'You can't?' But this time the dubious word play jarred on Merrill. For we are not, he thought, like those marvellous magpies riding the sky because love and procreation whirl them to their natural joys; this was at once more sluggish and more febrile; and furtive. 'You'll find out', he said briefly, and pushed out from the beach. Soon they had caught the breeze, but he was no expert and found himself fully busied with the patched red sail and tiller. The water was a hard clean greeny-blue, but behind them they left an unhealing weal which curved as he tried to keep course. Mrs. Absalom was unusually silent. She must feel herself committed now, he thought—a trifle grimly for the occasion—but was surprised suddenly to see her smiling behind her hand. God, he told himself, what a fool I am to think she'd do anything except her pleasure. She trailed her fingers overside, so that inches under the surface there were frothy lime-green bubbles exploding upwards. 'It's cold', she cried. 'You've no idea how it's cold! You won't tip us over, will you?'

'That isn't the idea', he replied. 'I can't swim. And a death by drowning's too good for me.'

'If only the Seiat could see me now, Mr. Merrill!'

'If only the Seiat could see you in an hour's time!'

She giggled. He expected her to counter with a question but instead she began to hum a lively tune that soon struck down to the minor. 'No', she said; 'It's sad on the water, because you always think how cruel it can be. Don't you think we should be kind one to the other, Mr. Merrill?'

He could think of no reply fatuous enough for her. Instead he was watching the Island. 'We ought to make for the south side', he declared. 'That's where the beach is. I wish I was a bit cleverer with the sail. Still . . .' The boat turned more into the wind. 'We'll make it all right.'

The rocky eastern face rose twenty to eighty feet above the sea. At the lower levels there were concave hollows of moss-blackened grass sinking rather suddenly from the skyline right to the cliff edge. But as they rounded the south-eastern spur they saw how a shelving beach of dark-grey gravelly sand gave them their landing-place, while behind it a grassy cleft went upwards and inland. 'There!' he shouted, and in his excitement pulled the tiller the wrong way, almost spilling himself overboard. 'All right', he cried, 'don't tell me! I know what I am.' And straightening course he ran the boat gently on to the sand. 'Nothing to tie her to, but the tide'll go out for hours yet. And I'll pull her up a bit too.'

He pointed up the cleft to where an outcrop of blackish rock was clamped to its own shadow. 'That's the place for lunch. Or look, there's a little cave that end of the beach. What a lovely Island this is!'

She watched him carry their things ashore. 'Why, what a boy you are, Mr. Merrill, and I always thought you so—what shall I say?'

'Yes', he admitted, 'I am a boy since I stepped ashore here. There's no age, no time, there's nothing except the Island and you and me. That's how I've thought of it; that's how I've wanted it; that's how it is.' He put the basket down where the grass met the beach, threw his jacket alongside it. 'It's like elastic', he said, treading the tough spongy turf. They began to walk diagonally along the left bank of the cleft, climbing where the angle was easiest. There was a peppering of rabbit pellets and once only the open mouths of a burrow. The sun was very hot on their backs when at last they topped the rise. A furlong or so ahead was a swell of ground where rock broke the surface, and this except for some of the eastern cliffs seemed the highest point on the Island. When they stood there at last a great stretch of coast swam up at them east and north, but Ffald-y-Brenin was as yet hidden; westwards a second rift dropped to toothy rocks and a gravel-spit. The sea out west was taut as a skin, with creeping greys and greens in the sapphire blue, and one huge patch of maroon where weed rose near the surface. Turning, they could see their own beach and their boat twenty feet from the water. There seemed to be no bushes or trees on the Island, but a pair of yellowhammers, of all birds, chased from one small rock to another in short quivering flights, never turning their mustardy heads towards the humans but observing them all the time.

'When we go down we'll bathe', said Merrill. Catching Mrs. Absalom's eye, he laughed.

'Oh', she cried, 'so that's what you meant about the Seiat. Well indeed, Mr. Merrill, if I'm not ashamed of you!'

'Go on', he said. 'Think of all that nice water around you.'

'It would be very improper. Besides', she added after a moment, 'it would be very cold.'

He grimaced at her, holding her hand as they left the mound. 'And you a Baptist!' But at the beach her scruples held firm, so instead of bathing they ate their meal and he smoked a pipe and threw crusts into the air for the screaming whiteheaded gulls, and they made guesses and bet half-pennies on where the cor-morants would reappear which were diving for fish off the lengthening south-eastern spur. They could see the air trembling against the rocks, the gravel was like hot needles against his soles when he walked back from the boat. As he sat down again he had the sensation that Ynys Las was nodding like a gigantic tired head. The illusion strengthened with the heat, nodding, nodding, nodding, the grey cliff-eyebrows sagging downwards, everything softened and loaded with sleep. But how could an Island . . .

He opened his eyes. It was Mrs. Absalom, carrying her shoes and stockings. 'I wasn't asleep. I was thinking. Thinking what nice toes you have.' He rolled over against her as she sat down, his face pressed against her, his arm across her lap. The glossy grass-daggers fused and dimmed, through his lashes he saw one tiny orange flower on Mrs. Absalom's frock bloat bigger than the headland, the weft of the material grow to furrows. Then he felt her fingers in his hair, heard her speak with all the tenderness of her singing; there were Welsh words he knew: *cysgu*, sleep, the gentle diminutives, *f'anwylyd*. For a moment only his blood stirred, his heart hammered, then he was falling towards unconsciousness, nodding into the dark as the Island itself nodded under him.

'Did I sleep?' he asked confusedly. 'What has happened?'

'Yes, you slept.' The short black shadows had wheeled. The cormorants dozed on the weedy rocks. 'Nothing's happened.'

He sat up, his shoulder against hers, and kissed her clumsily. 'No', she said, 'not here. I couldn't here.' She looked guiltily out to sea as though they were open to the eyes of the world.

With no more spoken they began to climb the cleft as they had done at mid-day, carrying their shoes and she her stockings. As they hooked fingers at the steeper ascents he could feel the soft resilient pads under her fingers, the smooth callouses of the palm and inside the thumb. They were panting when they reached the top but went straight on to a smooth green hollow under the rock-scarred mound. 'Now', he said, 'now'. She motioned him to undo the back of her dress, bending her head as he fumbled with fingers suddenly stiff and awkward. 'Hurry, hurry!' she whispered. Then he saw the pure white of her upper arms, soon her dress and slip and vest had fallen around her hips, and from this coloured calyx there flowered her fleshy sides, the full white breasts, the gleaming shoulders, the dizzy column of her throat where he saw the throbbing of a vein. She looked at him with dry hard smouldering eyes, her arms had dropped to her sides, their palms towards him in a gesture of desire and surrender both; he saw and kissed those little buds of flesh which grew between the crinkled inside knuckle-joints. And while he thought all his senses bound up in hers, everything in sky and earth and water was like a book opening before him, whose message was the urge to mating and fruition. They sank to the ground, and with a somnambulist's eye he saw behind her head waxy transparent stalks of stonecrop, the pale pink petals not an eighth of an inch long, and in the heart of each blossom a blood-drop. A pinhead spider clawed his way down an invisible line, then up, then down, unperturbed by these colossi who shut him from the sun, exhausting and renewing their loves in a rhythm nature now imposed on them and they not at all on nature. He went on with his spinning, and later Merrill was to see, when he looked from Mrs. Absalom's bruised mouth and slumberous eyes, the long glistening outriders from blade to blade, the struts and cunning cross-pieces, then the sticky involutions of the web, and at its centre the spider, bunched and dry and brown. The spider, the stonecrop, themselves—he lay over on his back, wicketing his fingers across his eyes. It prevented self-importance anyway.

When he sat up—'Staring's rude, Mr. Merrill', said Mrs. Absalom, pulling her clothes across her body.

'And thinking's ruder, Mrs. Absalom.'

She put her hand to her breast. 'Ah, how my little heart beats, you'd never believe. And all your fault.' She drew his hand under hers, then smiled mischievously. 'You know what the poem says you hear there, Mr. Merrill? It's best in Welsh, but it's in English too.' Her voice changed, grew charged with a stylised emotion, lyrical but restrained.

> *'Place your hand, if still you doubt me,*
> *Under my breast, but do not hurt me;*
> *And you'll hear, if you but harken,*
> *The sound of the little heart that's broken.'*

'I don't think it's broken', he said sombrely. He was always embarrassed by the national trait of play-acting, and doubly embarrassed by this resort to poetry on what appeared to him no proper occasion for it.

'A cigarette?' he asked.

But she shook her head. 'It's not quite the thing, is it?'

He smoked silently, at her order looking away while she dressed. For that again was not quite the thing. And here, he thought, is where the difference begins. The stonecrop and the spider stay the same: no break, no end for them. But he would never return to the Island. He thought of his wife. The futile catchwords riddled his brain, preventing clear thought. It had happened— it was no one's fault—the failure, the humiliation—where there was too much pity desire died. And died, it seemed, for ever.

'I'm ready', said Mrs. Absalom.

He turned. Even her shoelaces were tied, and she sat facing him with her back curved and her forearms wrapping her dress under her knees. She looked sleek as a cat.

'Not yet', he pleaded. 'Don't let's go.'

'It'll be time.'

'No', he said hoarsely. 'There's a lifetime ahead, but it won't ever be like this for us again. There's time, there's heaps of time.'

'It's all the same', she said enigmatically. And when he reached for her she shook her head as she had done last night at Ffald-y-Brenin. 'It's foolish', she said, 'not to know when.' And when he persisted—'You'll spoil everything!' she said angrily, and moved away from him.

He lay with his face on his arms then, filled as much with regret as revulsion. Yet, he felt sullenly, who was she to lecture him? Suddenly he felt jaded and drawn; his head was shaking with the blood-beat in his temples. He was in no mood for scolding. She'd better not say too much.

But that wasn't her intention. She was saying nothing.

He pretended to doze. Then he began to notice the ticking of his watch, time audible. He stretched his arm, so that the watch was further from his ear, the dial upwards.

'It's getting late', he heard Mrs. Absalom say anxiously.

'There's plenty of time', he muttered, glad to break the strained silence. He got up, reached out a hand to pull her to her feet. 'You don't dislike me, do you?'

The corners of her mouth drooped just enough to notice. Her lower lip was swollen, her eyes heavy but placid. 'I'm tired out', she said.

'What about me?'

'Ah', she said, 'that's your own fault.'

They were walking towards the top of the cleft. As they came out of the hollow where they had been lying they saw first the sky-line and then the dim mountains of Pembrokeshire enclosing the Bay to the south. There was a dimness on the sea too, its colours faded and streaked with white and grey. They looked down the steep green banks to the cove. The cormorants were gone, the south-eastern spur was shortened by the incoming tide which swilled waveless against the dark gravel beneath them. 'Oh look!' he shouted, dragging at her arm. One frightened oath escaped him and then he was leaping madly down the slope. The boat was floating midway between the beach and the spur. Even as he ran he saw it spin gently in an invisible current. The next moment he stumbled and fell headlong. When he got to his hands and knees he was too dazed immediately to stand upright, he had bitten deeply into his tongue which was now a hard lump choking the right side of his mouth; a wet and fiery pain flooding his left ankle brought him near fainting. He shut his eyes, and when he opened them again masses of dark green swirled right, then left, before him. But at last he saw the sea and went haltingly forward. 'No', he said, or tried to say, 'I can't. I can't do it.' He sat down and the puffs of air made his sweat cold as ice.

'The boat?' he asked thickly. Mrs. Absalom shook her head frightenedly.

'It was foolish', she said, 'I said it was foolish.'

'It was the fall. Anyone could have fallen.' He stood up, taking all his weight on one foot. The boat was thirty yards out, spinning very slowly towards the end of the spur. 'Oh well!' He sat down again, gasping. 'A bit awkward.' He began to untie his shoe.

'Awkward! A bit!' She had raised her voice unpleasantly. 'You know what this means?'

'It means we can't get off the Island.'

'You and your Island!'

He found himself thinking very slowly. 'What d'you want me

to do? Wade after it? You know I can't swim. To say nothing of this ankle.'

Her mouth wrinkled like the bitch's that morning. 'What about me? What about Dafydd when he comes home to-night?'

'What about him? He'll have a bed to sleep in, which is more than we'll have. And look at this ankle!'

'If you thought more about me and less about yourself . . .' She tightened her fingers till her fists trembled. 'I'm afraid. Oh, I'm afraid, Mr. Merrill.'

'There's a towel in the basket', he said slowly, 'and here's a handkerchief. Go and wring them out in the water and bring them here at once.' He fought back his nausea as she did so. 'Now bind it tight. There's nothing to be afraid of. You changed your mind and came to the Island for a picnic. While we walked around it the boat drifted out. We'll wait till we see the headlights of the car, or we can see the house itself from the cliffs. Then we'll signal, make a bonfire, anything. They'll fetch us off in the morning, as soon as they get another boat, I'll say how sorry I am, and that'll be the end of it.'

'You think he'll believe that?'

'If he's wise', he said, rather too cleverly.

'If he's a fool, you mean. No, he won't! Not after last night.'

'He saw nothing.' But the same thought was troubling Merrill. But I'll go, he thought meanly, I'll clear out—that will be best for everyone. Great God, he told himself, how we are tumbled out of our dignity and ease. An hour ago I rode the lightning of the flesh, and look at me now. And Mrs. Absalom, frightened and ugly.

'She might come back in', he said; 'the boat, on the tide.'

Mrs. Absalom sat silent. She didn't even look at him. Yes, he thought, she's frightened all right. What a fool he'd been, what a gaping fool.

'I'm going for a walk', she said suddenly, her voice trembling. 'No, I'm going on my own.' He felt guilty when he looked at her, she was at such a disadvantage, and as she climbed the long green bank again he noticed how the spring and tautness had gone from her step. 'We're a sad pair of sinners now', he said aloud, jeering himself into confidence.

The sea was like wrinkled iron. A thick haze on the horizon was topped with cloud whose rims flashed silver. 'It's all very well her walking off', he said. 'We've got to sleep somewhere. We've got to eat.' He counted their store and it was more than he had expected. 'Pity we fed those gulls.' With these words he knew how hungry he was.

He sat there for more than an hour till Mrs. Absalom returned, resting his ankle, sometimes mumbling his tongue, thinking to no purpose. As she approached he stood up. 'Please don't be upset', he begged. 'It'll be all right.' He knelt and spread the tarpaulin they had taken from the boat to sit on. 'Sit here, do! It's bound to be all right.'

'For you', she said shakily.

'For you too.'

'You don't know Dafydd!' He tried some vague comforting sentence. 'No', she cried, 'that's not right. He's—oh, he's deep. He could be—horrible.'

'You came for a picnic', he repeated slowly. 'We weren't here more than a couple of hours—just as the tide was turning. I was a fool, I didn't pull the boat in. We'll signal as soon as he's back, and if he can't fetch us off to-night that's hardly your fault, or mine.' He went on talking, rounding out the story they must tell, till she just had to grow interested, add details, approve omissions, even invent dangerously. 'There you are', he chided. 'Why, you're smiling again!'

'I'm not smiling inside', she answered truthfully. 'Only anything's better than thinking.'

'Could you eat now?'

She shook her head. 'No—or yes, I could. The way I feel— yes, let's eat now, now.'

And afterwards, he went on, there must be a signal fire, they must decide where to spend the night if they were not brought off. They just had to be sensible. But not in the cave—she shuddered —there'd be sea rats, huge ones, the sort you saw scamper towards the mill at Ffald-y-Brenin—what if they ran over your face? Laughing now, he patted her hand, her shoulder, welcoming the ascendancy again.

Then he hecked along with her, scrabbling in the sand and

hollow rocks for bits of stick, dry grass, anything that would burn brightly. 'Merrill, his crutch!' he shouted across to her, waving a narrow strip of sea-smoothed boarding. He was glad of it: his ankle was more troublesome than he had shown. 'If you can carry these, I'll catch you up', he told her. There was still the bank to be climbed.

It was a meagre bonfire they at last assembled on the cliff fronting Ffald-y-Brenin. Day was dead, except in the low west. 'I'm glad you've come. I was getting worried. Was there ever a place as quiet as this?'

'He should be at Felindre now. Perhaps he'll go on up to Cornel Ofan to meet you. If he does, then we'll see his lights.'

She stared forward. 'I wish Mrs. Merrill was coming back with him.'

He had thought the same thought. 'Put my coat on', he told her. 'Don't wait till you get cold first.'

'I wouldn't be surprised', she said presently, 'if Shan has her pups to-night. That's another thing that comes of larking about.' This astounded him, but she seemed entirely serious and he wondered whether she had just been thinking aloud. 'And where can we sleep? O dear, dear!'

'There's a place . . .'

Her face was growing still and mask-like in the bad light. Against her pale and shining skin the eyes were soft black hollows under charcoal eyebrows; the mouth was swollen and sensual. A cold unimplicated observer within him condemned the swift riot of his memory, speculated on the change that darkness brought. Yet, he thought, yet . . .

'Quick!' she said. 'The headlights.'

A wide weak beam of light played against the sky, then dipped and was reduced to two yellow balls as Absalom came down the track to Ffald-y-Brenin. 'Oh quick, quick!' she cried. 'Light it now.' Thin orange fingers of flame crept then ran through the grass and reached the sticks. By the time the lights reached the bridge and pointed straight towards the Island yellow flames were all around the edges of the beacon-fire, while its heart was a hollowed-out redness of stalks and ash. If he stops now and dips his lights, thought Merrill—but no, the car stopped, the headlights turned away from them, he was putting her into the shed for the night.

'Has he seen us?'

'He must have. But what can he do till morning?'

Many things, they both knew, and were in their different ways disheartened. A light came on in the house and shone bleakly against them, to increase their isolation. No long time after a lantern was carried to the workshop. They watched in silence till it returned, the light in the house went out but reappeared briefly upstairs, then Ffald-y-Brenin was lost in the darkness. The rising moon kept it long in shadow, and at last Merrill rose to his feet.

'He's gone to bed', said Mrs. Absalom bitterly.

And left his wife with me, thought Merrill; but what he said aloud was: 'Yes. We'd better go down. There's a place by the rock.' He saw her shaking her head. 'What else can we do?'

'I would give a million pounds if only I was out of this.' She broke into passionate Welsh in which he caught 'Ynys, Ynys, Ynys!' Well, he thought, it's no news if she's cursing the Island.

'I thought here', he said later, after a painful climb down. 'By the rock.'

When they lay down together she came into his arms for warmth and comforting. 'You don't want to be on your own?' he whispered. She turned half-heartedly and then consumingly to his will, but sometime, somehow, they fell asleep. He awoke cramped and aching. The moon, which had been clean as a cowslip, was now hidden by a spectrum of pink and green and sulphur-yellow. She made no movement and her breathing was regular, but he knew she was awake.

'Thinking again?'

'I'm thinking how bad it will be when Dafydd comes to fetch us.'

He withdrew his shoulder, eased his foot and ankle. It seemed better. 'Try thinking how bad it will be if he doesn't.'

She made no answer and when he woke again, an hour or so later, the words were still in his brain. Now, however, he wondered whether they had been as clever as he thought.

4

He wondered as much many times during the day. While the morning mists shredded and dispersed and the sea glowed like a hedge-rose, and the platinum sun deepened to the gold of midday; while the water crinkled in the afternoon breezes as though dapped with a million fingertips, and then hardened and blackened for an hour before the western sky splashed it with orange, gold and furnace-red. While shards of hard cloud pierced the sun, jagging his shafts, darkening him down, and at last pressing him into the sea, so that the air browned with approaching night, the cliff-edge blurred, and where the waves capsized on shore was just a wavering suddy line. Every hour and all the changes of the day were for Merrill tainted with the vulgarities of doubt and alarm—and discomfort and the beginning of hunger. Yet he kept a good front, lying and sitting endlessly as he was, feeling his ankle strengthen.

'It takes time', he said. Or, 'He can't do everything in a minute. He'll be fetching a boat from Abermaid.' Or, jocularly, 'You've got your story ready?'

But her answers were: 'You don't know him. I'm frightened. I'm hungry. Oh, I'm sick hungry!'

He grew tired of consolation, gave her her share of the food that was left, very, very little. She wasn't the only one hungry. He had plenty to worry about, without her whining. He'd be telling her as much.

But he always bit hard on the thought. It was rough on her, this. Rougher than on him. He could clear off—and would. She had Dafydd to live with.

He could read Absalom like a book. 'Like a book', he repeated, for Mrs. Absalom had gone up to look towards Ffald-y-Brenin. But it's no good to you, Absalom; you just can't do it! You can harass me, but you can't frighten me. You can frighten *her*, granted, and much good may it do you. All you can do to me is make me hungry.

Hungry. He flushed his pockets on to the grass. Not a crumb.

Then his face filled with glee. He had found a chip of a boiled sweet, fluff-covered and tobaccoed. It was like a symbol of things going well for him, and somewhat furtively he slipped it into his mouth and crunched it, dirt and all. His tongue was sore on the side but back to its right size and he licked lovingly around his gums after the short sweet swallow. He would have a cigarette now. 'Eh', he said, 'what's this?' For his lighter was sparking without taking flame. 'Dry', he muttered, suddenly furious. 'Damn you, Absalom!'

He struck the lighter once more and hurriedly lit his cigarette as the flame dwindled.

He could read him like a book. He was going to leave them another night and morning. Great God, he thought, it's absurd: who'd think of a thing like that except some damn stupid peasant, some idiot of a foreigner? It was too childish. Left so much out of account—after all, his wife was on the Island too, and if jealousy came into it, or even property,—he screwed up his eyes, thinking that Absalom might yet find it harder to see the thing through than he bargained.

A pity, he thought, Mrs. Absalom hadn't more brains, and detachment of course. He would like to explain the subtleties to her.

'Isn't it time', she asked when she came back to the cove, 'to light a fire again?'

He snapped his lighter, several times, till a yellow blob clung tiredly to the end of the wick.

'It's dry?'

'You can see.'

He hadn't meant to sound so irritable. 'I might have known', she said hysterically. 'You think of nothing, nothing, nothing.'

'Perhaps I was thinking of you.'

'You'd never think of anything except yourself!'

'Crying won't help.'

'How could you be such a fool?' she cried, her voice breaking with tears. 'And what a fool I've been to listen to you!'

He turned his back on her, staring at the dusky rock-spur. 'You made your own choice. You may as well face up to it. We are here for the night again. It can be better or worse, as we make it.'

'Look at the place we're in. Oh, look at the place!'

'It's not a hotel', he said. 'It's not solitary confinement either.'

'I wish to God it was!'

'You take me up on all I say. You can't see a joke.'

Her lip lifted. 'Joke!' He was reminded again of the bitch Shan. And if it came to that . . .

'Don't let's quarrel. That only makes it worse. I know it's my fault. I can't say fairer than that, can I?'

'You talk', she said angrily. 'Like a gipsy tinker you talk the hind leg off a donkey, for what good it can do. And what about your wife?' She felt the contempt of his silence. 'I said, What about your wife?'

'I heard you.'

'Then why didn't you answer me! But she's used to this, she won't mind, her ladyship won't.' She watched his back, vixen-like. 'Those washed-out ones never have any spirit.'

'Look here', he said, 'you'll keep your mouth shut . . .'

'Or what?'

His hands slacked. This wouldn't do at all. He made excuses for her. But one thing was settled; he'd clear off without compunction the minute he was off the Island. Shabby it might be, mean as misery, but he'd go.

'You didn't like that, did you?' she asked unexpectedly. 'Then be more polite to me. I've got feelings too.'

'We are tired', he said, 'and vexed. Oughtn't we to sleep? Or try to?'

'If I had a bed, and a roof over it. And food to eat.'

'You could smoke a cigarette—if we could get a light.'

'I'm worn out', she admitted, 'and that's the truth. If I thought to-morrow would be all right I'd sleep like a little child. But when I start worrying . . .'

'Leave the worrying to me. I'm not unused to it.' And: No, he thought, I said the truth; I'm not.

He had cut a pillow of turf for their place behind the rock. 'If only we'd brought a rug', he wished, picking up his water-proof, Mrs. Absalom's thin coat, the clumsy square of tarpaulin. 'Like Robinson Crusoe—and it's Friday too.' But she showed no sign of understanding as they settled themselves and tried to sleep. Despite her silence and depression, still more despite the ugly side of her nature revealed so short a time ago, he could feel a renewal of tolerance, even friendship, between them; she must have felt it too, as though their need for comfort and companionship was too strong for hatred in a narrow place. Further into the night they might grow wide-eyed and restless, but now exhaustion and reaction, the strain and boredom of the day welcomed the dark and the warm and the promise of forgetting. And so, while one moment they said they would never sleep, and the next knew only their weariness, everything was falling away from them, and first Mrs. Absalom was sighing and dozing, and then Merrill following her into long if broken slumber. When towards morning she awoke with a frightened cry he soothed her, muttering reassurances, thinking of her as his wife, not Mrs. Absalom at all, reality having grown so unreal. 'It's too early', he grumbled. 'Go back to sleep.' Confusedly, yet with deliberation, he refused to know things for what they were. He remembered her saying she was cold and pressed closer to her back, a gesture fraught with domesticity as a cat on the hob. Happiness and well-being were in his mind as he fell asleep.

'Ah', he cried, the light filling his eyes. 'What then?'

Mrs. Absalom was coming back from where a slow drip of cold water had served her as washbowl and breakfast. She carried a wet handkerchief in her hand, her cheekbones gleamed, her eyes glittered after her chilly toilet. 'If only we had coffee!' he called ruefully, doubling the tarpaulin away from his legs.

'*Ach y fi*, the old coffee! Tea', she said, 'with sugar, and fried bread and bacon.' She put her hands over her middle, groaned half in earnest. 'It's the sleep. It's done me that much good it has. Only it's silly to talk of food.' She hadn't looked so cheerful since the boat drifted out. Waiting with his hands cupped for water and then rubbing away at his face and neck he thought: She's tumbled to some trick for fooling Absalom. 'Cunning', he grunted. 'Or they think they are. In his place . . .' But he couldn't be sure he was in Absalom's place, try as he would. The quality of mind was different, and flatteringly different at that.

'Got an idea for a smoke', he told Mrs. Absalom. He snapped

his lighter in vain. 'Watch.' He unscrewed the base-plug and with a borrowed hairpin coaxed out the wadding, sniffed at it, smiled, and struck a spark into it. The sudden flare scorched his fingers before he could throw the wadding down, but he said nothing of this as he drew on his cigarette. 'From this', he said solemnly, 'I can light a piece of paper, and from the piece of paper I can light my pipe, and from my pipe I can light another piece of paper, and so on till the boat comes.'

She had finished sleeking her hair and was making little pinches at her lips to redden them. 'I look so shabby. You think it will come?'

'You look very nice. Of course it'll come.'

'No, I'm a sight. You know I am!'

He began to chaff her, despite his hunger conscious of a cockerel gaiety. 'That's a trick', he cried, 'pinching your lips, just look at you.'

She pouted at him. 'You are the one to talk. They'd be black and blue if you had your way. When Dafydd comes now . . .'

'Yes?'

'Oh, nothing. Will it be this morning, you think?'

'Or this afternoon.' He held out his hand. 'Come on, my ankle's fine; a last trip round the Island.'

'It sounds like a holiday at the seaside, doesn't it?'

'It is the seaside.'

She giggled. 'Only the holiday's over.'

They climbed the green bank, though it made him wince to do so. 'Only two days', he said; 'it shows how relative things are.' The word went over her head but she nodded agreement and looked wise. And there, he said inside him, is the hollow and the crushed stonecrop, and if I had the nerve to go on my knees and look I'd find that same spider's web and perhaps a silly fly in it. He looked covertly at her as they went past to the rocky central mound, but she was avoiding any glance at him or the hollow. For the holiday's over, he reminded himself. But, 'See', he said, 'what's left of the bonfire. It looks terribly small, doesn't it? All odds, it was, and ends.'

He looked towards Ffald-y-Brenin, half expecting to see a boat on the water between them. But there was no other boat at

Ffald-y-Brenin, and Absalom would have to go up or down the coast to borrow one. Again he tried to enter Absalom's mind: He'd not ask for help, have others enjoying his tangle. What had to be done he would do himself.

The coast, he noticed with surprise, was both bold and indistinct. Its masses and outline were plain enough, but the details— the yellow stroke of low-water sand north of the estuary, the black mouths of caves under Eryl Môr, a shawl of charlock miles inland—these were rather remembered than seen. The soft pulpiness of heat had dried out of the air, which was now hard and deceptive as glass. Yet it's June, he thought with foreboding— June! as though the name were a key to unlock the sun out of heaven, gaol the winds, manacle the great rain. Temporarily he had the illusion that Ynys Las rode the water as the moon rides cloud, movement and no movement. He closed his eyes and when he opened them again avoided sight of the sea.

'There's so little to do on an Island', Mrs. Absalom was saying.

'When the holiday's over.'

'When the holiday's over', she repeated brightly. 'Tell me about yourself, Mr. Merrill.'

'There's nothing to tell.' Good God, he reflected, a man would feel a fool in broad daylight, in the morning above all, babbling.

'You mean you can't think up good lies in the light?' The words were perfunctory, not sharp. She was sitting with her back to the coast, shiny-eyed, stroking the wrinkles in her dress, beginning to hum the tune she had sung at Ffald-y-Brenin. When she sang the words it was in English, as though for his benefit.

> '*A simple country swain am I,*
> *And love should be my pleasure;*
> *The whitening wheat I watch with care—*
> *Another reaps the treasure.*'

It was a song of love without possession, the bride lost to another. 'She died for him', said Mrs. Absalom tenderly.

'Who did?'

'Ann Thomas did. The Maid of Cefn Ydfa. It's a beautiful book, Mr. Merrill. It makes you cry all the time.' Her voice caressed her words, fluting the vowels like a blackbird's song.

'What a lovely man that Wil Hopcyn must have been. He loved her but they made her marry another. It's very sad, you'd hardly believe, Mr. Merrill.'

She knows what she's doing, he told himself. She's listening to every lift and intonation of her voice, her eyes and mouth move as puppets dance. Why the devil can't they be honest: she, Absalom, that old fake at Cornel Ofan?

'Wouldn't the world be lovely if we were all friends?' she asked, out of her self-made sentimentality. He yawned, deliberately. He wasn't going to be drawn into that kind of fatuity either.

'If only the boat . . .'

She took off her mood as easily as a stocking. 'Yes, the boat. We mustn't forget the boat.' Standing up, they saw the sea move sluggishly into the land. 'You can feel the power', he said; 'you can feel it in the Island, coming up into your body. I've never felt it before.'

'It's a meal we want, not power.'

'No, it's not hunger. It's the Island.'

She looked at him curiously. 'Why, Mr. Merrill, you've always sounded a bit daft about the Ynys. But I thought you'd got over it, now.' The stress on the last word was faint as she could make it.

'The Island and you.'

'That's just making fun of me, Mr. Merrill.'

'It isn't.' Taking her hand he stepped down from the skyline. The slow throb of the tide was in his veins. 'You', he repeated clearly. 'They said it was a magic island.' Her eyes smouldered, he saw her face change as her lips parted, her hand melted in his, and he could see and feel her breasts burn towards him through the clothes she wore. It was but to blow on red ashes; they were consumed in a flame of their own making. Yet a little meanness came in: somewhere in his mind was room for the thought that he was revenging himself on Absalom, whom he had begun to hate.

'I don't know, I'm sure', she said dreamily at last, 'why we did this'. She smiled slowly, her eyelids closing. 'When the holiday was over. Can you see the boat?'

As she fumbled behind her for a button hole he saw her breasts swell against the stuff, the broad nipples. Over, he thought; that's over. If the boat would come now, this instant, make an end! Good-bye the Island, Eryl Môr, and Ffald-y-Brenin. And good-bye Mrs. Absalom. Cynically he wondered: Is the word good-riddance?

But they must wait. He thought he had spoken aloud but she showed no sign of hearing. 'There was a spider's web here', he said boldly, as they went back past the hollow. 'Still is, I expect.' He drew his fingers over the grass. 'A little brown spider. They are lucky.'

'It's the red ones are lucky. They bring you money.'

'One the size of a boat would be lucky. With a pair of oars on it.'

'The waves are louder', she replied, tangentially. But as though afraid of deduction, she added: 'Than yesterday, I mean.'

'We can only wait', he said slowly. Every minute he felt change, the renewal of weariness and depression. As he stood on the top of the mound and saw the south-west horizon as though through smoked glass, doubt and fear smote him like axes. She must have been watching him closely. 'Oh', she whimpered, 'Oh, Mr. Merrill, what is it? What's the matter?'

He could hear the indrawn breath shudder through his nostrils. Christ! he thought, if only I were on my own. And anywhere but in this cursed place.

'Nothing's the matter', he said roughly. 'What the hell should be the matter?' It was the first time for him to use an oath to her.

However, he wondered, did I find her all milk and roses so short a while back? An end of hair had fallen loose behind her ear. Like a rat's tail, he thought venomously. 'Your hair's down', he said, his tone, gesture, expression, betraying him.

Her jaws hardened with anger, but her fingers caught instinctively at the loose strand. Vanity was too strong for her; almost humbly she tucked, patted, pinned.

'That's better', he praised. 'It's pretty now.' He was ashamed of himself, would wish this to be his peace-offering, but she was walking away, silently down to the cove, leaving him there uncertain whether to follow her or not. At last he saw her standing by the water's edge and wearing her coat. From where he looked down he lost all idea of her identity as Mrs. Absalom: for an enlightening moment he saw a lonely, frightened woman, a stranger to him, but her loneliness and fright a challenge to all he could give her of kindness and help. But the quixotries, the extravagances that crowded into his mind brought in their wake disillusion. 'There's nothing I can do', he complained. 'Swim like a dolphin with her on my back—go down and kiss her shoe. Bah!'

He began to curse Absalom foully for doing him so much wrong. Words of the Wise Man's and words of his own wife's sounded on his ear: Dafydd was no fool, they'd said. Words of Absalom's too. Suddenly they seemed all around him, these childish treacherous ones he'd thought such clowns. 'But if he saw us', he muttered, thinking of the night they returned from Cornel Ofan, 'would he have let us come?' Hunger and fear— how sick they made him! He sat down, holding his head tightly, for what he could see, clearer than the grass, the rocks, the sea, was Absalom sitting on his round of cherry tree inside the shed at Ffald-y-Brenin, his axe chucking at a porridge spoon, his glance now and again for the Island; and the Wise Man on the top of the hill peering out like some old druid, nodding benignly, and going back down to where the blue and gold enamelled musical box threw into the murk tinkling handfuls of notes, notes of a ridiculous and maddening sweetness that told of birds in a gilded cage. And his wife—where was she? From what door or window, what corner of the garden, was she staring west to Wales? They were all smiling at him, wagging a finger. 'I told you so; I told you so', they were saying.

He opened his eyes and stood up. This was weakness. Strength was to see things as they were. Absalom wouldn't bring them off till his wife returned on Tuesday. Three more days. His stomach craved at the thought. And from the south-west, across thousands of miles of black water, a storm was coming, the slashing gale of early summer.

But even this was not strength. Strength was to recognize that his wife might not return on Tuesday. He tried hard to recall her words but the exact edge of expression avoided him. 'But if you don't come back', he said aloud, then—'No, by God, Absalom wouldn't risk that!'

When he went down to the cove it was to find the cormorants gone from the spur and the gulls screaming and planing low. Mrs. Absalom at once moved away from where she had been sitting. 'I'm sorry', he said after her. 'I can't say more than that.' She had been crying, he could tell it from her reddened eyes, but when she still didn't answer and went to sit near the drip of fresh water he hardened to her at once. 'He won't come, you know', he shouted, thinking with brutal satisfaction: Sulk that off, if you can!

Nor did Absalom come. For long and sullen hours he watched the sea change and move. By the end of the afternoon the waves in the cove were freighted and slow, the ground-swell rolling them up like metal tubes before they exploded into the gravel and seethed treacherously forward. To see them was to see the mid-ocean heaping up its waters under the mallet-blows of a cyclone and then shovelling them away to the western coasts of Europe. And every separate drop of this titanic flood had within it the violence and malice of its origin, though these polished, sucked-under waves on Ynys Las resembled the deep-troughed mid-Atlantic combers as a kitten's paw the talons of the tiger. But soon now some flick or offstrip of the storm would reach the Island, cut it from the mainland for an hour, a day, a week, the water piling high into the Bay, the wind funnelling through the cwms and broken valleys, tearing at the mountain heads, drenching all Wales with sea-spray and rain. High overhead cloud came driving in, the air grew colder, white water bounced and fell from the rocks. 'Now', he muttered, 'it's coming now.'

One moment there was a breeze, the next the wind coughed and shouted in the cliff hollows, and then as Mrs. Absalom ran to the shallow cave and he pressed against the rock where they had slept, the wind and the rain were one, grey, harsh, and slanting. The shower snapped like a whip, while the sky grew blacker and the sea smashed harder at the beach. In a dry minute he hurried over to where Mrs. Absalom was sheltering. 'You can't stay here. It'll be filled at high water. But there's sand behind the rock. We could scoop a better place. Please come!' She seemed about to pull her arm away, but instead let him take it and lead her across. 'It could be worse', he said eagerly. It was such relief to break silence. 'It's got the high ground behind it, and if we could only protect this corner. . . .' He couldn't finish because she was choking with terror and grief. 'Oh God,' she wept, 'why, why did I ever come!' He drew her face to his shoulder but she twisted away from him. 'I'm hungry', she sobbed, 'God help me, I'm hungry!' But what can I do? he kept asking himself, and along his blood beat the words, Three days, three days, three days.

'Sit down', he said at last. He *must* do something besides think. With the big blade of his knife he began ripping out pieces of sand-hung turf, stacking them to flank their shelter. He carried sand and gravel in his waterproof, sheltering when the rain slashed in, talking to her. 'You see', he urged, 'it's better than nothing. With the tarpaulin fixed. . . .' He could never finish his sentences; he had looked seawards and the wind filled his throat. It made no difference. She was huddled now in silent misery. He felt a new grievance that she hadn't stirred to help him.

Crying doesn't improve a woman, he grumbled; real crying like hers. Features, complexion, the informing spirit, all smirched and smutted and bedraggled. Then he remembered what he had said about her hair and was ashamed.

His arm around her shoulders, pressed back against the rock, they waited for the end of day. 'I don't want to see it', she muttered once, turning her face from the grey quaking walls of the cleft, shuddering at the wind which roared and ruffled and screeched overhead, the thud and hiss of the breakers. But was darkness any better? You could believe the elements alive, pitiless, gloating. Yet better, because you hoped to sleep, to awake from the dream, to find it ended. At the worst, there was forgetting for a while.

They were awake for hours before it grew light. After a time he began to tell her ramblingly about himself, his home, his wife, his job. There was peace between them again. He was aware of her sex only in so far as it made it easier for him to talk, almost to confess, about these simple and yet momentous matters. 'Oh', she commented oddly, 'we'd never have done that, Dafydd and I.' He had spoken of his marriage in a registry office. 'I was married from the Hall, in a very old church. It seems more respectful somehow.' He thought she meant respectable. No, he said, there were no children. Yes, his wife had always wanted them—no, he didn't himself. But he'd been willing. It was the way things worked out.

Even as he spoke he knew he would bitterly regret his confidences later. 'Everything went wrong. I can't believe it. That it happened to us.' There had been a miscarriage, a long, long illness,—'Years', he said. 'We were young. God in heaven, years!' Then a second illness. 'My fault', he said bitterly. 'Or no one's fault—what's the difference? Our life broke up on that.' How clearly he was remembering: he could have torn the world in two for her, destroyed it that she might be well and happy. 'She says she's better. The doctors say she's better. But it's too late. You live on pity long enough and everything else goes dead. I'm not making excuses. I've done some shabby things, and this is one of them.' He went on talking, telling her what he had never told anyone. 'She wants us to start again—or she'll leave me, she says.' How bald and unjust that sounded in words—he was overcome by longing to put his wife in the right, himself wholly in the wrong. And at the same time to win himself sympathy not blame.

But he'd been a fool to talk. There were no confidences in return. Abruptly he grew quiet, eaten by unease. The relief he had temporarily felt ebbed from him. For no one particular reason he grew convinced that Mrs. Absalom was now stronger and surer of herself than he.

The same great wind was blowing sheets of rain over the Island, the sea still crashed and lathered the beach behind them. So far the tarpaulin had kept them dry and the narrow coffiny patch under them, but the wall of turfs was sodden and must sometime collapse. With daylight he came to loathe lying still, yet to shrink from the notion of stirring. There was a knot of hunger in his stomach. He avoided looking at his watch as long as he could, for those early hours were the most unbudging. Yet the hands crawled round to eight and nine and ten and eleven o'clock. 'It's stopping', he said. The sky had lightened a little, the spray-filled mist was thinner, and they stood up to rub their limbs, work their shoulders free of cramp, walk about again.

For a while he watched the waves flung huge and bristling against the black western edge of the cove, whence they bounded back to make a maelstrom of the centre. Then this whirl of waters yielded to the whaleback flow from the outer Bay, was borne high and tossing to the beach and flung in headlong till the ground trembled up into his legs. As it ground backwards, brown with gravel, the next wave would be bursting off the west face, hanging it with waterfalls, swilling to the centre where in its turn it felt the lift and drive of the tide and came hurtling inshore. It made him giddy to watch, increased his sense of helplessness, so he went despondently back to patch the turf wall and cut narrow drainage channels.

'What on earth have you done to your hat?' he asked, when Mrs. Absalom walked back to join him.

She held up a round of wire unsmilingly.

'Well?'

'Rabbits', she said, and her tongue came out to touch the middle of her lips. 'When we were children . . .' She began to twist the wire.

'But we haven't matches. We can't cook it.'

Her glance was cold humourless contempt, but she said nothing. Three or four hours later, during another break in the rain, she was searching for a stick at high-water mark. All this was beyond his knowledge, she explained nothing of her purpose though she borrowed and kept his knife, and he had the impression he was no more than a dog at her heels as she went up the grass bank, seeking a run that had been recently used. When she plugged the stick almost to its head in the ground his eyes widened, she was breathing hard through her nostrils as she tightened the noose and gave it its last touches. Some words in Welsh she spoke to herself, but when he stood staring she said sourly: 'We won't catch anything by standing here. Let's go down out of the way.' He followed her without argument. It was her affair, this.

The rain had stopped now. Twice during the evening they climbed to the snare to find it empty. A third time they had started up the bank when they heard a squeal. 'Quick', she cried, 'run! Oh God, God!' His heart jumped at every stride, his ankle suddenly folded sickeningly. In the snare he saw a blue-grey scut, a struggling grey-brown body. The stick was coming up out of the ground, he thought, and he grabbed at the creature, pulling up the whole snare. 'I've got it!' he shouted, and groaning with pain turned to where Mrs. Absalom clambered behind him. At that moment the rabbit was convulsed in his hand, he lost his grip, it fell to the ground and ran madly towards the top of the Island. 'I had it', he said stupidly, gaping at the empty noose. 'It was in my hand. I had it.'

Mrs. Absalom screamed with rage and disappointment. Then a torrent of filth burst from her lips and she struck him violently in the face. He felt her nails hot as fire from his eye to his chin. She was quite mad. It was all he could do to control her arms. When she stood glaring at him afterwards—'You mad ugly bitch', he snarled; 'I'll never forgive you for this.' With trembling fingers he reshaped the snare and thrust the peg into the earth; then after one look of disgust and defiance he hobbled in agony to the top of the Island. The wind threw him off his balance as he tried to see the mainland across a desolation of lunging water, and soon he was forced to the hollow where he lay flat on the wet grass for shelter while the wind, like air turned fluid, went over him in a guttering roar. He retched with the pain of his ankle and must have fainted, for the minutes which had been so slow had somehow rushed on to dusk when he decided he must go downhill. Much of the way he levered himself down with his hands and right leg, half-sitting and forced to constant halts. When he came to the rock he could see that Mrs. Absalom was lying there under the tarpaulin, so stubbornly he sat against the rock not far from her feet. He felt the wind cut like a knife to his sweaty chest. Like an animal, he went on repeating; like an animal. He touched the long hot scratches on his cheek. Like an animal.

He was awake and aching and chilled in heart and limb. Dazedly he went to the tarpaulin and crept under. He must have warmth. He lay close against her, shivering, put his arm around her. 'Leave me alone', she said evilly. 'It's all you think of.'

'No', he said. 'I'm cold. I think I'm ill.'

But she sat up violently, thrusting at him. She had been awake all the time. Everything that was cruel in her rushed to her tongue. 'If you've spoiled one woman, you can't spoil me. Get out', she said shrilly. 'Don't you touch me!' He dragged himself round the corner of the rock; he had no will against hers.

Sunday night, he thought wretchedly. Christ, how I hate her, and how I hate the Island. The rain was beginning again, rattling against his clothes, splashing into his eyes. He licked his lips as an animal licks its hurts. Through the dark he could hear the boom and swashing of the sea and the wind scuffling off it. The ground began to heave and swing as he stretched himself out and huddled into the rock. 'I shall be lucky', he said suddenly, 'if I come out of this alive.' He longed for sleep, but when at last it came he was to fall through the night into frightening dreams and panic awakenings. The Island, the snare, his wife, Mrs. Absalom's words and lunatic face, his pain and hunger interwove, changed rôles, clogged him awake and asleep with nightmares. When, he cried, oh when will the light come again?

5

Five days later a motor-boat approached the Island from the south. In it were two men and a lad of fourteen, who saw to the engine. The men were the ex-collier Thomas who had recited 'The Explosion', and the Wise Man of Cornel Ofan; the boy was Thomas's son. The morning was blue and white, the sea reflected the sky in greys and whites and creamy bluey-green; in front of them the Island was glazed and unreal, as though crumpled out of cloth. The boat rode the swell buoyant as a bird and threw white thrashes of spray high into the air. All three of them wore oil-skins.

'We shall soon know now,' said the Wise Man.

His companion nodded. He was enjoying himself, he was greatly interested, but he had seen too much in the pits, in warfare, in slump, to get over-excited by what had happened to these love-me-quicks. When the Wise Man came for the boat he responded as he had responded in the old days to the call for a rescue party; you didn't ask Who, Where, Why—you caught up your cap and went. He touched the food packet with his mutilated hand, felt for the hot flasks with his right. 'His missus', he said, 'she seemed very nice, that one did.' He winked at his son, turned his wrist so that the coal-pocked thumb-ball rolled upper-most. 'The blueness of a wound cleanseth away evil', he quoted— a family joke evidently, for the boy grinned before ducking his head to the engine.

The Wise Man nodded approval of them both. He liked an improving sentence even if it wasn't much to the occasion. 'A very nice lady', he agreed. 'A man would like to do her a good turn. Now that other one . . .'

'But hunger is a good cure', said the ex-collier, with the con-viction of one who has tried it.

'It is sometimes a lesson', said the Wise Man sceptically.

'The buckle-end of a belt is also a lesson', said Thomas. He had dropped his voice confidentially. There were things children shouldn't hear. 'That Merrill now—a man wouldn't mind giving a clever buggarr like that a belting.'

'He is not so bad neither.' The Wise Man nodded into his oilskin collar. 'We shan't need to leather him off the Green Island, I venture.' He laughed, without Thomas quite knowing at what.

They were drawing close to the south-eastern spur. The tide had run down to low water and the cormorants were fishing from the rocks or slanting their long brown throats ecstatically sky-wards. A few minutes more and they were entering the cove, sliding in to the dark-grey gravelly beach. All they could see was the spur to their right running like a jawbone into the water, the harsh wall of rock to their left, and the dark grassy sides of the cleft running up to the top of the Island.

'Oi-oi-oi!' shouted the ex-collier. 'Who's about here?' The Wise Man followed him stiffly on to the sand. Almost at once Mrs. Absalom came into sight, scrambling down the bank. She carried her crumpled hat in her hand, and ran to them sobbing and trying to talk all in a breath. 'Give her a drink', ordered the Wise Man. The boy in the boat looked on marvelling as she gulped and sucked. She rubbed her chin where dribblings had run, then licked the fingers and back of her hand. 'Now give her food.

Where is this Merrill with you?' he asked. She pointed to the black outcrop. 'He's ill. He's very bad.' He saw how her eyes changed. 'We caught a rabbit. He couldn't eat it. He let one go. I ate it though. Take me off the Island! Oh for Jesus' sake take me off the Island!' She screamed and beat with her fists at the Wise Man's chest, but he set her aside and went over to the rock.

Merrill was lying there under the tarpaulin. His face, when they drew the tarpaulin down, was greatly altered since the Wise Man last talked with him. But he was conscious and when they had poured hot tea into his mouth he opened his eyes on them.

'I knew you'd come', he whispered. His eyes filled with tears of weakness and self-pity. 'She had food', he whispered, 'chocolate and bread, but she wouldn't give me any. There was tea and milk, and she had meat and butter, but she wouldn't give me any.'

'Then we will', promised the Wise Man. 'Only tell us later, not now. Now you must drink this.'

'It's lies!' cried Mrs. Absalom. 'There was nothing, thanks to him. Only the rabbit. He couldn't even twist its neck, the soft fool he is.'

The Wise Man nodded. Of course it was lies. 'Eat more—a little more', he told her. 'We must get to the boat.' There was neither pity nor condemnation in anything he said or did. Nor even surprise. Things, you could gather, had gone much as he expected.

Thomas's one eye peered at Mrs. Absalom, swung up to the skyline, back to the rocks. He made his deduction. 'It would get a man down on here, after a time or two.' He appeared to deal with what might be, rather than with what was.

'And where's the boat you had?' asked the Wise Man. He listened to angry explanations from Mrs. Absalom. 'There now!' Watching him, Merrill saw only a humorous appreciation in his face. 'That was a poor trick for a college-trained man, Mr. Merrill?' Thomas gave one brief hard bark of a laugh. Let them, thought Merrill, let them. Wasn't he eating their food? Cunning satisfaction took the place of a beginning rage.

But anger was to come. As the boy and Thomas took him to the boat they discovered how bloated his ankle was. 'And what's

this on you now?' asked the Wise Man. Mrs Absalom told him,
contemptuously this time. 'Well to be sure!' His words and gesture
carried with them the tolerant but wondering comment: And
what next shall we find this silly man has been up to? But it was
a weak anger Merrill felt, tempting him to tears.

They brought off the tarpaulin and spread it for Merrill to lie
on, put his coat over his shoulders and Thomas's oilskin over his
legs and feet; the boy started up the engine. The smell of hot oil
came to Merrill's nostrils as the loveliest smell he had ever known,
the sourness of the boards was precious to him. 'And how many
rabbits did you catch?' he heard the Wise Man asking. As though
she'd tell, as though she'd ever confess to what she'd eaten on the
sly, not sharing with him, throwing the pelts over the cliff.
'Very clever too', said the Wise Man. 'A good thing that one
wasn't in charge, I fancy.'

Thereafter they were talking in Welsh, and he noticed the
change that was coming over all their voices. Contact was being
re-established between them; Mrs. Absalom's voice moved on
levels of excitement, grief, despair; whatever her story, it lost
nothing in the telling; the Wise Man's questions were free from
that smug condescension he had shown on the Island; the com-
ments of the ex-collier, which in English had been so indifferent,
so unrelated to his own awareness of starvation and strain, grew
eager, appreciative, astonished. Thomas's was the only face
Merrill could see, the eye sunken and glittering, the mouth so
impatient to speak that sometimes throughout a whole diapason
of the Wise Man's his lips would be a-bubble. He too had been
beleaguered in his time, let no one forget it. Several times they
mentioned 'Mr Merrill'—he knew it, he was a million miles from
them, right outside their Welsh world. There was something of
Dafydd too. But whereas they spoke his own name often with a
pause before it, as though they were jerking a hand or head at
him, and always with some change of tone, Dafydd's flowed
smoothly into the current of their talk. To them Dafydd was
calculable. Even if he left two people on an island to starve, and
whatever his plans for one of them now—they had the feel of him
in their fingers. They were of a kind. But he, Merrill—only his
resentment kept him from weeping. A man who might have died,

would have died, wasn't he entitled to pity, a word of kindness, something better than jeers?

The firm outline of his thoughts wavered. Why trouble anyway? To be from the Island was enough.

He found himself thinking of his wife, confusedly and with distractions. For he thought also of food and comfort, and he felt safety, as an animal feels it which breaks from the trap and turns to its lair and scents the well-loved pungencies. And he was puzzled why he should be so weak and Mrs. Absalom so strong. They don't know her cunning, he thought, they don't know how she starved me all the time. His mouth watered, and he was toiling towards food from one corner of the Island to another, hopeless as a dog on a treadmill.

He groaned and saw the Wise Man's face, huge and benevolent, hanging over him. Hating his weakness before these cunning strangers he tried to struggle up, but the old man's hand steadied his shoulder to the tarpaulin. 'You will feel better when you see your wife', he soothed. He patted him as he would an animal he was tending, and Merrill felt suddenly eased as those animals did. Unexpectedly, he smiled. 'And what would be wisdom for me?' he whispered. But the Wise Man shook his head craftily, then bent to his ear: 'To preach from the text: And Adam was not deceived, but the woman being deceived was in the transgression.' His shoulders shook as at some famous joke.

He's a cruel old devil with it all, thought Merrill; and wondered what verse he had found for Mrs. Absalom's case. It could hardly be complimentary to him, Merrill. What a humbug he was, with his scripture and quackery and posing!

The boy had cut the engine. The boat ground softly into the Ffald-y-Brenin shingle. They were taking him up, lifting him to land. Dafydd Absalom had come to look at him. 'Duw, duw, Mr. Merrill', he was saying blandly, 'and me thinking you were in London where the beds are soft.' The lift of his eyebrows was at once quizzical and cruel. He watched Merrill's face closely, nodding with satisfaction, once or twice stroking his chin. 'Fancy me being so fullish!' He turned to speak to the Wise Man at his side. 'I might have guessed, him being so fond of the Island out there. And there's nice to see the wife again.'

Merrill closed his eyes. He could hear Mrs. Absalom's voice in low, passionate explanation, and a dog whistling and whining its pleasure. 'That's a bad bag she's got there', came the full bass of the Wise Man. 'You let the milk come down, Dafydd. That was dull of you.' The bitch squealed but grew silent as the Wise Man examined her. 'See', he said, 'see? I'll bring you some ointment for it, in a brown box—very good it is—you rub it in this way . . .' Mrs. Absalom had stopped talking; he knew they would all be standing round the man and beast. For him, Merrill, they had no place, the foreigner, the outsider.

Before he opened his eyes again he knew his wife was with him. 'I knew you'd come', he whispered. 'I know it's you.'

'Don't talk.' She fondled his hand, terrified by his thinness. 'We are going up to Cornel Ofan.' He shook his head. 'I've been there for days. I was frightened when I found only Dafydd here.' Again he shook his head. 'They have been good to me. He really is a Wise Man.'

'And I am a fool.'

She put her hand to his face and felt the hot tears there. At that moment she believed it possible to gather up the shards of their two lives and make them one. At worst, it could be tried.

'But why don't they move you?' she asked anxiously. When she looked round it was to find them all ignoring her.

'Mr. Jones', she called; 'Mr. Jones.'

The Wise Man looked up. 'Yes, my dear?'

'We must move my husband—at once.'

He waved his hand in a casual, almost reproving way. 'In a minute', he said, and went on with his explanations in Welsh.

'That's how they've all been treating me', whispered Merrill. 'That's why I won't go to Cornel Ofan to be laughed at.'

'We'll see', she told him. 'Mr. Jones!'

'In a minute, a minute!' he answered testily. 'I am very busy, as you see.' She reddened at his rudeness; through Merrill's weakness there flared both indignation for his own sake and anger for hers. 'She is a nice bitch', the Wise Man was adding, as though this were full explanation. 'She deserves care.'

'And doesn't my husband deserve care?' she retorted furiously.

'In God's good time.'

'Are you mad?' she asked. 'Are you mad, all of you?'

He stood up, shrugging his shoulders, inviting sympathy. The bitch lay at his feet, wagging her tail, the others formed a row behind him. The barrier, less of hostility than incomprehension, was complete between them. In the Wise Man's case she was lost. The ex-collier, battered and peering; the gaping boy; Mrs. Absalom, white and ill-looking but smirking that her welcome had been no worse than it was; Absalom, his face never more branded than now with the inexplicable contradictions of his nature,—from these she was prepared for indifference, even callousness, but the Wise Man! All her hopes had been on him; but now she felt her husband and her forced together, to answer a threat on their own.

Of them all, she appealed to Absalom. 'I'll give you',—she fumbled in her bag—'I'll give you anything I have to drive us to Abermaid.'

He hesitated, his cheekbones suddenly glowing. 'Go on, Dafydd', counselled the old man; 'you couldn't do a better thing for yourself, and he could never walk it.'

He looked from one to another of them and then amid their silence went to the shed and brought out the car; he backed her round to where Merrill was lying, the tyres scuffling in the sand. 'Take him to the old doctor's in Teilo Street', said the Wise Man. 'He is not as good as the *dyn hysbys*, but he is no fool neither.' Seated beside her husband Mrs. Merrill gave him a glance of bitter reproach, but he ignored it and held out his hand. 'No?' he said, as the Merrills stared at him without taking it.

'Hold the dog!' called Dafydd. 'One fool's enough at a time.' The gears ground, slipped, then caught. After a jerk or two the car moved slowly off, and Mrs. Absalom walked into the house.

The Wise Man took off his oilskin and threw it into the boat. 'I am sorry Mrs. Merrill has so bad a notion of me. It is for the best, but a poor thing to think of all the same.'

'You are a deep and depthy man', said the ex-collier. 'He'll be all right?'

'Why not then?'

'If I was her', said the ex-collier emphatically, 'he wouldn't be worth a po-tatto to me.'

The Wise Man chuckled. 'You are a great one for morals as well as the reciting, I can see.'

The boat backed out and turned in a swirl of green and white. The old man stood there for a while, watching it chug and spit its way south. There was a last wave of hands. Mrs. Absalom was still indoors. As he passed the workshop door the bitch grovelled her pleasure, the mongrel Twm drummed his paws, thrusting up his ugly bucket-head. 'Did a little girl's bag hurt then?' the Wise Man crooned, and she followed him past the bridge to the beginning of the trees. When he turned he could see the long black roof covering the house and workshop, the black wheel, the untidy pebbly shingle and its broad glittering channels. From the beach the sea spread gay and apple-green, but out past the headland it was shaded to a dark foamy blue, and the sky was blue above it. Breaking the arc was the glossy seal-like bulk of the Green Island.

'What of it?' he asked suddenly, and louder than he had intended.

The bitch Shan, thinking she was spoken to, pressed against his leg, and he looked down. 'Home you go, little Shan', he told her, and docilely she went. His lips pouted, made a wise little round red hole as he studied the awkwardness of her movements. For the Wise Man was a healer: he felt his power to cure her drip like fat from his fingers.

As he took the track between the Ffald-y-Brenin oak trees he was thinking equally of the Merrills and Absaloms and of Shan. He saw no reason why she should suffer for any of them. Then he sighed. His wife, he knew (that unsurprised, farsighted lady with the formal manners and the work-worn hands) would want a full story, and he was the man to tell it. But first things must come first.

His brows sagged under their load of learning. Should he put a little more or a little less lard in the bitch's ointment?

When next he turned he neither saw nor wished to see the Island.